SANTA, THE BILLIONAIRE

by

SERENITY WOODS

Copyright © 2021 Serenity Woods
All rights reserved.
ISBN: 9798777936301

DEDICATION

To Tony & Chris, my Kiwi boys.

CONTENTS

Chapter One 1
Chapter Two 9
Chapter Three 16
Chapter Four 24
Chapter Five 33
Chapter Six 40
Chapter Seven 46
Chapter Eight 55
Chapter Nine 62
Chapter Ten 69
Chapter Eleven 78
Chapter Twelve 85
Chapter Thirteen 92
Chapter Fourteen 100
Chapter Fifteen 107
Chapter Sixteen 116
Chapter Seventeen 124
Chapter Eighteen 132
Chapter Nineteen 141
Chapter Twenty 148
Chapter Twenty-One 152
Chapter Twenty-Two 161
Chapter Twenty-Three 168
Chapter Twenty-Four 176
Chapter Twenty-Five 182
Chapter Twenty-Six 189
Chapter Twenty-Seven 198
Newsletter 205
About the Author 206

Chapter One

Nick

It's been a very long day.

My daughter, Kora, has been in labor since dawn. It's now nine p.m., but according to the midwife it's still going to be at least an hour before we see the first baby.

I'm used to the wait. All of Olivia's labors were long, especially when our twins were born, so I've done the worried father routine four times for my five kids.

I wish it was easier now I'm the grandfather rather than the father, but it isn't. Kora is my only daughter, and she will always be my little girl. It might have been different if her mother was still here, but now Olivia's gone I feel I have to fill her role as well as my own. It's only been worse since my father died, too. Mum might still be alive, but I'm the head of the family now. It's a cool role, and I'm not complaining, but it does come with some responsibility.

Callum, the dad, comes out of the room, stretches and yawns, then walks down to the waiting room to join me. Kora's been uncomfortable the last few weeks of her pregnancy, so I doubt either of them have had much sleep.

I put down the magazine I'm reading as he stops by the coffee machine and slots some coins in. Someone has decorated the room with stickers to get in the Halloween mood, mainly to entertain any siblings of the newborns, I would think. Pumpkins, ghosts, and witches adorn the walls and the window, and orange and green streamers decorate the table and the water cooler.

"Hey. How's it going?" I ask my son-in-law.

"Everything's fine, according to the midwife." He presses a button, and the cup underneath begins to fill with steaming coffee. He runs a hand through his hair, which is already ruffled and sticking up at the front. "Apparently the incredible pain is normal."

I give a short laugh. "Yeah. Not helpful, eh?"

"Kora's still refusing an epidural. I don't get it, myself. If it was me, I'd be yelling 'give me drugs!'"

I can see the frustration beneath his forced attempt at humor. "I'm guessing she's concerned about prolonging the labor."

"Yeah, apparently it can make pushing more difficult. Still… I wish she'd take it. I hate seeing her in pain."

"It's tough being the fella at times like this. You feel so powerless."

There's no point in giving him platitudes, in telling him that women's bodies know what they're doing, or that they're in good hands with the midwives, who've seen it all a thousand times before. It might be natural, and there might be one hundred and fifty babies born in New Zealand every day, but it's Kora's first labor, and he's terrified. Like most modern fathers, he's read all the books and gone to all the classes with her. It's scary when you read how many things can go wrong, even in this modern day, with all the technical equipment and medical knowledge that exists. For men, pain isn't natural. All pain we experience is a warning that something is wrong, and it's impossible for us to understand how excruciating pain can be a positive thing.

"Evening." Someone comes into the waiting room—it's Lucas, my second-oldest son. He's obviously come straight from the office as he's still wearing a suit. "How's she doing?" he asks Callum, shaking his hand.

"As good as can be expected for someone in agony," Callum replies.

Lucas gives a short laugh. "Yeah. How much longer, do you reckon?"

"A few hours yet, I think. Don't feel you have to stay, guys. I'll soon be waking you all up once the twins are here." Callum grins.

"I'll head off soon," Lucas says. "I just wanted to touch base. Give her my love, won't you?"

"Yeah, will do." Callum raises a hand, then heads back to the delivery room with his coffee.

Lucas looks at me, smiles, and comes over to give me a hug. "You staying here?" he asks, going back to the coffee machine.

"Yeah, I'll see it out. I'd like to be here for Callum, if nothing else." I nod as he gestures to the machine. "Cappuccino, please."

He slots in some coins and presses a button. "It's all going okay?"

"Yeah. I think Kora's more worried about the twins being born on Halloween than anything else."

That makes him laugh. "It'd be strange if one was born at five to midnight and the second one at five minutes past. They'd have different birthdays."

"I hadn't thought of that."

"Twins." He shakes his head, takes out one cup, and presses a button for another. "I can't imagine having one baby, let alone two. It must be hard work. Was it easier or harder, do you think, for you and Mum, having had two kids before you had Theo and Kora?"

"Oh, harder." I accept the cup as he brings it over to me and sip the hot cappuccino. Hospital coffee machines are traditionally awful, but this one isn't bad at all. "Ben was four and reasonably well behaved, but you were going through the terrible twos and were a handful."

He chuckles and sits beside me. "Some things don't change. It wasn't easier having been through it before?"

"It never got easier. It's always terrifying."

His lips twist. "Yeah, I can imagine."

I smile. Like all my boys, he's a good-looking lad. Taller than the others. Leaner and less stocky. He used to look quite geeky when he was younger and wore glasses and was always reading, but he's a bit more sophisticated now.

"I'm still waiting for you to give me a grandchild," I inform him. "Don't snort. You'd make a great dad."

"Gotta find the mum first."

"Still no luck on that front?"

He gives me a wry look. "I'm working on it."

"So I understand."

"What's that supposed to mean?"

"I hear things."

"Do you, now?"

"Are you trying to work your way through the female population of Wellington?"

"Someone has to."

"If you're looking to settle down, it helps to go out with a girl for more than one date," I advise.

He leans forward, elbows on his knees, his coffee cup dangling in front of him. "I can't think about it now. Work's busy. I've got a lot on my plate."

"Yeah, I know." I'm conscious I've taken my foot off the gas this year. Ben's been tied up with his project, the South Pole theme park. Kora's been absent a lot as she's settled into married life. Theo and Jacob are both heavily involved in the marketing and creative side, but less so in the financial. We're all there to support Lucas, but I know it's fallen on him to do a lot of the heavy lifting. This afternoon he was on a Zoom call for several hours with the directors of a couple of our Aussie stores, and he obviously stayed late catching up on work.

I should take some of the responsibility off his shoulders. I am the CEO, when it comes to it. The problem is, it's not a role I enjoy. My father was the one with the business acumen, and Lucas takes after him. I don't have a business brain. I'm like Ben and Theo and Jacob, more creative, more interested in how and why products sell than the cogs and wheels behind the scenes. As the oldest Prince, apart from my mother, who has never been interested in running the company, it was the logical step for me to take over when Dad died. But I'm not a natural for the position. In fact it's been a burden at times, but that's not something I like to admit when I lead such a privileged life.

I'm distracted from my thoughts by someone else walking through the door. I nod as I recognize her. It's Elena Hunter, my personal assistant. I know she prefers to stay at the office until we've all gone home and, like Lucas, she's still in her working suit, so she must have stayed there until he left.

Elena is five-foot-six, although she looks taller because she's always in heels—I've never seen her in flats. Today she's wearing a pair of black slingbacks that must be three inches high. She's also wearing a white blouse beneath a dark-gray suit, the skirt a little loose around her waist, the jacket also looking maybe a size too big. She's lost weight over the past few months.

I know she's forty-nine because her birthday is on New Year's Day, and I heard her telling Kora that she's fifty on the first of January. There's no gray in her blonde hair, though. She's had it cut in a chic bob ever since I've known her, which is nearly twelve years now. When she doesn't have her contacts in, she wears dark-rimmed rectangular glasses and, together with the suit, she looks every inch the professional PA.

She met Olivia soon after moving to Wellington, and they swiftly became best friends. It was Olivia's suggestion that I hire Elena as my PA while I was still Marketing Director, after my first PA moved away. I objected at the time, but Olivia wasn't to be put off, and when I couldn't come up with a convincing reason why, she eventually talked me into it.

Elena is a hard worker, very professional, but when I moved into the CEO's office after my father became ill, I was all ready to leave her behind and take on Dad's PA as my own. But Sally decided it was time to retire too, and after that, it would have been cruel not to give Elena the job.

Despite the fact that we've worked together for so long, I know practically nothing about her personal life. Olivia reserved her friendship with Elena for going to the theater or the cinema to see shows I wasn't interested in, and clubs to discuss books I wouldn't have read, so we didn't socialize much together. She's single, and although I'm guessing she's had male friends, I've never seen her with a guy, and she's never talked about any. She keeps to herself, and I'm more than happy with that.

"Hello, you two." She smiles as she spots us and comes over. She's carrying a supermarket bag, and she puts it on the table and extracts the contents—a couple of boxes of sandwiches, a bunch of bananas, a few apples, two packs of cookies, and several chocolate bars. "Thought you might be peckish," she announces.

"Thank you, I appreciate that." I ate in the hospital café a couple of hours ago, but I'm already hungry again. I pick up a banana and peel it.

She looks over her shoulder at the delivery room. "Do you think Callum or Kora want anything?"

"Callum comes out every half hour or so," I tell her. "I'll ask him then."

She takes off her glasses and massages the bridge of her nose, then looks at me. She has bright-green eyes, very striking. "What about you two?" she asks. "Is there anything else you need?"

"I'm going home soon," Lucas advises. "So I'm good."

I hesitate, and she glances at me. "What?" she asks. "Whatever you need, I don't mind. I can't help in any other way."

"I could do with a change of clothes," I tell her. I came to the hospital from the office this afternoon, and I haven't yet been home.

"Callum said he'd call you," Lucas says to me. "You don't have to stay. There's nothing you can do here."

"I know."

"He wants to stay," Elena says softly. "Just in case his baby girl needs anything." She smiles, showing me she's not being sarcastic and she understands. "It's okay, I'll call in and pick you up a couple of things if you like."

"That would be great. I think there's a pair of track pants and a tee hanging over the chair in my bedroom."

"Okay. I might call home first. I'll be back in half an hour?"

"Terrific, thanks."

She nods at us both and heads out.

I peel back the cellophane on one of the boxes of sandwiches and offer one to Lucas. He checks the wrapper—cheese and pickle—and takes one, and I munch on the other.

"Nice of her to do that," he says.

"She's my PA," I reply. "It's her job."

"A bit beyond the call of duty, isn't it?"

I frown at him, and he holds up a hand. "Sorry, I know it's none of my business what you ask your staff to do."

"No, it's not."

"It's just that sometimes you're a bit… abrupt with her."

I eat the last mouthful of sandwich and get up to throw the wrapper in the bin. "I don't know what you mean."

"She's very professional and a hard worker. She's worked for you for a long time, but I know you were reluctant to take her with you when Sally left. It's odd, that's all. I don't get why you're so cool toward her."

"I'm not cool. She's a member of my staff. It's good to keep a professional distance."

"I know what you're saying, but…" he smiles. "I think she likes you."

"You're wrong," I snap.

"I don't think so. And she's lovely—elegant, intelligent, efficient, funny. I would have thought you might find her attractive."

I fold my arms and lean against the wall. "Well, I don't. Your mother was the only woman for me, Luc."

"She's been gone a long time now," he murmurs.

"Twenty-two months, fourteen days, five hours, and about… seventeen minutes."

His expression softens. "I know."

"That's not long in the big scheme of things."

"Long enough," he says. "For you to move on."

I stiffen. "Look—"

"Dad, you know none of us would mind if you started seeing someone else, right?"

I glare at him. "I don't want to talk about it."

"Nobody expects you to stay single for the rest of your life. Mum wouldn't have. She'd have wanted you to be happy."

"You don't know what you're talking about," I snap, "and I'd rather you keep your thoughts to yourself."

A silence falls in the room. Lucas has a great poker face that he uses all the time at the office, but right now it fails to work, and his expression flickers with hurt.

"Fair enough." He gets to his feet.

I walk forward. "Lucas…"

He holds up a hand and I stop. "It's none of my business."

"I'm stressed," I tell him, which is partly the truth. "I'm worried about Kora, and it's getting to me."

He gives me a direct look. "You don't get stressed."

"Of course I do."

"Not like that. You're the calmest guy I know. You'll have told yourself that what Kora is experiencing is perfectly normal, and you won't worry until there's something to worry about. You don't want to talk about your personal life, and that's fine. Just don't hide behind Kora."

Somehow, he manages to make me feel ashamed, even though I'm twenty-seven years his senior. "You're right," I admit. "I don't like talking about my personal life. It doesn't feel right. I was married to your mother for a long time, and I loved her very much. I promised to love her forever."

"You promised to love her until death parted you," he reminds me. The words stab me, and I wince. "Sorry," he adds. "But it's the truth."

I don't know what he wants me to say. We stand in the middle of the waiting room, in the harsh overhead lights surrounded by pumpkins and ghosts, as silence settles around us. Along the corridor, a woman's sharp cry echoes, and Lucas's head whips around.

"It's not Kora," I tell him.

He looks back at me, his eyes startled, like a rabbit in the path of an approaching car. "I'm going home. There's no place for me here."

"Son…" I sigh. "I miss her, that's all, and I'm not comfortable talking about other women."

"I get it." He picks up his phone and his car keys. "Make sure you or Callum calls me when the babies come, okay?"

"Of course."

He nods and strides off down the corridor.

I sink back onto the chair, feeling exhausted. Lucas was right in that I rarely get stressed, but I am worried about Kora, even though everything seems to be progressing normally.

But that's not why I snapped at him.

I like to think I'm an honest man. And that means being honest with myself, as well as with others. I'm not an ostrich. I don't bury my head in the sand. I face up to my problems and tackle them head on. You can't be head of a successful business by doing anything else.

I got angry with Lucas because it's nearly two years since Olivia died, and I'm lonely.

I miss her. Of course I do. But whereas in the beginning, I saw her everywhere I looked, now whole hours go by when I don't even think about her.

And I hate myself for it.

I made her a promise, and I intend to stick to it. I'm a man of my word, and I'm loyal to those I love. Nothing will ever change that.

Even if I am in love with someone else.

Chapter Two

Elena

The Prince family home is shrouded in darkness.

I've never considered myself superstitious, but it's Halloween, and it's late, and it's really dark all around the huge mansion. I feel as if I'm in a Stephen King novel.

Okay, maybe mansion is stretching it, but to a woman who lives in a tiny one-bedroomed apartment, Buck House, as it's affectionately known by Ben and the others, is as palatial as the residence of the English royalty.

I've been there several times over the years—to pick up Olivia when we used to go out in the evenings, once or twice for a party when they've entertained everyone at the office, and more frequently over the last two years to carry out errands for Nick, such as dropping off his dry cleaning, and letting in the plumber when there was a leak in the downstairs bathroom and Nick was busy and couldn't make it home. But this is the first time I've been here alone.

After turning off the alarm, I insert the key in the lock and go into the large entrance hall. I've been home and changed out of my office clothes, and my sneakers squeak on the tiles, loud enough to make me jump. I walk across the entrance hall, bypass the huge living room with its high ceilings and the gleaming kitchen, and take the hallway down to the west wing of the house where I know the master bedroom is situated. The house has wings! It always makes me feel as if I'm visiting someone famous when I come here.

Unnerved by the darkness and the silence, I flick on a light switch, illuminating the cream-carpeted hall and the photos of the Prince family on the walls. I stop and look at one of Nick and Olivia on their wedding day. They were in their mid-twenties at the time, Olivia looking shy but beautiful in a straight satin gown, Nick handsome as ever in his suit, with his baby-smooth face and dazzling blue eyes, gazing at her with adoration.

I walk on, past the many photos of the children—Ben, Lucas, Theo, Kora, and Jacob—some with one or both of their parents. School photos, family vacations, graduation pictures, and at the end, a photo of Ben and Heloise holding baby Estella. Poor Olivia never got to hold her first grandchild. She'd have adored the sweet, good-natured baby.

At the end is a picture of Nick, taken three or four years ago. He's been growing a beard for a while, and it's odd to see him clean shaven again. It was Olivia's favorite photo of him, one she took herself, which might be why it's still hanging there, or maybe he walks past these so often he doesn't even see them anymore. It reminds me of the painting of JFK; Nick's wearing a gray suit and standing in a similar pose, arms folded, looking down, but, unlike the president, he's laughing at something she's saying. It's a lovely photo and captures him perfectly—happy, in love. The way he was with her.

Not the way he is with me.

I turn away, and walk on.

At the end of the corridor, the master bedroom leads off to the right. The door's open, and I flick the light switch on and go inside.

My eyebrows rise as I look around. It's immediately clear that Nick isn't using this room. The bed is made, the duvet and pillows pristine and untouched. The bedside tables are free of the personal paraphernalia that sometimes litters his desk—reading glasses, piles of books or half-read magazines, tie pins and cufflinks, old coffee mugs. An old-fashioned dressing table that could have been where Olivia sat to do her hair and makeup is empty of the bottles and hairbrushes and tissues that would have littered it back in the day. No clothes hang over the backs of the two chairs by the window.

I cross to the walk-in closet and open the door. It's empty, and it smells faintly of Olivia's favorite perfume. Frowning, I close it and leave the room.

I know there are five bedrooms in the other wing, which is where their children's rooms were, but there's one other bedroom here. I think it was originally the nursery, and the youngest child stayed here until they were old enough to join the others. I would have thought it would have made a good study as there isn't one in the house as far as I know, but Olivia told me they turned it into a spare bedroom 'just in case'. She never explained what she meant by that, but I wondered whether they sometimes slept apart.

Crossing the hallway, I open the door of the spare room. I can see straight away that this is where Nick is sleeping. He's pulled the duvet over, but it's rumpled, and the pillow still shows an indentation where his head rested. Discarded clothes are draped over the back of the chair. I open the closet door, revealing a line of shirts—white, light blue, pale pink, striped—a rack of ties, and his suits at the end. The scent of his body spray reaches my nostrils. I inhale, then close the door.

This time the bedside table bears the items I was expecting—spare reading glasses, the biography I've seen him reading at work, his iPad, an open notebook with a pen resting on a page half-filled with his small writing, and an empty glass tumbler. I pick it up—it's heavy bottomed, and when I sniff it, I smell whisky.

I put it down, suddenly feeling like I'm intruding. I didn't come here to sneak around like a stalker. But it's a unique chance to gain a glimpse into the life of the man I've worked for all this time.

Being a personal assistant is a strangely intimate job, especially when working in the private sector for a wealthy CEO. I've been a PA all my life, and the role varies widely from company to company and boss to boss. When I was training, I was told the job is to free an executive's time from administrative and organizational chores so they can concentrate on strategic tasks. These chores can include organizing events and conferences, booking and arranging travel and accommodation, liaising with staff and clients, anything I can do to leave my boss with more time to spend on the big picture stuff. I also oversee the other PAs and head secretaries in the building.

But that's not all. Some bosses require their PA to do more personal tasks, such as booking appointments for doctors or dentists or hairdressers, or organizing cleaners or maintenance work at their home. I know where Nick gets his hair cut, and the name of his GP. I remind him when it's one of his children's birthdays, and occasionally I've researched gifts for them, although he usually buys them. I know his tastes in food and drink, and which sports he likes to watch. And because Olivia was my best friend, she also gave me a few other little insights, like when she told me he's a bad sleeper, and she sometimes woke to find him gone in the night, and found him on the deck with a glass of whisky, looking out over the harbor.

But there's so much about him I don't know. Despite the oddly intimate nature of our working relationship, we're both aware of the line separating our professional and personal lives, and we never, ever cross it. He might ask me if I'm doing anything interesting at the weekend by way of conversation, but he's never asked me about my social life, or if I'm dating anyone. He's commented once or twice when I've worn a new suit, but he's never complimented me on my appearance, and he's never touched me inappropriately; he's never even looked at me in a way that could be construed as improper.

I can predict his actions in a given situation, but I can't tell what he's thinking, and I certainly have no idea what he's feeling. If I'm perfectly honest, sometimes I'm not even sure he likes me. He's never rude, and he's always polite and respectful. But he's… distant, in a way he isn't with other people.

My fingers brush the notepad next to the whisky glass. I shouldn't… I mustn't… But I'm consumed by curiosity. What was he making notes on late at night, while he was in bed? What couldn't wait until the morning? Was he jotting down something business-related that sprung into his mind, so he didn't forget when he woke up? Writing to a friend?

I pick up the pad. The lines of writing contain words he's crossed out where he's obviously been playing with different phrases. Beneath these, he's re-written them with the new words. With some surprise, I realize it's poetry. Before I can think better of it, I read a few lines.

> You haunt me in the dark hours.
> I paint pictures of you on the canvas of my mind
> To fill the lonely hollow inside me.
> I hunger. I ache. I yearn for you.

I put it down hurriedly. It's obviously about Olivia. It's filled with raw emotion, and it portrays the pain he feels about losing her that clearly isn't diminishing with time.

I turn away, wishing I hadn't read it. It's time I got going.

I walk over to the chair, pick up the track pants, tee, and the sneakers beneath, pop them in the bag I brought with me, and leave the room.

After flicking off the lights, I walk back down the corridor, out the front door and lock it behind me, and reset the alarm. Then I get in my car, put the bag beside me on the front seat, and start the engine.

The car makes an unmistakable squeal as I turn the corner, and I blow out a breath. I think the brake pads need changing. Great, just before Christmas.

I feel unsettled and guilty. I scold myself as I drive, my hands gripping the wheel hard. I haven't done anything terrible. He's the one who asked me to pick up his clothes, and it's not as if I had a soak in his bath or curled up in his bed. The only thing I did that I shouldn't have was read the poem.

In the middle of the night, when I'm lying awake staring up at the ceiling, I admit I've harbored the fantasy that he's ready to move on. I've imagined him calling me into his office. He'd be sitting on the edge of his desk, and his blue eyes would meet mine as he'd ask me to close the door. He'd tell me he has feelings for me, and has for a long time, but he finally feels able to express them. And then he'd kiss me, something I've dreamed about for a long, long time.

Clearly, though, he's not done with his grief.

And yet, why is he sleeping in another room? Why not stay in the room he shared with his wife, if he wants to feel close to her? Unless maybe it's too difficult. It's hard when you're that obsessed with someone and yet you know they're out of your reach.

Hell, I should know.

I pull up in the hospital car park, wincing at the squeal of the brakes. I turn the lights and engine off, and sit there in the dark.

I could write a novel—a whole series of novels—about obsession.

How long have I been in love with Nick? Well, how long have I known him? It'll be twelve years on December the first. So... eleven years and three hundred and thirty-five days, then.

It's a long time to be in love with someone, and not have it returned.

I met Olivia first, shortly after I moved to Wellington, and we established a firm friendship before she told me her husband was looking for a new PA, and she thought I might fit the job perfectly. I can still remember the moment I met him. She took me up to his office and knocked on his door, and he stood up as we went in and smiled at me. Just like I'd read what happened in books, my heart skipped a beat.

At first, all I knew was that I found him attractive. I didn't have any concerns about working for him when I felt that way. It was clear he was devoted to her and she to him, and I had no worries about anything untoward happening. I like to consider myself professional, and I would never date a boss. And anyway, I wouldn't initiate a relationship with a married man.

But time passed, and gradually my feelings toward him deepened, and I fell in love with him without meaning to. He's handsome and kind, warm and funny—to others, anyway—and good to his family. I couldn't help myself.

I've never told him, and I never told Olivia.

But I'm the most horrible person in the whole world, because one of the first things I felt when I heard she'd died was a tiny swell of hope because Nick was free.

Straight afterward, grief hit me like a sledgehammer, and it's been there ever since, twisted up with guilt to such an extent that it's prevented me from telling Nick how I feel about him. Still, I hoped that eventually something might develop between us.

But seeing the poem has made me feel as if I've read his diary. It was so intimate. I knew he missed Olivia. Of course he does. She was his wife, and I saw them together enough times to know it was a good marriage. I hadn't realized the depth of his grief, though. It's been nearly two years. I thought he was getting over her. But clearly, he's nowhere close to doing that.

I pick up the bag, get out of the car and lock it, then walk over to the maternity ward. It's pointless to think about him in a romantic way. I've trained myself over the years to push those feelings away, and although sometimes I fantasize there can be something between us, I've got to keep my feelings locked down, or I'm going to go mad.

I go through the main doors into the brightly lit corridors, hugging the bag to my chest. Nick might not be able to move on, but I'm going to have to eventually, for two reasons.

The first is out of my hands. I'm worried about my sister, and it's too expensive to fly up to see her all the time. I need to move closer to her so I can be there when she needs me.

But the second reason is because of how I feel about Nick. If I don't leave, I'm still going to be here when it's time for me to retire. I'll still be single, and I'll still be alone, because I'll never be able to stop hoping something will happen between us while I work there, and deep down I know it's never going to.

If I leave, maybe then I'll be able to put him out of my mind and get on with my life.

Musing on that, I open the door to the waiting room, and go inside.

Chapter Three

Nick

I look up from the magazine as someone appears in the waiting area and, like a cartoon character, I do a double take. It's Elena, but she's not wearing her suit and high heels. Now she's dressed in a light-blue T-shirt beneath a casual jacket and navy yoga pants with white sneakers. She's also pulled her hair back into a ponytail.

I can count the number of times I've seen her in civvies on the fingers of one hand—once or twice at a party, and a few times when she's called at the house to pick up Olivia. All those times she's been dressed smartly in a blouse, slacks, and heels. I've never seen her like this.

It's hardly unusual clothing, but she looks younger and sexy and hot, and she takes my breath away.

"Hey." I put the magazine down and get up.

She comes over and holds out the bag in her hand. "Change of clothes. Any news?"

I take it from her, trying not to stare at the different shape of her face now she's pulled her hair back off it. "Apparently she's fully dilated. It's not going to be long now."

"Oh, how exciting." She smiles. "I might have to wait for the big moment."

"It'll be cool to have someone to celebrate with. I'll go and change."

"Want a coffee?"

"I've already had about a dozen, but yeah, why not?"

I head to the Gents', where I take off my suit, put on the tee and track pants, and pull on the sneakers. I stuff the suit in the bag. It's about time it went to the dry cleaners anyway.

I pause on the way out and look in the mirror. My eyes have dark shadows under them, and they look haunted. I feel as if my guilt shines out of them like a beacon, so bright everyone can see it.

But they can't, of course. I need to get a grip. My daughter is about to give birth. I have to concentrate on her and put everything else out of my mind.

I head out to the waiting room, toss the bag onto a chair, and take the coffee Elena holds out. "Thanks."

"Are there many other women in labor tonight?" she asks, taking the seat next to mine.

"Two, I think. One of them is screaming a lot." My brow furrows. "That must be tough for her husband."

"Mm. How's Callum doing?"

"Okay. He'll be glad when it's over. That's when the fun'll start."

She chuckles. "Yeah."

I study her profile as she looks into her coffee cup. She has pale skin that catches the sun easily, and more than once she's come to work with a sunburned nose in the summer, so I know she must spend time outdoors when it's warm. Her drawn-back hair exposes the delicate skin behind her ears and the curve of her neck. Usually her lips bear a dark-pink or coral-colored lipstick, but tonight they're a natural pale pink.

In the office, over the years I've been careful to avoid talking about anything too personal. It seemed inappropriate, and with all the stuff in the news about sexual harassment nowadays, it makes sense to keep working relationships as professional as possible. But here, tonight, with Kora struggling to bring life into the world, the moon hanging in the dark sky outside, the rich smell and taste of the coffee, and only the two of us in the quiet of the room, it feels oddly intimate, and suddenly I have to ask.

"Did you not want children?" I ask. "Or could you not have them?"

She lifts her gaze to mine, surprised. For a long moment she studies my face. I think I've shocked her.

"I'm sorry," I murmur. "I shouldn't have asked."

"No, it's okay. It's just… you've never asked me anything like that before."

"I know. I apologize if it's inappropriate."

"It's not inappropriate, Nick. Not tonight, with your little girl giving birth in there." She gives a small smile, then takes a deep breath. "I wanted them. My husband didn't."

I feel a twist of pity deep inside. "Oh… I'm sorry."

"It's okay. I made my peace with it a long time ago."

Should I press her further? I have to admit, I'm curious about her marriage. I know she was single when she moved to Wellington, but I know nothing about her ex. I asked Olivia about him once, but she said she didn't know anything, and that Elena didn't like to talk about him.

"You broke up with him before you came to Wellington, didn't you?" I decide that if she gives me any sign of not wanting to talk, I'll back away.

She props her feet on the small table. "Yes. We'd been married for ten years."

"That's quite a long time."

"Yeah. The tin anniversary. Not very exciting." Her lips curve up, and then she sighs. "If I'd known he didn't want children at the beginning, things would have been very different, but I don't think he knew himself until I pushed the issue."

"Then he admitted it?"

"It took a while. He kept saying he wasn't ready. It wasn't until I was in my mid-thirties that I started to get impatient, and one day I made him sit down and talk about it. And he admitted he didn't want them."

"That must have been hard."

"Yes." She sips her coffee. Silence falls between us, but it's not an awkward one. I can see she's thinking about what to say. "It was a difficult marriage," she says eventually, slowly. "Kids were just the last on a long list of problems between us."

I lean forward, elbows on my knees, and sip my coffee. "Marriage can be hard even when things are relatively smooth. It makes it a lot harder when one party has issues."

"Oh, he had a lot of those." She speaks fervently, with feeling. "Not that I'm perfect," she adds hastily. "I'm not saying it was all his fault. I understand it takes two to tango."

"Yes, that's true. But in my experience one party often works harder in a relationship to make it work."

She meets my eyes then. "Are you talking about yourself or Olivia?"

I look into my coffee cup. I've never spoken about my marriage to anyone. Not my kids, not a counselor, not a friend. But it seems to be the night for confessions. "She also had a lot of issues stemming from her past. She wasn't an easy person to be with at times." I look back at Elena, at her forest-green eyes. "I'm not trying to say your experience was normal, just that I can empathize, a little."

"I never realized," she whispers. "You always seemed… happy."

"I was content. That doesn't mean it wasn't hard work sometimes. She was a free spirit, and I had to learn there were many things she didn't want to talk about, and there were times when I had to let her be alone. It didn't come naturally." I think about the many occasions early in our marriage when I tried to convince her to talk to me, and all it did was make her cry. "But in the end I had to choose between taking what she was prepared to give me, or moving on. I chose to stay, to accept that marriage isn't about owning the other person or forcing them into a mold of the perfect spouse." I realize how that must sound. "I'm not criticizing you, by the way. I know sometimes it's too big an adjustment to make and you have to walk to stay sane."

"I know, it's okay. I had to make the choice of whether to accept his decision and stay, or whether to leave. At the time, I thought it was possible I might meet someone else and still have children. It was why I walked, in the end. Not that it did me much good." She gives a sad smile.

"You never met anyone else you considered having a family with?"

She sips her coffee and lowers her gaze. "No."

I'm not sure what to say about that. It seems odd to me that she hasn't met a single suitable guy. She's beautiful and intelligent, and I'm sure she'd be a warm and loving companion. "I'm surprised men aren't falling over themselves to get to you," I tell her softly.

"There was someone," she admits. "But it didn't work out."

"Why not?"

"He was married." A touch of color appears on her cheekbones.

"I'm sorry. That must have been hard."

"Yeah." She finishes off her coffee and clears her throat. "Do you believe in soul mates?"

"No."

She looks up at me, clearly surprised. She was expecting me to say 'of course,' and that Olivia was mine.

I lean back and stretch out my legs. "I can't remember who said it, but a famous actor who'd been married four times said he didn't have three failed marriages—he had three successful ones that came to an end. People change over time, and a couple can grow apart. That doesn't mean they weren't right for each other when they got together. I think the term soul mates was invented by people who had been together a long time and knew each other intimately, and couldn't imagine being without one another." I shrug. "And I think men have lower expectations than women. Girls look for the perfect guy, the perfect relationship, wedded bliss. Men just hope to find someone willing to put up with all their faults."

She smiles at that, the skin crinkling at the corner of her eyes. "Do you think you have a lot of faults?"

"Oh, hundreds."

"I know you well enough to know that isn't true," she scoffs.

"You'd be surprised." I smile back. "I'm sorry your marriage didn't work out. You'd have made a great mum."

She swallows hard. "That's a nice thing to say."

"I didn't mean to upset you."

"It's okay, I'm not upset. Like I said, I've made my peace with it all. In the beginning, I hated him a lot. But as time's gone on, I've grown to understand that he never meant to hurt me. He'd had a terrible upbringing, and he was very confused."

"Confused?" It's a strange word to pick.

She gets up then, throws her coffee cup in the bin, and goes over to the window. After a while, I realize she'd not going to reply.

"Is he still up in the Bay of Islands?" I ask. I know that's where she comes from, and where her family still lives.

She turns then, folding her arms, and leans against the wall. "No. He took his own life shortly after I left him."

My jaw drops. "Oh Jesus, Elena…" I stand up and walk forward, stopping a few feet away from her.

She looks up and meets my eyes. "It's all right. It was all over a long time ago."

I have so many questions. Did he kill himself *because* she left him? I sense she's not telling me everything. But something in her manner stops me from asking. She's confessed a lot today. I don't think she's comfortable revealing anything else.

"Did Olivia know?" I whisper.

She nods. "She didn't tell you?"

I look down at my own coffee cup, finish the last mouthful, and toss it in the bin. "No."

Clearly, my wife kept other people's secrets as well as her own.

Elena opens her mouth to reply, but at that moment footsteps echo on the tiles, and I turn to see Kora's twin, Theo, and my youngest son, Jacob, coming into the waiting room.

Theo comes up and hugs me first, and then Jacob follows. "Any news?" Theo asks.

"It's not going to be long now," I assure them. My head is still spinning from Elena's revelation. I want to ask for more details, but she moves to kiss Jacob's cheek, and the moment's gone.

Maybe it's for the best. I have other things to think about right now.

I smile at Kora's twin. The two of them have a special bond, and I'm not surprised he's here. "Where's Victoria?" I ask him, referring to his wife.

"At home," he replies. "She's been working hard today and she's tired, so I said I'd ring her when the babies are born."

His wife has been organizing the decoration of her new health spa near the Abel Tasman National Park. She's been working flat out, so I'm not surprised she's exhausted.

"I can't believe it's nearly time," Jacob states. "All that waiting! And now the babies are nearly here. How's Kora doing?"

"She's good," I reply. "First labors can be longer with twins, so I imagine she's pretty tired, but Callum said she's staying positive."

At that moment, the door to the delivery room opens, and Callum strides out. "They can see the baby's hair!" he declares. His eyes are wide, a little wild. Then he turns around and runs back in.

Jacob chuckles. "The proud father," he says.

"Can't believe she's got to go through it twice," Theo comments. "Poor Kora."

"Poor Callum!" Jacob grins. "Kora's got a firm handshake—I bet she's crushing his hand every time she has a contraction!"

We all chuckle, and then I begin to pace the floor. I know I'm only the grandad, but suddenly the anxiety is more than I can bear.

Elena watches me as the two boys chat. I try not to look at her.

Luckily, it's only another five minutes before Callum comes out.

"It's a girl," he says, beaming. "I've got a daughter!"

We all cheer. Relief washes over me, pure and simple, at the thought that Kora has delivered one of the babies successfully. To my surprise my throat tightens, and my eyes prick with tears.

Theo and Jacob rush up to give Callum a bearhug. I turn to Elena, not really surprised to see her eyes shining. She laughs and blows her nose on a tissue, then comes up and puts her arms around me.

I hug her back, filled with emotion.

"Congratulations," she murmurs.

"Thank you."

She moves back a little to look at me. Her green eyes shine. Her lips part. They look beautiful and soft, and suddenly I feel the weight of the past two years of being alone lying heavily on my soul. I like kissing. I miss it.

And I can't think of anyone I'd rather kiss than Elena.

Without thinking, I lower my head and press my lips to hers.

I feel rather than hear her inhale. I move back and look at her, but she doesn't lower her arms, and she doesn't move away. So I kiss her again.

It's an innocent kiss, just a touch of our lips, and it only lasts a few seconds.

Then awareness of where I am and who's standing nearby hits me. I pull back, and she lowers her arms as the others walk up to us.

Something has changed between us tonight. It's my fault; I turned the conversation intimate. I kissed her. Now, with my boys standing before us, I feel a strong sweep of guilt. I criticized their mother. I said I didn't believe in soul mates. I was married to Olivia for thirty-four years. Surely she deserves more loyalty than that?

Smoothly, Elena turns to Callum and reaches up to give him a kiss on the cheek. Jacob grabs me for a hug. And the moment passes without anyone noticing.

"I'd better go back in," Callum says. "I just wanted to let you know."

"Good luck." I watch him stride off, back to the delivery room.

"How long did it take between Theo and Kora's births?" Jacob asks me.

"About fifteen minutes, as I recall."

Elena clears her throat. "I'd better get going, guys."

"Aw," Theo says, "don't you want to wait and see what the other one is?"

"Text me when you find out," she says. "It was lovely to be here for the big moment." She smiles at them and picks up her handbag. "Bye, Nick. See you tomorrow."

"Yes, see you." I force my lips into a smile.

She turns and walks away, out of the room.

"A girl," Theo states. "I have another niece!" He already adores his brother Ben's little girl, Estella.

"Kora wanted a girl," Jacob replies. "I wonder what the next one will be?"

I leave them talking, and go over to pour myself a cup of water from the cooler.

My hand is shaking a little.

I kissed Elena. God, what was I thinking? I was caught up in the moment, that was all. It was a celebratory kiss, and it meant no more than the kiss on the cheek she gave Callum.

Except of course it did. Don't fool yourself, Nick. I knew perfectly well what I was doing. It was born out of the intimate moment we exchanged. And it had more than a little to do with the feelings I've had for her for a long time, if I'm honest with myself.

But she's gone, and it's done. I have to put it to the back of my mind and concentrate on Kora.

In just over fifteen minutes, Callum comes back out to announce the second baby has been delivered successfully, and it's a boy. Fraternal twins, the same as Kora and Theo, and the same as Olivia and her twin, Margaret, who died when she was twenty-one. History repeating itself, an echo through time.

I hug him, and then half an hour later, I go in and see my daughter, and get my first cuddle of my new grandchildren. I hold the baby boy in my arms, and I can't help but think back to when Theo and Kora were born.

I feel so guilty that I said Olivia wasn't my soul mate. I was married to her for a long time, and that wasn't fair. I loved her with all my heart, and I told her I'd never love anyone else. I'm not going to break that promise now.

My first loyalty will always be to my family. I can't change that. I won't change that. Tonight was a slip, and I won't make it again.

I put it firmly out of my mind, and kiss my grandson's head.

Chapter Four

Six weeks later

Elena

It's the week before Christmas, Friday the seventeenth of December, and the day of the office party. The whole building is in a festive mood. The secretaries have erected a huge tree in the main office, and all their desks bear tinsel and dancing Santas and other glittery knick-knacks.

I have a tree in my office, the same one I use every year, a realistic dark-green plastic conifer that sits on a square table in the corner, with warm-white fairy lights and red and gold decorations. I also have a big bowl of potpourri on my desk. Usually I make my own, but this year I bought it. The dried slices of orange and lemon, sticks of cinnamon, cranberries, twigs of rosemary, and cloves make the whole top floor smell festive.

It's one p.m. Officially, office hours end at five-thirty, but because it's the office party the merrymaking will begin around four p.m. and go on well into the evening.

Traditionally, I pop my head into the main office when I finish work, have a drink with the head secretaries, then leave them to it. The youngsters don't want their boss hanging around, and their music isn't usually to my taste anyway, as I'm a jazz girl first and foremost.

The top floor is quiet. Nick and the boys are in a meeting in the conference room. I've caught up on my dictation, letters, and filing, finished my phone calls, and completed the staffing report I needed to do.

I figure I can sneak out for half an hour and grab myself a drink and a sandwich at the nearby coffee shop. After letting one of the other secretaries know I'm going out, I grab my jacket and bag and head to the elevator.

Within fifteen minutes, I'm sitting at a table by the window overlooking the waterfront, sipping an iced coffee and nibbling on a turkey and cranberry sandwich.

It's a beautiful afternoon, and the summer sun dazzles my eyes as the rays bounce off the ocean. Most people sitting at the other tables have bags of Christmas presents at their feet. Normally I love this time of year, with the knowledge that I have a week off coming soon. I can visit my family without stressing about being away from the office, and I can also relax on my own and recover from the stress of the pre-Christmas weeks. Usually I'm buzzing with excitement about buying presents and researching recipes for Christmas food.

But right now I feel flat and uninspired. I've bought and wrapped my family's presents, but whereas normally I spend hours tying them up with ribbon and making my own gift tags and cards, this year I've used basic paper and shop-bought cards, and at home I don't have a single decoration up, not even a tree. I haven't been able to muster the enthusiasm to do it.

I look out at the couples walking along the quay, hand in hand, and watch a young guy grab his girl by the waist and kiss her. She laughs and pushes him away, but doesn't object when he does it again, eventually sliding her arms around his waist and cuddling up to him.

They're so young, and they seem so in love. They have all their lives ahead of them, years of being engaged, married, having kids, growing old together.

They have no idea how lucky they are.

When Nick kissed me on Halloween, the night his daughter gave birth to Jamie and Rachel, the twins, I thought my heart was going to leap out of my chest, run down the corridor, and bounce all the way out of the building. I'd been dreaming of it for so long. And even though it was brief—just a peck, no tongues—it was as terrific as I'd hoped.

It was the culmination of an intimate moment, a sharing of hearts, and as I walked away, I was filled with hope that it might mean Nick was ready to move on.

I came into work the next morning nervous and excited. I spent all day waiting for him to call me into his office to discuss the kiss.

I waited the rest of the week. And the week after that.

By the end of November, I realized it wasn't going to happen.

Either the kiss hadn't meant anything to him—it truly had been a spur-of-the-moment thing born out of relief after the news that Kora's baby had been born. Or it *had* meant something, but afterward he'd regretted it, and had decided not to take it any further.

I went home that night and sobbed my heart out. And then a ball of fury began to grow in my stomach, and spread out through me until all I felt was resentment and indignation.

What was wrong with me? I no longer expected children, but didn't I deserve to be loved? How dare he string me along for a whole month? In fact, for twelve years?!

Of course, he hadn't strung me along—he'd never given me any indication that he was interested in me, apart from that kiss. It was my own fault I was still sitting there, waiting for him, like a dog sitting by her master's table, begging for scraps.

I turn my gaze back to my iced coffee and stir it vigorously. I sound pathetic, and I hate it. I've never been the sort of person to feel sorry for herself. Whenever I feel myself sinking into self-pity, I've always pulled myself up by the bootstraps—or slingbacks in my case—counted my blessings, and taken some positive action. I need to do that now.

Come on, Elena. What's wrong with you?

My phone buzzes where it sits on the table, and I glance at it. The screen reads 'Liz'.

Concern immediately shoots through me. I ring my sister every morning at ten, when I know she's gone to the shops on her own. She hardly ever rings me, especially once she's home.

I slot my bluetooth headset into my ear and answer it. "Hello?"

"Ellie. It's me." She's whispering. I can tell immediately that something's wrong.

"Hey, where are you?"

"I'm at home. I'm in the bathroom."

I go cold. "What's happened?"

"He found the money I'd been putting away for Christmas. It's all gone, Ellie. All of it." She bursts into tears.

I cover my face with my free hand. "Oh, Liz…"

For a long moment, we don't say anything. I wait as she tries to stifle her sobs, my brain working furiously.

My brother-in-law, Keith, used to be a good friend of mine. He was generous, funny, and rather loud, an extrovert who thought it was his place in life to put everyone at ease and make them laugh. He and Liz have been together since she was twenty-five, and they had a strong marriage with hardly any bumps in the road, as far as I know. The two of them looked after me when my husband took his own life. I'm not sure I'd still be here now if it wasn't for them.

And then, two years ago, Keith had an accident. He was cleaning the gutters at home, and he fell off a ladder. He damaged his spine, and ended up in a wheelchair.

His fury at the injustice of it all overwhelmed him, and it gave him a chip on his shoulder the size of Australia. He's changed so much, he's unrecognizable from the genial man he used to be. He's angry at the world, and resentful of Liz, because she can walk and he can't. He's become rude and aggressive, and even though he's not physically abusive toward her, as far as I know, he makes her life an absolute misery.

He demands our attention and help because he thinks he deserves it. And it's impossible to argue, because how do you tell a disabled person who is in pain and has their freedom curtailed because of their injury to pull themselves together and buck up? The truth is that Liz can walk and lead a normal life, and he can't, and he can always throw that in her face.

I know he's obviously got PTSD and severe depression, and we've tried to help with that, to take him to see various doctors who've prescribed a plethora of drugs. But he refuses to take them, preferring instead to drink his problems away. When he's not yelling at Liz, he's zoned out and just sits there watching TV. And she lets him, because he's just so hard to deal with otherwise.

The worst part of it is the money. Before his accident, he was a carpenter, and quite a good one, but he's unable to work now. Unable, or unwilling—the truth is arguable. I know I'm bitter about it, but I'm sure there are ways he could use his skills to make a little money. Even if crafting furniture was too difficult, he could do carving, or make dolls' house furniture or something. I like to think I would have, if I was in his position, with a family to support. His only son is grown now, but he's at university, and struggling for money, like all students do.

He gets a small state disability pension. Liz is unskilled and works two cleaning jobs. So they have very little income, much of which Keith spends on alcohol. Liz hides the rest of her earnings and does her best to manage, but I have to help her out a lot, because otherwise they'd have no roof over their heads and no food to eat. I also help their son when I can.

Our parents exist on the state pension and a small private pension my dad has, so they wouldn't be able to help. Not that they know much about what's happening. Neither Liz nor I have ever been very close to either of them, and I don't blame her for wanting to keep the details to herself.

Liz was putting a tiny amount aside out of their allowance to have a nice Christmas dinner with her son. And now it's obviously all gone. It's not the end of the world. I can just about afford to buy them a turkey. But it's the principle of it. Things have been gradually getting worse, and I knew eventually she was going to break.

"I'm so sorry," I murmur. "I wish there was something I could do." I fly up to the Bay of Islands where she lives as often as I can to give her moral support, but it's not cheap. My savings have been whittled away, and now I'm scrimping and scraping to make ends meet as much as they are.

And now this.

"Liz, you have to do something," I tell her, somewhat tearfully. But I know it's pointless. For ages I've been telling her the same thing. I've tried to convince her to leave him. To move in with me, or even to go to a shelter. I know his abuse will never, ever stop until she proves she's not willing to put up with it. But she won't. She says marriage is 'for better and for worse,' and what kind of person would it make her if she walked out on him after his terrible accident?

"I just need a little cash," she says. "The rent's due on Monday, and I don't get paid until Friday."

I close my eyes. "Okay."

"I'm sorry," she whispers.

"It's all right. I'll come up, and I'll bring the money." I could just transfer it into her account, but it's a joint account, and I run the risk of him seeing it and withdrawing it before she can. I've tried to convince her to open her own account, but she sees it as a betrayal of her loyalty to him. I don't get it. But I love her, so I try not to let it make me angry. Plus I want to see her. I know she feels better when I'm there.

"Are you sure?" she asks. "I know the flights are expensive…"

"Don't worry about it. I'll give you a call when I'm organized. Until then… are you going to be okay?"

"He's been drinking for a few hours and he's practically comatose. I'll keep out of his way. I'll be fine."

"All right. Speak soon."

"Thank you, Ellie. I am so very sorry."

"Love you." I finish the call and pull the headset out of my ear.

I feel a sweep of hopelessness as I search on my phone for available flights for tonight or tomorrow. There are a couple of seats left, but the cheapest, even with carry-on only, is three hundred dollars each way. Sheesh. There's no way I can afford that. I'm going to have to drive up. That sucks. It's around twelve hours from Wellington to the Bay of Islands, and I don't really want to drive all that way with my car's brakes squealing.

When I left Ricky, and I stayed with Liz and Keith, they helped me through it, dealing with all the practical side of things as well as supporting me emotionally. Without my sister especially, I'm not sure I would have made it. I owe her big time. I've been considering moving back to the bay for a while, and now I need to make the decision.

I look out at the couple who are still kissing on the quay, and I think of Nick. I don't want to leave him. But I have to, for my mental health, for financial reasons, and to help my sister. There's no decision to be made anymore.

I pull up my emails and study the one sitting at the top of my inbox. It's been there for two days. I've hit reply more times than I can count, but each time I've closed it down before I can send it.

I press reply. Then I type a short message.

My finger hovers over the send button. Then, before I can psyche myself out of it again, I press send.

I wait for the panic I'm sure is going to sweep over me, but oddly all I feel is relief that I've finally made a decision. It's done. I'm going to move on. Start a new life. Even though I'll miss my old one, there is something exciting about starting again. I've stagnated here. A new challenge might be just what I need to give me a new lease of life.

I put the remainder of the sandwich and the coffee cup in the bin. Then I make my way back to my office.

*

At five-thirty p.m., I turn off my computer, wash up my coffee mug, and collect my handbag and coat.

The office is nearly empty. Kora's still on maternity leave, and because it's Friday night, Ben has flown home to be with Heloise and his daughter. Theo left early for a dinner date with Vic. Both Lucas and Jacob have gone downstairs to the party. Only Nick is still here, finishing off something in his office, with the door closed.

I've waited until the end of the day to speak to him because I'm a coward, and I know this is going to be a difficult conversation. At least, I think it will be. It's possible he'll listen, then nod and go back to his laptop. I wouldn't be surprised by anything he says or does at this point.

I fold my coat over my left arm, take a deep breath, and knock on his door.

His voice comes through muffled. "Uh…"

I frown, my hand on the door handle. "Nick?"

"Just a minute."

"Are you okay in there?" He's had the door shut for about ten minutes, which is fairly unusual, unless he has a meeting.

"Yeah…" He mumbles something, and then I'm sure I hear him swear. Finally, he gives a big sigh and says, "Come in."

Cautiously, not sure what I'm going to find, I open the door and enter.

He's standing in the center of the room in a Santa costume. A complete one, the red jacket and trousers trimmed with white fur, a black belt, and black boots. A red hat sits on the table. The long, naturally white beard he's been cultivating completes the look.

His hair is all ruffled, and he looks harassed.

"Checking your list twice?" I ask.

"Very funny." He huffs another sigh. "I'm delivering toys to Auckland hospital tomorrow and I was trying it on. The zipper has stuck." He tugs at the hidden zipper on the front of the jacket. The strip of material that covers it is stuck in the teeth.

I press my lips together, trying not to laugh, and fail.

"Yeah, yeah," he grumbles. "Laugh at my misery, why don't you."

"Come here." I put down my coat and handbag, go up to him, and take the zipper in my fingers. Carefully, I wiggle the material to try to release the teeth.

"What do you want for Christmas, little girl?" He waggles his eyebrows at me.

"That sounds creepy. I hope you're not going to say that to the kids."

He chuckles. "Maybe not. I do like playing Santa though. I wish I could make wishes come true for real."

I think about what I'd wish for, and how he could make it come true if he really wanted. But I could never ask him.

I finally release the fabric from the metal teeth and slide the zipper down.

Underneath the suit, he's not wearing a shirt, and my fingers brush his bare chest. Ooh. That makes me go all melty inside.

"I thought I was going to have to go home like this." He sighs, lets the jacket slip down his back, and hangs it over a chair.

Wow. I've only ever seen him without a top several years ago at a pool party he held at his house. And it's an entirely different experience seeing him up close. I know he still goes to the gym, and he looks good for a sixty-year-old, lacking the usual soft paunch that accompanies guys of his age.

"You need a bit more padding," I point out. "Santa's supposed to be fat."

"I'll eat a few more Mars Bars before the big day." He grins. He toes off the big black boots, then slides off the red trousers. Luckily he's wearing his own trousers beneath the Santa suit or I might have fainted. He pulls on his shirt and does up a couple of buttons. "I keep meaning to ask—have you got the Grayson file?"

"Oh yes, sorry, I meant to return that to you." I run out to my desk, retrieve it, and walk back. He's followed me, and he's leaning against the doorpost, doing up the rest of the shirt buttons.

"Thanks." He takes the file. As he does, something makes him glance up, and he stills. I follow his gaze. A twig of mistletoe hangs from the frame.

I blink at it. Then I stare at him.

"I forgot that Kora put it there," he says, sounding embarrassed. She came into the office this morning to show off the twins.

"I... um..." I hadn't noticed it before as it's pinned to the inner door frame.

"Seems a shame to waste it," he murmurs. Then he smiles. "Merry Christmas, Elena." He steps closer, bends his head, and presses his lips to mine.

I'm so surprised, I just stand there. He kisses me once. But he doesn't move back. Instead, he lifts his head to look at me.

We study each other for what feels like an ice age. I'm too shocked to do anything but stare into his bright blue eyes.

I wait for him to move back. But he doesn't. Eventually, he turns and tosses the folder onto a nearby chair. Comes back and holds me by the upper arms. And kisses me again.

This one is not the kind of kiss one colleague gives to another when they find themselves under the mistletoe—a quick friendly peck, or a cheeky smacker that earns them a whack on the arm. It's not even like the kiss he gave me on Halloween—a gentle press of his lips against mine held for the extra few seconds that implied it was more than a celebration.

He tilts his head to the right, changing the angle, and kisses me properly. Okay, there are still no tongues, but it's not a peck. It's not cheeky. And it's not brief. It's a long, sensual smooch that makes my heart beat a rapid tattoo on my ribs and sucks all the air out of my lungs.

When he finally lifts his head, the look in his eyes gives me goosebumps. His gaze holds a touch of amusement, and a whole heap of heat. This Nick is clearly anything but saintly.

I've waited so long for him to look at me like that. Months, if not years. But it's too little, too late.

I swallow hard, and say, "I quit."

Chapter Five

Nick

I stare at Elena. "Sorry?"

She clears her throat and takes a step back. "I resign, Nick. I'll work out my four-week notice, and then I'm leaving."

My jaw drops, and horror fills me. Holy shit.

Despite my intention to wipe it from my mind, I've relived our Halloween kiss over and over again for the last six weeks.

I know it was wrong of me to kiss her out of the blue like that, without making sure it was what she wanted. She could have slapped me at the very least, sued me for sexual harassment at the worst. But she didn't, and neither did she push me away. Instead, she gave a beautiful little sigh as she leaned into me, resting her hands on my chest.

The softness of her lips, the subtle smell of her perfume... they've haunted me every night as I lie awake in the dark. It's driven me mad. And when she came into my office tonight, and she was standing there beneath the mistletoe, I gave in to the desire that's been simmering and kissed her again, convinced it would be well received.

Boy, did I get that wrong!

"Jesus, Elena... I'm so sorry... I totally misread the signs. I thought it was what you wanted." Is she really quitting? "Please don't leave. I won't do it again, I swear."

She picks up her jacket and hugs it to her. She looks pale and upset. "It's not because of the kiss, Nick. I came in here to hand in my notice."

A silence falls between us. It wasn't the kiss?

"Why?" I whisper.

She bites her bottom lip and looks down. I'm suddenly conscious I'm not wearing shoes and my shirt is undone. I've been so fucking inappropriate. Jesus, Nick.

She doesn't answer. I wonder then whether it had anything to do with the first time I kissed her. I assumed because she didn't react badly that she'd been okay with it, but has she been worrying about it since that night?

"Is it because I kissed you on Halloween, when the twins were born?"

Still, she doesn't say anything. Her mouth opens and closes as if she's trying to speak, but the words refuse to come.

I feel a flare of anger. Why has she waited so long to voice her objections? "Elena, please. We're both grownups. Let's talk about this."

She winces. "It's partly because of that kiss."

"If you thought it was inappropriate, you should have told me."

"Don't be angry with me." She stops, and her eyes fill with tears.

I'm so shocked, I can only stare at her. In all the years she's worked for me, I've never seen her tearful. Occasionally I've come across one of the other secretaries sitting in her office with her, sniffling into a tissue. But even when she's had to deal with difficult customers, or when bad news has come like Rebecca's accident or the death of my father, she's always remained calm and in control.

When Olivia died, I rang her at home to tell her, half expecting her to burst into tears. Instead, though, she asked me how I was and how the boys and Kora were doing, and then we discussed the funeral for a few minutes. She asked if there was anything she could do, and made me promise to call her if I needed help. But I still never saw or heard her cry.

"I'm not angry at you," I tell her with feeling. "Of course I'm not. I'm furious with myself. I shouldn't have done it. I'd say it was a spur-of-the-moment thing, but we both know it wasn't, and it's been coming for a while. That doesn't mean I should have given in to it, though."

She looks up then and meets my eyes. "What?"

I feel a flash of impatience. "Come on, Elena. I've tried to ignore it. I can't pretend any longer. I have feelings for you—you must know that. And I think it's possible you might have feelings for me. I can't fight it anymore."

Her eyes still glisten, but now fury fills them. "I must know that? Of course I didn't know! I wasn't even sure if you liked me!"

I stare at her. "What?"

"You've always kept your distance, Nick."

"I'm your boss, I've had to."

"Yes, but… you never gave me any sign you were interested, until Halloween. And then, I thought maybe the kiss meant something, but it's been six weeks. I've been waiting for you to say something. But you've not given any indication that it's been on your mind. Why have you waited so long?"

"I… don't know." Suddenly, I have no idea, and I feel a touch of panic. "I wasn't ready."

"Because of Olivia?" Her eyes blaze.

I don't say anything, but I can see she takes that as a yes. I don't know what to say. I can't explain my reasoning to her.

She turns away, but she doesn't walk out. Instead, she drops her jacket and bag back onto the chair and goes over to the window. Folding her arms, she stares out at the late afternoon sun for a moment. I study her back, feeling helpless. Finally, she turns back to face me.

"I know you loved your wife more than anything," she says, her voice so low it's almost inaudible. "And you always will. I do understand that."

"Elena…"

"Before she died, did she make you promise never to love anyone else?" Clearly, that's what she's been thinking all this time.

"No." I walk forward to stand a few feet in front of her, push my laptop aside, and perch on the edge of the desk. It's time I told her everything. She deserves that, at least.

"Did you know that Olivia had a twin?" I watch her eyebrows rise at the unexpected turn to the conversation.

"No," she whispers. "She never told me that."

"A fraternal one, like Kora and Theo, and like Kora's twins. Her name was Margaret—Maggie. She died on their twenty-first birthday."

"Oh no."

"Yeah. Olivia was so distraught she tried to take her own life."

Her expression softens, pity lighting her eyes. "Oh, poor Olivia."

"It's the reason why the family made the decision to move to New Zealand."

"Do the kids know?"

"They didn't, until recently. Kora found out when she went to the UK."

Some of the tension goes out of her. Her shoulders drop, and she perches on the edge of the table that holds my printer, a few feet away. "That must have been difficult," she says.

"Yeah, it was. Kora was very hurt that we'd never told her everything. I explained that Olivia didn't want them to know because it was part of her old life, and it was the only way she could cope, by shutting it out."

"I knew she was a troubled soul," Elena murmurs. "But I never knew why."

"Well, her birth mother died from a brain aneurysm. And there's something else, but I need to ask you to promise that you won't tell Kora and the boys."

"I promise," she says immediately.

"Maggie died in a motorbike accident—her boyfriend was driving. But what they didn't find out until the autopsy was that Maggie had suffered a huge brain aneurysm at the same time. They think it might be why her boyfriend came off the road—perhaps she suddenly felt a sharp pain, and cried out or something, and he got distracted. We'll never know. But it meant that there was a high chance it would happen to Olivia someday."

Her mouth forms an O. "So she lived with that permanently hanging over her."

"Yes."

"Did she tell you when she met you?"

I study my feet in their gray socks. "No. She kept that little nugget of information to herself for quite a few years. She didn't tell me until she turned fifty and she began having migraines. I assumed they were related to the change in hormones with the menopause, but one day after a particularly bad one, she told me about her mother and Maggie."

"That must have been so hard for you," Elena says.

"Yeah. To say the least. I was very angry with her for keeping it a secret. I wanted to take her to the hospital for a scan, but she refused. She said she didn't want to know. That really upset me. I said it wasn't fair on the kids, and that if a scan showed an aneurysm was forming, the doctors could do something about it. But she still refused. It drove a wedge between us for those last few years."

Elena's green eyes study me. "I never knew."

"I loved her still, of course I did. And in the end I had to respect her decision, because it was her body, and you can't force someone to go to hospital. And it's not as if she'd always been an easy woman to live with up until that point. You just said she was a troubled soul; you know what she was like."

She nods. "I knew there were things in her past that haunted her. I wondered whether she'd been assaulted or something. Somehow you didn't ask Olivia personal things like that."

I give a small smile. More than anyone, I know what she means. "Anyway. I guess you're wondering what all this has to do with you. The thing is… You became very close friends. She knew that you and I liked one another. And she wanted me to promise that, if and when something happened to her, we would get together."

She stares at me. Her jaw drops. "What?"

"She said to me, 'I know you like her, Nick. I know you find her attractive, and you both get on. You'd make the perfect couple.'"

"Oh my God."

"What was I supposed to say to that?" The frustration and anger I felt at the time floods me now. "She was my wife. She obviously thought she could drop dead at any moment, and yet she refused to be treated for it. And now she's trying to fix me up beyond the grave? I got very angry and told her she was being ridiculous. She tried to make me admit I liked you, and I denied it—vehemently."

"Of course you did." Elena's words placate me a little. She understands.

"But the thing is… I did like you. I was attracted to you. I have been from the first moment I saw you."

Her jaw drops again. She looks completely shocked. That amuses me, a bit. Is she really surprised?

"But I was married," I continue. "I had five kids. I was a loyal husband. I loved my wife with all my heart, and I would never have had an affair. So I ignored my feelings. And I made sure never to show any sign of how I felt."

We study each other for a long moment. She swallows, but she doesn't say anything.

I inhale, then blow out a long breath. This confession doesn't come easily to me. I've spent a long time keeping secrets. "And then she died."

Elena presses her lips together, and her eyes shine again.

"For the first year," I say, "I just reeled from grief and shock. Everyone said it would get better after the first anniversaries. First birthday without her. First wedding anniversary. The anniversary of her death. But it didn't. For several months after, I still hurt every day. And then…"

I pause as I think back to the moment. It was last Easter. As a company, we try to do fun things throughout the year to make the workplace more pleasurable. We'd bought everyone an Easter egg, and Kora, the boys, and I took turns to deliver them around the building. "I gave you an Easter egg," I tell her softly. "I called you into the office and thanked you for all your hard work, and I gave you the egg."

"I remember."

"You were standing almost exactly where you are now, with the light behind you. You laughed and said it was your favorite chocolate. You looked… beautiful."

She rubs her nose.

"I knew then that I was over the worst," I tell her. "I was moving on. And then the guilt hit me. I felt disloyal, traitorous, even. Because if I admitted I liked you now, it meant admitting I lied to Olivia when I told her I wasn't attracted to you. And that made me feel awful. So I ignored it. And I continued ignoring it." I get up from the desk and take a step closer to her. "But I'm not going to ignore it any longer."

I'd hoped my long, heartfelt confession would put to rest the heartache I'd felt over the past few years, and explain to her why I'd waited so long to tell her how I felt about her. I thought she'd maybe cry, and I'd put my arms around her, and she'd tell me everything was okay, and of course she understood.

But she doesn't.

Instead, she gets up and takes a step back. "Stop," she says.

I stop walking.

"You're too late," she continues.

I blink a few times. "Elena, please… I've tried to explain why I waited…"

"It doesn't matter." She speaks simply, her eyes wide and clear. "I've waited too long for you. I do understand, but it doesn't make any difference. You've… you've killed any feelings I had for you."

It's as if she's cracked open my chest, taken my heart in her hands, and squeezed it until it oozes between her fingers. "Ah, no, don't say that…"

"I've moved on, Nick. I've got another job. Last time I was up in the Bay of Islands, I had an interview. I got the job, and I've just accepted it today."

"Take it back," I tell her immediately. "Stay here, with me."

But she shakes her head, and her eyes are hard. "It's too late. And anyway, I've been excited at the thought of doing something different. I've stagnated here, Nick. I've done the same old job for so long, I do it now without even thinking about it. I need a change. I'm fifty on New Year's Day. And I'm done with my old life."

I can't believe it. Right at the moment I'm brave enough to open up to her, she closes me down and crushes me under her foot.

But I know she hasn't done it out of spite. I can see the hurt in her eyes, and I can sense her frustration. She has real feelings for me, and I've kept her waiting so long that she's afraid to trust me. She thinks I'm oblivious to her pain, and she's right. I was. I've only been thinking of myself. I'm a selfish bastard, and I don't deserve her.

How cruel life is.

Chapter Six

Elena

My head is spinning, and I feel a little dizzy. Oh no, please don't let me faint like a Victorian debutante. It's because I didn't eat my lunch. I've only had a bite of a sandwich today, and the shock has upset my system.

I sway, and immediately Nick is there, taking my hand and leading me toward the nearest chair. "Careful," he says. "Hold on, I'll get you some water."

He goes out, and within ten seconds comes back with a cup from the water cooler in my office. He hands it to me, and I sip it slowly.

"I'm okay," I insist. I brush a hand over my face. "I should go."

"You're not going anywhere until you've got some color in your cheeks."

I want to argue with him, to say he can't tell me what to do, but I don't have the energy. I slump in the seat, and I feel a wave of desperate despair.

Nick studies me for a second. Then he goes over to his desk and opens the top drawer. He extracts something, comes back, and pulls over another chair so he's sitting facing me. Then he reveals the object in his hand—a bar of chocolate. He opens it, breaks off a cube, and hands it to me.

I can't help but give a little smile as I take it from him and pop it in my mouth. The rich, creamy taste of the chocolate floods my mouth, grounding me, and the dizziness eases.

"You're too thin," he tells me. "You're not eating enough."

I poke my tongue out at him, and he gives a short laugh.

He has a piece himself, then leans forward, elbows on his knees. "There's something you're not telling me," he states. "I know it's none of my business. We've cultivated this relationship over the years where we've carefully ignored each other's personal lives, and it's possible you don't want to start now. But if you want to talk, I'd love to know what's bothering you, and if I can help."

When he said, *I have feelings for you—you must know that*, I felt a surge of anger and frustration, because I had no idea. How was I supposed to know that when he never gave me any sign?

But now, I can see how foolish I've been. The very fact that he's carefully kept his distance should have told me. He's so warm with everyone else. With other people—family, friends, customers, even other work colleagues, he's generous with his hugs and kisses on the cheek. He remembers details about their families and always asks after them. If I really think about it, it's only me he keeps his distance from.

Oh, I'm such an idiot.

Clearly, he's picked up on the fact that there may be another reason why I've decided to leave. After the way he confessed what Olivia asked him to promise—and that's blown my mind so much, I'm going to have to think about it later—I know I owe him an explanation.

In the distance, music begins playing, accompanied by a loud cheer. The party has begun downstairs. But Nick doesn't move, and his blue eyes are concerned.

I can't think where to start. How do I even begin to describe why my life is such a mess?

Nick thinks he isn't a great businessman. He tells everyone that Lucas is the brains behind the company, and he's just at the helm, keeping everyone on track, but it's not true. He might not have the financial brain that Lucas does, but Nick is very astute, just like his father before him, and he's incredibly good at reading situations.

"Is this about your sister?" he asks. I look up in surprise. "You said you've got a job in the Bay of Islands," he explains. "That's where she lives, isn't it?"

I nod slowly. "Yes. I need to be closer to her. I've been flying up there once a month, but it's not enough, and it's too expensive to fly more frequently."

He frowns. Does he understand? How do you explain to a billionaire that you only have eighty-four dollars in your account to last you until you get paid again?

"Is she unwell?" he asks.

I've never told him anything about Liz. Occasionally I've mentioned that I'm visiting her, but that's about it. But what's the point in keeping it a secret now?

"My brother-in-law is disabled." I accept another piece of chocolate from him. "Two years ago he fell off a ladder and injured his spine. He hasn't worked since then. He's in a lot of pain, and he's severely depressed, but he refuses to take medication. He drinks instead, and he steals the money my sister earns to pay for it. I give her what I can, because otherwise they'd be on the streets." I sigh. I might as well tell him everything. "I've used up my savings, and now I can't afford to help anymore. So the only thing I can do is be there in person to support her." I suck the chocolate, having squished my whole sorry life into a few simple sentences.

For a while, he doesn't say anything. I have another piece of chocolate, and sip my water.

Eventually, he leans back in his chair and looks out of the window. I follow his gaze, seeing the rays of the late afternoon sun turning the ocean to molten gold. Seagulls whirl and dip on the currents. I envy their freedom.

He brings his gaze back to me. "Elena…" The way he says my name gives me goosebumps. "We all make choices in our lives, and we have to live by those choices. If your sister has chosen to stay with her husband, even though he makes her life difficult, that's not your fault, and it's not your responsibility to fix her."

I stiffen in the chair. "I know. But I love her, and I can't bear to see her struggle. She feels strongly that her marriage vows mean she owes him her loyalty. For better or for worse, right? That's how she sees it, even if it doesn't make sense to you and me."

"I get it," he says, and I wonder then how difficult those last few years were with Olivia. It must have been so hard for him when she refused to have a scan to check for an aneurysm. I can only imagine how angry and frustrated that made him, especially because he would have needed to keep from his kids. And yet he stayed with her, because he's loyal and steadfast.

"I owe Liz," I say softly. "She was very good to me when Ricky died. I… I fell apart, and she was there to pick up the pieces. I wouldn't have made it without her. I love her a lot, and I need to help her now. Please understand that."

"I do." He reaches out and squeezes my upper arm. "I won't question you again. I'm sorry." He lowers his hand, and my arm tingles where he touched it.

"Thank you."

"She's very lucky to have you," he murmurs. "Are you going up there for Christmas?"

"Her son is home from uni, and I was going to let them have a family Christmas. Unfortunately, though, she rang me earlier to tell me that Keith has just spent the money she'd put aside for Christmas dinner."

Nick looks appalled. I love him for that.

"I'm driving up tonight to see her," I continue. "She needs money for the rent. I don't have much to give her, but I can be there to give her moral support if nothing else."

I don't know why I'm blurting everything out. I've spent a lifetime keeping things to myself. But it feels oddly good to share at last.

"Why are you driving?" he asks. "Aren't there any flights?" I just look at him, and he has the grace to look embarrassed. "I'm sorry. I didn't think. But it's such a long way."

"I know."

He gives a long sigh. "Look, I have a suggestion. I'm flying up to Auckland tomorrow to see my cousin, Brock King, and play Santa at his hospital. Why don't you come with me, and we'll go on to the bay after the hospital visit? It's only a thirty-minute flight."

"Oh, Nick… I couldn't…"

"Elena, we've known each other long enough, and I want to help. I'd give you money, but I know you won't accept it. I'm going up north anyway. Come on, I feel bad enough as it is. If I'd got my head into gear earlier, told you how I felt, maybe things would be different right now. But I didn't, and you have other priorities, I understand that. Let me help you."

My mouth opens and shuts like a fish's. It's a very generous offer, and it's too good to turn down. My car might not make it all the way, and I haven't been able to renew my membership to the recovery service this year, so if I were to break down, I'd be stuck.

He and the boys and Kora fly around New Zealand all the time in their private jet, but I've never been in it. I'm sure it's the height of luxury. But it means being alone with him, after everything he's said, and after that wonderful kiss…

"Please," he prompts.

"I don't know…" I feel that I have to protest. "I have my pride, Nick…"

He gives me an impatient look. "'Proud people breed sad sorrows for themselves.'"

That makes me smile. It also makes me think of the poetry in his bedroom. *I hunger. I ache. I yearn for you.* He said he's done with grieving, but if that's the case, why is he still composing such beautiful, heartfelt lines to her memory? It's none of my business, and it's irrelevant.

"Nice words," I manage to say.

"They're Emily Brontë's, but I agree with the sentiment. I'm flying up anyway. If you refuse, you'll be cutting off your rather beautiful nose to spite your lovely face. Where's the sense in that?"

I give him a wry look. "Stop flattering me."

"I'm being truthful. I'm determined to help, and it'll be foolish to refuse me."

I bristle a bit at that. I don't like being called foolish. Rich people have no idea how hard it is for poor people to accept help. But I know he means well. And he's right; there's no point in refusing him. Life is hard enough as it is without me turning away such generous offers.

"All right." I sound begrudging, and I try again. "Yes, thank you, you're very kind."

"Kind, shmind. It's the least I can do."

"What time are you leaving?"

"Eight a.m."

"Shall I meet you at the airport?"

"I'll pick you up at seven thirty."

I hesitate. He's never been to my apartment, and I have no intention of him seeing it now. But it will save me an Uber fee, so I nod and give him my address.

"Okay. How are you feeling now?" he asks.

"Better, thank you. I'd better be going." I get to my feet.

He stands as well. "Are you going to the party?"

I pick up my jacket and bag and turn to face him. "No, not this time. I'm not in the mood for celebration, and I don't want to cast a shadow on the festivities."

"You'll be missed. Both at the party and at the firm. You're a huge part of this company. It runs like clockwork because of you, and we're all going to miss you terribly. I hope you know that."

My throat tightens, and I swallow hard. "Thank you."

"Elena… I am sorry." His brow furrows. "For everything. For not telling you how I felt until it was too late. I can see I've really hurt you, and that's killing me."

Tears prick my eyes. "I never expected anything… you were my best friend's husband. I loved her too, and I miss her every day. I can only imagine how hard it's been for you. It's all such a mess."

There are only about six feet between us, but it feels like a chasm. My heart aches with the knowledge that things could have been so different. And the worst thing is, it's nobody's fault. It's not Olivia's. It's not Nick's, because he was grieving for his wife, and I can't blame him for that. And it's not my fault either. If I'd thrown myself at him, he'd have turned me down because he wasn't ready, and that would have been embarrassing for both of us. It's just one of those things. Ships that pass in the night and all that.

It doesn't make it any easier to deal with though.

He looks down at the Santa outfit on the chair. If he was the real Saint Nick, I might have made a wish in the hope that he'd make it come true. But he's not, and there's not enough Christmas magic left in the world to put everything right in my life. There won't be any fairytale ending for me.

"Tomorrow, seven thirty," I manage to say. He nods, and I turn and walk out.

I scurry down to the underground car park, barely able to see my car through the blur of tears.

I'm sad, but I'm conscious too that it's a release of emotion. It felt good to tell him everything. Well, almost everything. And even though it makes it harder in many ways, it's also wonderful to know he feels the same way I do. He likes me. He's attracted to me. There is something between us.

Or at least there could have been.

Finally, I let the tears fall, no longer able to contain them.

Chapter Seven

Nick

At just before seven thirty a.m., I arrive at the address Elena gave me the night before. The sliding glass doors of the apartment block require a key to open, but as I walk up, a young businessman in a striped suit comes out, and I'm able to slip inside. I go up in the elevator to the third floor and walk down the corridor to apartment 303. I knock on the door.

Footsteps sound behind it, followed by a female voice saying, "Who is it?"

"It's Nick," I reply, smiling.

She mumbles something under her breath. Then she says, "I thought we were going to meet outside."

"Someone came through the front door as I arrived, so I thought I'd come up." I have the sudden, horrific thought that she has a man in there with her. Surely not? "Would you rather I wait in the foyer?"

She gives a big sigh and then opens the door. She's wearing a pair of fawn slacks, a silky cream vest, and a pair of very sexy high-heeled sandals. Her toenails are an elegant light bronze color.

I drag my gaze up. Her blonde bob looks freshly washed. She's not wearing her glasses, which means she has her lenses in, and I can see her amazing green eyes.

"You look nice," I tell her, the understatement of the year.

She looks startled. "I'm not used to you saying things like that to me."

"Well, I've thought it for years, I just haven't said it." I glance past her. There's no sign of a man. "Can I come in?"

Somewhat reluctantly, she moves back to let me pass, and I walk into her apartment. Once in, I stop and look around. Shock filters through me. It consists of one room that serves as a bedroom, living room, and kitchen, with a small bathroom visible through a partially closed door. The double bed is neatly made and topped with contrasting cream and purple cushions. There's a two-seater sofa, a coffee table, a tiny TV, and a desk with a chair. To one side, the kitchen consists of a sink and draining board, an oven, and a set of cupboards. Everything looks neat and well ordered, but it's tiny. I've stayed in bigger hotel rooms.

I thought I was paying her a generous wage for her position. She must really be giving every last cent to her sister and nephew if this is all she can afford.

She clears her throat, obviously conscious of my shocked silence, and picks up a small travel bag. "I'm ready. Shall we go?"

I gesture for her to precede me, and we make our way out of the apartment. We go into the elevator and ride the carriage down in silence. She studies the floor, nibbling her bottom lip. Now I understand why she wanted to meet me outside. She's embarrassed and maybe even ashamed of where she's living. It's not a bad apartment block, it's clean and tidy, and it's also very close to town, so it must be convenient. But after our conversation about money, she must be self-conscious about the size of the place.

I had no idea how bad things were for her. Obviously, a lot of people live in accommodation like this, particularly when they're young. But normally by her age, most people are married or living with someone in a home with more than one room. Olivia once told me that Elena used to talk about spending her free time on her flower beds and veggie patches. She must have moved since Olivia died, probably having to downgrade because she's given all her money away. She must miss her garden terribly.

I think about the fact that I often send her to my house to let tradesmen in, or to drop off my dry cleaning. I feel embarrassed to think about how the place must look to her. We've always called it Buck House in jest, but even I know it's big. It didn't seem it when we first bought it, when the kids were young. With five children under ten running around, the place was always filled with noise and laughter. Now, though, it's very quiet, and I rattle around in the rooms. I hardly ever go over to the west wing, where the kids' bedrooms were.

I have considered selling it, and mentioned it once to Ben, but the look on his face made me pause. For my children, it's their family home, and at the time I don't think he'd gotten over his mother's death, and he saw the selling of the house as a betrayal of her memory. Maybe I'll address it again now a bit more time has gone by.

The elevator door slides open, and we make our way out of the building to where my car is parked.

"Isn't Colin with you today?" she asks, referring to my chauffeur.

"No, I didn't want to disturb him for the short trip. I'll be leaving the car at the airport, and thought he could have a lie-in."

I open the boot, put her suitcase in, and we get inside.

It's not the first time I've been in car with Elena, but something has definitely changed between us. In the past, my brain has been in business gear, and I've deliberately not let myself think about her as anything but my PA. Now, though, I'm acutely conscious of the way the material of her trousers stretches across her slim thighs. I can smell her perfume, something delicate and flowery with a hint of orange. She smells summery and Christmassy.

"Are you ready for your performance this morning?" she teases as I steer the car into the traffic.

"My Santa suit is in the boot. I've also had a couple of boxes of toys sent to the plane. Brock is sending a van to pick them up from the airport when we arrive to take them to the hospital. I can give them out to the kids then."

"It's so nice of you to deliver them in person," she says. "You could have just couriered them up."

"Well, Brock and his brothers often go around the hospitals delivering toys with the medical equipment. I stayed with Brock once when he did it, and I went with him and helped him out. I enjoyed it so much that since then I've done it every year. It's nice to be able to give something back."

It's something I've always said, but for the first time I'm embarrassed by the words. I sound superior and privileged—maybe because I *am* superior and privileged. What on earth must Elena think of me?

"What is it?" Elena asks.

I glance at her, surprised she's picked up on my mood. "I was just thinking about what I said. And how I asked you yesterday why you were driving and not flying."

"Let them eat cake?" She smiles. I recognize the quote—it was what the French queen Marie Antoinette was supposed to have said when told her people had no bread to eat. It showed her complete lack of understanding of what it's like to be poor.

My lips twist. "Yeah, that's about right."

"Oh Nick, I'm teasing you. I didn't mean it. You're the most altruistic man I know. It's not your fault that your family has money. All of you are so incredibly generous with it."

"That's nice of you to say, but I know I can never really understand what it's like to struggle for money. I've never had to worry about paying rent. I've never had to walk around the supermarket and count the price of the items in the trolley. My kids never wanted for anything, and although Olivia and I worked hard to make sure they were well mannered and polite, I know we spoiled them."

"Who wouldn't if they had the money? Are you supposed to give every cent away and live as paupers?"

"No doubt some people would say so."

"Well, I'd like to see them do it if they had your bank balance."

I take the road to the airport, the water in the harbor to our left sparkling in the early morning sun. It's nice of her to say so, but it makes me feel uncomfortable talking about money when she has so little, so I change the subject.

"I didn't see any Christmas decorations in your apartment. I thought you loved the festive season?"

"I haven't been in the mood this year." She looks out of the window.

At work, she's always one of the first to decorate her office. In the past, she's made little boxes of home-made chocolates for the secretaries, and she's left a huge Christmas cake on her desk so staff can have a slice with their morning cup of coffee. It's only now I realize she's not done it this year. I can't believe I haven't noticed how low she's obviously been.

Musing on that, I drive the rest of the way in silence. I park in the short-term car park and pay at the meter, and we carry our bags over to the domestic terminal.

Elena goes toward the main counters, then remembers at the last minute, laughs, and follows me to the private desk. The jet is ready and waiting, and Tim, our flight assistant, assures me the boxes of toys are loaded. He takes our cases, and we make our way out onto the tarmac and over to the plane.

She's still quiet, and it occurs to me then that this must be the first time she's flown on a private jet. Our family plane seats eight, and it has luxurious cream leather seats with burgundy cushions and throws for the cool days, polished wooden tables, and a light-gray carpeted floor. Tim is waiting as we board, and he takes her flight bag and slides it into the overhead locker, then shows her to one of the seats by the window. I say a quick hello to Jock, the captain, then come and sit opposite her, buckling myself in, and she does the same. Within ten minutes, we're taxiing down the runway, and then we're heading up into the cornflower-blue sky. Jock informs us on the intercom that we'll be touching down in Auckland in just under an hour.

Elena leans on the table, her chin on her hand, and looks out as Wellington disappears beneath us. "What a lovely day."

I'm too distracted by the view in front of me to follow her gaze. Her pale cheeks are touched with a light rose. Is she warm? Or is her blush to do with being near me? I like to think it's the latter.

"Beautiful," I say, and I'm not talking about the weather.

She brings her gaze to mine, and the rose-pink hue on her cheeks deepens. So it is a blush. She told me I'd killed any feelings she had for me, but I think that was a lie. She looks away, though, and I feel a touch of sadness. It doesn't matter what we feel for each other. The moment has passed, and life has moved on without us.

I force a smile on my face as Tim hovers nearby. "It's a bit early for champagne," I tell him. Elena's eyes nearly fall out of her head. I was teasing; not even I drink champagne at eight in the morning, but I can see she thought I was being serious. How the rich live! I can only imagine what she's thinking.

"Coffee?" I add hastily, reminding myself not to joke about money when I'm with her.

"Please."

"And for breakfast?" Tim asks. "Continental or full English, ma'am?"

Her jaw drops. "Oh, um…"

"Maybe some toast and preserves?" I ask gently. "As it's not a long flight."

"Yes… that would be lovely."

Tim nods and withdraws to the kitchen area, leaving us alone.

"Relax," I scold. "You're wound so tight you're going to break something."

"I'm nervous."

"About seeing your sister?"

"That as well." She flicks her gaze up to me, then looks back down at the table and scratches at an invisible mark.

I'm puzzled. "We've worked together a long time. We know each other well. Why are you nervous about being with me?"

"This is very different, Nick, especially after our… conversation yesterday." The pause is long enough to tell me she's referring to the kiss. "And we don't know each other well, not really. How often are we really alone at work?"

I think about it. She's right, of course. When we are alone, it's in my office or her office, and we're talking about business—about files, typing, the staff, the workload, or customers. It's not… I struggle for the right work. Intimate. Yes, this feels intimate. Just me, her, and the clouds for company.

I don't know if it's the fact that she's on a private jet, that she's having to accept charity to get up to see her sister, or whether it's everything going on between us that's making her uncomfortable, but she clearly is. She's examining her nails as if they're the most interesting thing she's ever seen.

At that moment Tim arrives with a plate of toast, a dish of butter slices, a selection of tiny pots of preserves, and two steaming cups of latte. We help ourselves, smearing strawberry and raspberry jam onto the crunchy toast.

While she's concentrating on her breakfast, I sip my coffee and let my gaze caress her, studying little details I've never noticed before. The tiny chickenpox scar on her forehead. The subtle color of her eye makeup—caramel over her lids, a thin line of black on the top lid sweeping up at the edges, black lashes carefully curled. Her bob is parted on the right, and she tucks the right side behind her ear, letting the longer left side fall forward to partially hide her face. Elegant pearls adorn her ears. Everything about her is elegant, actually.

It's difficult not to compare her to Olivia. My wife was striking rather than beautiful, with long dark hair, a full mouth, and expressive gray eyes. She dressed in a bohemian way—long colorful skirts, bangles on her arms, dangling earrings. She was moody and artistic, emotional and expressive. Elena is very different, and I like that.

I don't like her being nervous around me. Well, I charm people for a living—it's all part of the job. If I can't get her to relax, I've severely underestimated my talents.

"So where does your sister live in the bay?" I ask. "I haven't been north of Auckland very much."

She proceeds to tell me about where Liz lives in Kerikeri, and then we talk for a while about Waitangi and the new museum they've built there. Gradually the tension goes from her shoulders, and the ready smile appears back on her face. We continue to talk about places we've been in the Northland, and it's not long before Jock's voice comes through stating he's beginning his descent.

Tim clears the breakfast items away, and Elena reapplies her lipstick. I watch her smooth it over her lips as she pouts at the hand mirror, and I can't help but think about kissing her. I want to kiss her again.

I tear my gaze away and look out of the window as the City of Sails appears below us. I mustn't think about it. I'm only torturing myself.

A car is waiting for us when we exit the airport, organized by Brock. Tim assures me the van with the boxes of toys will meet us at the hospital. I reply that we'll be back at the airport by one p.m. at the latest, and we head off into the city.

The hospital isn't far from the central business district, near the large domain and the University of Auckland. The driver drops us off by the entrance to the Starship Children's Hospital, and I text Brock to tell him we've arrived. It only takes him a couple of minutes before I see him walking into the main waiting area.

I've known Brock since we were kids. My father and his mother were siblings—she married William King, meaning my side of the family are Princes and Brock's are Kings, which often leads to much amusement. I spent a lot of time with Brock and his brothers, Charlie and Matt, and we've stayed in touch.

He grins as he approaches, and we exchange a bearhug. He's a big guy, solid and muscular, an inch or two taller than me. Our age shows in the color of our hair—his is gray, mine is white, although he's clean shaven. He chuckles as he moves back and gestures at his face. "You decided to go for the Santa beard for real, eh?"

"Thought it would be less itchy than the false one." I grin and gesture at the woman standing quietly at my side. "This is Elena

Hunter, my PA. After our hospital visit we're going up to the Bay to meet some of her family."

"Lovely to meet you at last." Brock shakes her hand. They've spoken many times on the phone. "Good to put a face to the name."

"Likewise." She smiles at me. "You never said how alike you both are."

"I didn't realize we were," I reply with surprise. "In what way?"

She clears her throat. "Do I have time to visit the Ladies'?"

"Of course." Brock indicates the sign across the other side of the waiting room, and she excuses herself.

He looks back at me and raises an eyebrow.

"Don't start," I tell him wryly.

"Good-looking woman," he says. "Is she really just visiting her family?"

I sigh. "Yeah. I've kinda missed the boat on that one. Left it too long to express my interest and she's moving on, leaving after Christmas. Fucking idiot. Me, not her."

His brow furrows. "You've told her how you feel?"

"Yeah, but she says it's too late. I wasn't ready before, though. You know how it is."

"Yeah," he says. He was a lot younger—in his thirties—when his first wife died, but he had the same period of mourning before he finally started dating his current wife, Erin. "Can't you talk her around, though?"

"She's got another job up here. She wants to be nearer to her sister, the one we're going to see later."

He nods. "Doesn't mean you can't fly up to see her at weekends though, does it?"

"A long-distance relationship?"

"It's less than a two-hour flight, Nick. I'd hardly call that long distance, not when you have your own jet." He looks amused.

"I hadn't thought of that," I say honestly. "I wouldn't have thought any woman would want a relationship where you're apart all week."

"You might be surprised. Think about it, anyway. I know you're probably thinking lightning never strikes twice where love is concerned, but if it does you really have to grab the opportunity with both hands. If you want her, you might have to make some sacrifices."

I look across as she exits, thinking about his words. Brock's right: travel isn't so much of an issue when you have your own jet. Nowhere is very far away in New Zealand. It would mean a big lifestyle change, though.

I suppose it depends on how much I want to be with her.

I watch her walk across the room toward us, noticing the slight sway of her hips, the way several other men glance at her as she passes.

Hmm.

Chapter Eight

Elena

I'm totally unprepared for the emotional impact the next couple of hours have on me.

When you don't have kids of your own, it can make you a bit nervous being around babies and small children. I have my nephew, and I played as big a part in his life as I was able, but it's not the same as caring for your own child day in, day out. I don't know what to do when they're upset or unwell, and visiting sick children is not something that has ever been high on my wish list.

I therefore follow Nick and Brock into the children's ward nervously, unsure what part I'm expected to play.

I needn't have worried. The two guys are the stars of the show, with Nick ho-ho-hoing around the place, chucking kids under the chin and dishing out toys, and Brock acting like a magician's assistant, the perfect supporting act as he introduces Santa and lines up the kids to receive their presents. I get to sit amongst the children as they show me the toys they've unwrapped, and I ooh and aah over the teddy bears and help them sort out the pieces for the LEGO sets, while their parents and nurses hover nearby in case any of them feel unwell.

It's tough to see the little white faces, the bandages and casts, and the hairless heads, but I try to look past them at the children who manage to remain cheerful and playful despite their obvious illnesses.

Two hours fly by as we move from ward to ward, and it's with some astonishment that I realize it's midday as we say goodbye to the last group of kids and return to the nurses' station where Nick goes off to get changed back into his ordinary clothes.

"All done," Brock says to me as we wait for him. "Did you enjoy it?"

"It was very rewarding. I have nothing but admiration for you, working with these kids day in, day out." Brock is a doctor specializing in respiratory infections and he's worked super hard through the years, although he's semi-retired now.

"It can be tough," he admits. "But you learn to take a step back emotionally. You're no good to the patients or their parents if you're sniffling in the consulting room. They want reassurance and help, not commiseration."

"I see your point." I've always liked Brock's easy manner on the phone, his deep voice and the way he likes to tease, but I like him even more in person. "I can tell you're related to Nick," I tell him.

He smiles. "Oh, really?"

"You both have a way of making people feel as if they're your favorite person in the whole world."

He chuckles. "Well that's probably because you *are* Nick's favorite person in the whole world."

My face warms, and then burns as a hot flash takes the blush and turns it up to eleven. Brock notices and has the grace to give me a regretful look. "Sorry," he apologizes.

I touch a cool hand to my face. "It's okay—it's my age. Mostly. I… I'm sure that's not the case, anyway."

"He told me he has feelings for you," he says softly.

"Oh! Really? Well… um… even if that is the case, unfortunately I've just handed in my notice. I'm moving up to the Bay of Islands in the New Year, so it's too late for anything to happen."

"We'll see," he says mysteriously, and then he smiles as Nick comes out in his jeans and shirt, carrying the bag with the Santa suit. "Thanks for coming up," Brock says. "I appreciate it, and you could see that the kids and their parents did, too."

"Great time, as always," Nick replies, shaking his hand. "Give my love to Erin, and Charlie, Matt, and all the kids."

"Will do." Brock waves a hand and walks away.

Nick turns his attention to me. A remnant of my blush lingers on my face, and he studies it for a moment, but doesn't comment on it. "Ready?" he asks.

I nod, and we make our way out of the hospital to wait for the car, which is on its way.

It's always warmer in Auckland, and I close my eyes and let the subtropical summer breeze blow across my face, bringing it a touch of humidity with the scent of jasmine from the gardens. As hospitals go, this one isn't the worst.

I open my eyes to see Nick watching me. I wonder what Brock meant by *We'll see*. If he thinks I'm going to change my mind and stay in Wellington, it's not going to happen. My family has to come first, even at the expense of my own happiness.

The car pulls up, and soon we're heading back to the airport. By one p.m. we're in the air, on the way to the Bay of Islands.

This is a short flight, so there's no time for lunch, but Tim brings us a coffee and a chocolate muffin, which will be enough to stave off my hunger until dinner.

It's only when I think about the evening meal that I realize I haven't discussed with Nick where he's going to stay tonight. I stay in Liz's spare room, but there's no room for Nick, and I can't imagine he'd want to stay with her anyway.

"I should have asked before," I say, "but where are you going to stay tonight?"

"I've got a room at a B&B near Rainbow Falls," he informs me.

"That's not far from where Liz and Keith live."

"Well that's perfect, then. Can I come and meet them?"

I hesitate. I hadn't considered that he might want to do that. The house is in a decent area. It has four bedrooms and a large-ish lawn. But it's old now, a bit rundown, because Keith can't get out to paint it, and they can't afford to pay someone else to do it. Liz does what she can, and I do a few jobs when I visit, but it needs a lot doing to it. It's one of the things I hope I can help with when I move up here.

I realize I'm ashamed of what Nick might think, and that makes tears prick my eyes. How can I be ashamed of my sister when she's having such a hard time? "Of course," I say immediately. "I'd love for you to meet her."

He nods, although he narrows his eyes a little. I know he's astute, and he misses very little. It strikes me then that he might want to size up the situation for himself, maybe to see how bad things are, to test whether I spoke the truth in my need to move up here. Does he think I said I have to move because I want to get away from him? That's not the case at all. But then I did tell him he'd killed any feelings I have for him. It was a lie, of course, but he wasn't to know that.

We've just finished our muffin and coffee when Jock announces he's beginning his descent. Tim clears up our cups and plates, we buckle ourselves back in, and within fifteen minutes the wheels touch down at the Bay of Islands airport.

Up in the Bay, it's even warmer than it is in Auckland. I don my sunglasses as we walk across the tarmac, glad my moisturizer has factor thirty built into it.

I have to admit, as we walk into the quiet airport, it's wonderful to travel on a private jet. No queues, no waiting, no being squashed into seats and bumping elbows with strangers. I've seen the way the Prince family lives, but I haven't experienced it much for myself. I could definitely get used to having money.

We exit the airport, and Nick informs me he's hired a car from the local rental service. "I didn't think you'd want us pulling up in a chauffeur-driven limo," he says with a grin. "Or was I wrong? I can still arrange it."

"No, no," I say hastily, imagining the neighbors' faces. "Rental is fine."

It might not be a limo, but he's booked a sleek S-Class Mercedes that's a hundred times more gorgeous than anything I could afford. I slide into the beautiful cream seat, afraid to breathe in case I mark any of the gleaming interior.

"You shouldn't have done this," I scold, buckling myself in as he gets in the driver's side. "We could have gotten a taxi."

"I thought you deserved a treat."

"The private jet wasn't a treat?"

"Another treat." He turns on the engine, then pulls away, and the car purrs like a big cat as he takes the road into town. "Talking of which, I'd like to take you, Liz, and her husband out tonight to dinner."

"Oh Nick. That's very kind of you, but no thank you."

"Why not? Everyone has to eat, and it might take some of the tension out of the air if we go out."

I realize he has no idea what the atmosphere is going to be like in Liz's house. Liz would enjoy the treat, but she wouldn't go without Keith. Even if he was in a fit state to eat out, which is unlikely, Keith would be embarrassed at having his meal paid for by another man, and his resulting anger would make for an unpleasant couple of days.

"You'll see when you get there," I mumble, now regretting my decision to let him accompany me. He glances at me, but he doesn't say anything.

I direct him to take State Highway Ten, and we sail effortlessly along the road, flanked by palm trees and ferns, and kiwi, feijoa, mandarin, and persimmon orchards. At the roundabout, we turn right, and I point out the turnoff for Rainbow Falls where he'll be staying before directing him to Liz's house, not far from the Kerikeri inlet.

He parks outside, and we get out. Ooh, it's so warm and humid. Everything around us is lush. Huge silver ferns tickle our skin as we pass, their new, unfurling fronds bearing the distinctive koru shape. Palms whose trunks look like huge pineapples bear large leaves that arch overhead. I also recognize Nikau palms, Bangalow palms, and Palmyra palms. Purple and orange bougainvillea climbs up the wooden trellis on one side of the front garden, while orange and blue birds of paradise add even more color.

The grass on the lawn is desperate for a mow, though, and the house hasn't been repainted for years.

I make my way to the front door and knock. Nick waits beside me, his hands in his pockets. I glance at him, and he meets my gaze and winks. I drop my eyes, but not before a seed of warmth settles in my belly.

About twenty seconds pass. I frown and knock again. I can't hear the TV, or indeed any noise from inside.

Finally, I hear footsteps. Then the door opens, just a crack.

"It's me," I say at the sight of one of Liz's eyes peering out. "What's going on?"

She looks at Nick, and her eye widens.

"This is Nick. He's a friend," I state.

She looks back at me, and her eye turns glassy.

"Liz? You're frightening me. Let me in."

Her fingers tremble where she's holding the door. Then she moves back.

I step into the hallway. It's south-facing and there's not much natural light here, so at first I don't get a good view. But then she moves to close the door behind us and moves down toward the kitchen, and when she turns, I get the first good look at her face.

I gasp. The right side bears a huge purple bruise, and her eye is swollen.

Nick obviously spots it too, and goes still.

She lifts a hand and pulls some of her hair forward to try and hide it, which doesn't work. "I don't suppose you'll believe me if I say I walked into a cupboard," she attempts to joke.

"What happened?" I whisper.

She wraps her arms protectively around her middle. "I heard from Carl." He's her son, who's twenty-two and in his last year of a degree at Otago University, in Dunedin at the bottom of the South Island. "He told me he's not coming home for Christmas. He's staying with friends. He said he doesn't want to be around Keith during the holiday. I begged him, but he refused. Keith found me crying, and I was so angry I yelled at him that he'd driven our boy away."

"So he hit you?"

She shakes her head. "He threw a bottle at the wall. It knocked the lamp, and as it fell it caught my temple. I'm not making excuses for him, but he didn't mean to do it." Tears form on her lashes, then tumble onto her cheeks. "Sorry," she whispers, embarrassed to be crying in front of a stranger, and also ashamed, I'm sure, because I've warned her all along that this might happen.

"When was this?" I ask her.

"A couple of hours ago. He's asleep now, out on the deck. He won't wake up for a while."

"Oh, Liz…"

Suddenly, as if her legs won't hold her up any longer, she slides down the wall, sits on the floor, and bursts into tears. "I can't do it anymore," she says between sobs. "I just can't."

"You don't have to." I drop to the floor beside her and put my arms around her. "It's all right. It'll be all right."

I'm so shocked, I can't feel anything. I'm conscious of the shafts of light coming through the high windows, falling across us, highlighting motes of dust dancing in the air. It smells a bit musty, and the whole place feels dark and unhappy.

I look up at Nick. He's looking through the house toward the deck, but his gaze comes back to me now. "Do you want me to talk to him?" he asks me.

I shake my head. "I think we should just go."

He nods. "Why don't you pack her a bag?"

"Yes." I kiss the top of her head, then get to my feet. "Come on," I urge her. "You're leaving."

She lets me pull her up, and together we stumble through to her room. "A bag," I instruct. "Do you have one?"

Still crying, she pulls out a large bag from a cupboard. I open some drawers and pull out her underwear—well-worn and cotton—a few bras, and socks, and stuff them in the case. She sits on the bed as I add a pile of tees, jeans, shorts, and a pair of sneakers. I go into the bathroom and scoop as many bottles as I can into another bag and put them in too.

"Phone?" I ask her.

"In the kitchen."

I leave her for a moment and go through the house and out into the kitchen. Her phone rests on the counter, and I collect it with the charger. I glance up then, and look out at the deck. Keith is asleep on the outdoor sofa, snoring loudly, his wheelchair nearby, at an angle. To my surprise, Nick is standing over him. He's looking down at the sleeping man. His expression is unreadable. I'm not sure if he's feeling anger or pity toward him. Maybe both.

He glances up and sees me. Leaving Keith sleeping, he comes back into the house.

He looks down at me, and his blue eyes are blazing. Suddenly, without warning, he slides a hand to the back of my neck, bends his head, and kisses me. It takes me by surprise, although I don't know what I would have done if he'd have given me warning. It's hot and hard and quick, and when he lifts his head, I'm breathless and blinking with shock.

"I'll wait for you outside," he says, his words clipped. Then he walks out of the house, opening the front door with such force that it bangs on the wall.

I stand there, stunned, wondering what had prompted the kiss. My fingers rise to touch my lips for a moment, before I turn and walk back to help Liz finish her packing.

Chapter Nine

Nick

Elena leads Liz out of the front door by the hand, carrying her bag. Liz looks like a child—confused, bewildered, and upset.

"Is there anything else you want to bring?" Elena asks.

Liz blinks at her. "I don't know. Is there?"

"You're coming to stay with me," Elena says firmly. "For a while, until everything's sorted. I've packed clothes and you've got your phone. Is there anything else you think you might need?"

Liz just looks into the house, breathing heavily. "I should leave him a note," she says, and walks back in.

Elena glances at me, then follows her. I stay out on the porch, not trusting myself to go back inside.

There are always two sides to every story. Keith is obviously wracked with pain, guilt, and fury at his impotence—possibly both physical and sexual. He's hurting, depressed, maybe even suicidal. And we don't know what provoked the attack—maybe Liz mocked him, or perhaps she showed pity, not understanding it's the last thing he needs.

But none of that—NONE of that—justifies him hitting her, even if it was an accident, and I'm not sure it was.

I have no idea how able he is—whether he can wash, dress, look after himself, or cook his food and clean his clothes. But none of that matters right now. The priority has got to be to get Liz away from him.

It's only a few minutes before Elena and her sister reappear. This time Liz closes the front door behind her. She's pale, but she's stopped crying. She doesn't look back as she walks to the car and gets into the back seat.

Elena and I get in, I start the engine, and pull away, not sure yet where I'm going. I take the road toward the State Highway, and glance across at Elena. "What do you want to do? Do you want me to take you to a hospital?"

She looks over her shoulder. "Liz?"

"I'm okay," she says. "It's not as bad as it looks."

I think she's lying, but I guess she's not ready to answer a hundred questions about how it happened.

"Do you want us to take you to a hotel for the night so you can think things over?" Elena asks.

Part of me is expecting Liz to tell us to turn the car around. But to my surprise, when she meets my eyes in the rearview mirror, hers are blazing with fury. "No," she says. "Fuck him. I'm done."

Elena glances at me again, then back at her sister. "So shall we go back to the airport and fly to Wellington?"

Liz nods and looks out of the window.

Elena turns in the seat. "Is that okay?" she murmurs. "Is it all right if we go home today?"

"Of course. I'll call Jock and Tim and let them know." I've plugged my phone into the car already, so I bring up my call list, hit Jock's name, and when he answers, apologize and say we're on our way back to the airport. He's okay about it—he'd rather be at home at this time of year—and he promises to tell Tim. I inform him there will be one other passenger, and he says he'll let Tim know.

I hang up and concentrate on the traffic for a while. The two women are quiet; no doubt they'll talk more once they're on their own.

I glance across at Elena. She's pale, studying her hands in her lap. I can't imagine how horrible this is for her.

"I'm so sorry," Liz says. She's looking at me. "For all the hassle. If you'd rather drop me off in town, I'll understand. I can catch a bus somewhere, or something."

"Of course not," I say crisply. "I'm glad I can help." I take the turnoff for the airport. "What did the note say?"

Elena answers. "She said she'd had enough, and she was leaving him."

Well, that sounded fairly final. "Did you say where you were going?" I ask Liz.

She shakes her head. "He'll know I'm going with Elena, though. He'll call her apartment." She puts a hand up to her mouth. "Oh no. I think I'm going to be…" Her eyes meet mine, alarmed.

I brake hurriedly and pull the car over, just in time for her to wrench the door open and vomit onto the grassy bank. Elena scrambles out and runs around with a tissue, comforting her sister as she wipes her mouth.

I wonder if it was the thought of Keith trying to contact her that made her ill. Is she worried he'll talk her into going back? She needs to go somewhere he can't find her. A women's refuge is an obvious choice, but I can't imagine Elena being happy to let her sister go somewhere like that, especially at Christmas.

And it's then that the idea begins to form. I mull it over as the women get back in the car and buckle themselves in, and I head back onto the road. I can't imagine Elena agreeing to it. But maybe she will if it saves Liz's sanity.

Of course, the first thing I have to do is contact Daniel and see if he has space. It's a busy time of year, but he's an old friend. He might be able to organize something for me.

In less than five minutes I pull up at the airport, park the car, and drop the keys off at the desk. Jock's already on the plane and Tim's waiting for us. His smile fades as he sees Liz's face. He doesn't comment, but his tone is extra kind as he extends a hand to help her up the steps and show her to her seat.

I remain outside for a moment, and bring up Daniel's name on my phone. He answers within a couple of calls.

"It's Nick," I tell him.

"Hey. How're you doing?"

"Good."

"All set for the twenty-third?"

"Absolutely. Look, I have a favor to ask…"

*

Within ten minutes, I'm on the plane and Jock is taxiing down the runway. We take off, and once we're at a suitable height, Tim comes over and asks us if we'd like anything to eat. Elena tries to get Liz to agree to something, but she shakes her head.

"Maybe some sandwiches?" I ask Tim, thinking that maybe Liz might be persuaded to have a nibble.

He nods and goes off to make us all a coffee.

Liz and Elena are sitting side by side. I'm opposite Elena, by the window.

"Can I get you anything?" Elena asks her gently.

"I'm all right," Liz states. "Honestly." She gives me a small smile. "Thank you so much for this. I had to get away."

"Of course."

"I'm sorry… about being sick in the car. I don't know what happened. I suddenly thought about having to talk to him, or, God forbid, him turning up somehow at Elena's apartment, and I came over all cold and clammy."

"He can't afford to fly down, can he?" Elena asks her.

"He could beg for money from a friend," she states. "He'll be on to his mate, Stu, and I'm sure he'll want to help if he can."

"Whatever happens," Elena says calmly, "we'll deal with it. You don't have to go back unless you want to."

"I don't," Liz says immediately. "I'm never going back."

"That's fine, we'll manage," Elena says.

I don't know if it's my imagination, but I'm sure I can hear a touch of desperation in her voice. Maybe it's the thought of the two of them having to stay in her tiny apartment. They'll have to share a bed. All this hassle will be the last thing she'll want at Christmas, but I know her family comes first.

I guess it's time for me to speak. "I have a suggestion," I tell them both.

Their eyebrows rise. "Oh?" Elena says.

"First of all, I want you to promise you'll think about it before you say no," I tell her.

"You're not buying us a house," she replies wryly.

I chuckle. "No, that's not what I was going to say. Look, I know it's none of my business, but I want to help. I'm going away for Christmas and New Year."

"Oh… I'd forgotten…" Elena says. I'd already told her about my plans. She was surprised that I wouldn't be home for the festive season when I have a new grandchild and all my kids around me. I told her it was because I hadn't had a vacation in years and fancied some time to myself. It's partly true. I love my family to bits, but I've spent the last thirty years thinking about nothing else, and for once in my life I want to concentrate on myself for a few days. I have a project I'm working on, and I felt like escaping somewhere so I can devote all my time to it.

"Yes. I'm going on a fourteen-day cruise," I tell Liz. "The ship goes to Brisbane, then back to Milford Sound, and all the way around New Zealand."

"How lovely," she says with a genuine smile.

"We're not staying at your house," Elena replies.

"No, that wasn't what I was going to say. The kids are all going to be there—they're meeting up for Christmas. No, I have another idea. I'd like you to come with me."

They both stare at me. "What?" Elena asks eventually. "Where?"

"On the cruise," I clarify. "A very old friend of mine is the captain of the ship. I've just spoken to him, and he told me one of the suites is available after a cancellation. It's too late for him to fill so he's offering it to me at a reduced rate."

It's a lie—the cruise ships are always overbooked at this time of year, and I've no doubt he has a dozen people willing to take the cancellation. But we've known each other a long time—since secondary school, actually, and he was more than happy to offer the suite to me.

"It's a two-bedroomed suite," I tell them. "Fully inclusive, so you'd have nothing to pay."

Elena's jaw drops. "We couldn't possibly," she whispers.

"I'd leave you alone as much as you wanted. You'd have fourteen days to talk and relax and think about what you wanted to do—fourteen days where Keith wouldn't be able to contact you, even if he wanted to."

I look at Liz. Her bottom lip is trembling, and her eyes are brimming with tears. I don't know if it's the thought of Keith contacting her that's upset her again, or if it's my offer.

"Excuse me," she says, her voice little more than a squeak, and she unbuckles herself and rushes off to the toilet, past a startled Tim, who's carrying a tray with the coffee and sandwiches.

Elena doesn't say anything as he comes over and places the items in front of us. It's only after he's withdrawn that she leans forward on the table. Her cheeks are flushed, and her eyes are bright.

"Nick," she says, "it's a very generous offer, but we can't possibly take you up on it."

"I told you that I'd like you to think about it first," I say firmly.

"I don't have to think about it. I just couldn't."

"Elena, I like you—in fact actually I think I'm a little crazy about you. But that's not why I offered. I did it for Liz. It's clear she's terrified Keith's going to try to contact her. I don't have much experience in these things, but I'm guessing she's worried he'll guilt her into going back up there, and it looks as if she really doesn't want to do that."

"I've never seen her so adamant," she admits. "It's good, of course. I'm pleased in one way. But it's a huge break for her, and it won't be an easy ride."

"Of course it won't. He's her husband, and she'll continue to love him, no matter what he's done. He's pushed her past her limits, though, and she needs time away to process that. And to be honest, he needs time without her. I've no doubt he'll be mad at first. He'll say he can't cope on his own, and he'll try to blackmail her into coming back. At first he'll think it's just a matter of time. But maybe if she stays away long enough, he'll come to realize what a huge mistake he's made. It might change him, make him a better man."

Elena studies me, her eyes open and clear. "You think so?"

"I don't know the man. Maybe not. And maybe even if he does change, she'll decide it's over, and I'll completely understand that. But we need to give them both time to think about their marriage. And the best way to do that is to go away."

I reach out a hand to her on the table, palm up. She looks at it for a moment, and then slides hers into it.

"Plus," I say softly, "I think you both deserve a treat after everything you've been through. The ship is amazing. Think about it—two weeks of drinking cocktails on the deck as the sun goes down… They have a Michelin-star chef on board who serves these amazing meals. A spa where you can be pampered to your heart's content. There will be a fantastic Christmas dinner, and a party on New Year's Eve. You've had a tough time of it. Don't you think you deserve it? Doesn't Liz?"

She bites her bottom lip as it trembles. "It's such a generous offer. But…"

"No strings attached, Elena. I don't expect anything in return. I hate to brag, but it's peanuts for me. Maybe we could call it a going-away present or something. I don't know. I understand you have your pride, and taking money or gifts doesn't come easy. I don't quite get it because I've never been in your position. People seem to think accepting gifts or money is a failing, a weakness. I have no idea why. It's just paper and coin. Zeroes in a bank account. I have more than most. If I had a mountain of food and a person was starving, I'd happily give some of it to them."

"You're very sweet," she whispers. She brushes her thumb across my knuckles, sending a shiver right through me. "I'm sorry if I come across as ungracious. I really appreciate your generosity. But you're right; it is very hard to accept charity. I don't know why either."

"It's not charity. I feel…" I struggle to put it into words. "As a man, I'm thoroughly ashamed of what Keith did. I don't believe he's evil, and I do think he's obviously been driven to it out of misfortune and pain and misery, but there are no excuses that can condone what he did. I want to help Liz, to show her that what she's experienced is wrong, and to help her work out a conclusion going forward. And I'd like to give her a treat. After everything that's happened, all the unhappiness she's had… two weeks away doing absolutely nothing… don't you think she deserves it?"

Her expression turns wry. "Of course she does, but that doesn't mean I'm saying yes. We'll need to talk about it tonight. Can I let you know tomorrow?"

"Of course. Daniel will hold the suite until then."

Liz comes out of the toilet and rejoins us. "I'm sorry about that," she says, picking up her coffee.

"No worries," Elena replies. "I've said to Nick that we'll talk about it tonight and give him our decision tomorrow."

Liz nods, and her hand creeps toward the plate of tasty-looking sandwiches. I sip my coffee to hide my smile and look out of the window at the snow-topped peak of Mount Taranaki. I don't know whether I've managed to convince Elena. But I've done my best to try.

Chapter Ten

Elena

When we get back to Wellington, we walk out to Nick's car together, and Liz gets in the back.

Nick catches my hand before I get in, though, and pulls me to one side. "Just quickly," he says. "I wanted to let you know that I've transferred your Christmas bonus into your bank account. It's a special one, as this is your last Christmas with us. In fact, it's a personal gift for all your hard work, so no need to declare it."

I've already organized the Christmas bonuses for the staff, so I know it's just a cover. He's giving me some extra money because Liz is with me, and he didn't want that to be the reason we don't go away with him.

It would be rude to refuse it, and anyway, I desperately need the money. "Thank you," I say, as graciously as I can. "You are very generous."

"No worries. Do you want me to take you back to your apartment, or are you going in town first?"

"Somewhere on Lambton Quay would be great," I reply. "We'll pick up a few bits before going up to the flat."

"Okay." We get in the car, and Nick heads for the town center.

I want to check my bank account on my phone to see how much he's put in there, but I can't do it in front of him. In New Zealand, the average annual wage of a personal assistant is between fifty and sixty thousand dollars. Nick generously pays me seventy thousand, which would be a very decent living wage for most people, but it soon dwindles away when I divide it between myself, Liz and Keith, and their son. Our usual Christmas bonus is one-point-five percent of the staff member's wage, which normally works out at around a thousand dollars for me. It sounds a lot, but after tax it just about covers one flight up to the Bay of Islands. I wonder how much he's put in there?

I feel uncomfortable accepting the money. I wish I was strong enough to refuse it, but the thought of having a few extra dollars makes me weak at the knees. I hate being so materialistic, but all the way back on the flight I was worrying about how I was going to cope having to feed someone else. Now at least I should be able to afford a bottle of wine and something nice for dinner.

"Here you go." Nick pulls up not far from the cable car entrance and puts the handbrake on. "You know where I am if you need me."

"Thank you." I unbuckle my seatbelt, then look up at him. The memory of his kiss at Liz's house is still strong in my mind. Most of the time, he's warm, funny, and gentle, the perfect host both socially and at work. He puts customers and staff alike at ease, and he's always smiling. At Liz's house, though, when he was obviously angry about what Keith had done, he looked every inch the powerful billionaire CEO. His kiss had been hard, demanding. The memory gives me goosebumps.

I've thought often about what it would be like to be married to him, to have him share my life. To be with him in the evenings, cuddled up, watching movies. To accompany him to social events—to have him be mine. But I've never let myself think too much about what it might be like to be *his*. To be alone, to let him undress me. To slide under the covers, skin against skin. To have him touch me, to feel him inside me. That way lies madness, and I've carefully pulled my mind away from those thoughts as if tugging a naughty dog away from a discarded piece of food.

But now… the memory of that kiss makes me think of what he's offering. I don't mean the trip away, or the money, or the help for Liz. He called me beautiful, and said he has feelings for me. Can I really walk away from that?

Liz opens the car door and gets out, and my heart slowly sinks back down inside me. What other choice do I have?

"Thank you," I say. "I'll call you later."

He nods, looking regretful. I close the door, Liz waves at him, and we walk away.

"He's lovely," Liz says as we walk arm-in-arm along the line of shops. "And I think he likes you."

I don't answer, busy pulling up my bank account on my phone with my free hand. I stare at the balance, then click on the account. Holy moly. He's transferred twenty thousand dollars in there.

For a moment, I'm speechless. I can't possibly accept it. It's what I earn in five months after tax, but I don't need to pay tax on it because he said it's a personal gift, and there's no gift duty in New Zealand anymore.

Liz has stopped to look in a shop window, so she hasn't noticed anything. I quickly slide my phone into my bag and walk on with her. I'm not going to tell her about the money. I'm embarrassed, if I'm honest, especially after his generous offer of the cruise.

I thought she was looking at the clothing the mannequin is wearing in the shop window, but I realize she's studying her reflection, trying to hide the bruise on her face with her hair. My heart goes out to her—I'd forgotten about it.

"We'll just call into the supermarket and pick up a few things," I tell her, "and then we'll go home."

Within thirty minutes, we're trudging up the hill to the Terrace with a couple of bags of groceries. I'm going to make us a nice pasta dish with a fresh salad, and I've also bought some chocolate for later, and a couple of bottles of wine.

We go up to the apartment, and Liz sinks onto the bed.

"You look exhausted," I tell her. "Why don't you close your eyes for ten minutes while I make some dinner? Then we'll sit and have a chat."

"I couldn't," she says, but I make her take off her jacket and shoes, she lies back on the bed, and within five minutes she's fast asleep.

I study her for a moment, frowning at the sight of the large purple bruise on her right cheekbone. Her hair is a dark blonde, longer than mine, and it could do with a trim. We have the same oval-shaped face, the same angle of eyebrows and curve of our lips. I would have said she was prettier than me, but if I'm honest, the glow she used to have has vanished, and she looks tired and worn. I know she's battled with the symptoms of the menopause, which haven't really taken a grip on me fully yet. She's only eighteen months older, but she looks more than that. It makes me sad.

I leave her to it, take off my own jacket and shoes, and quietly put the groceries away. Then I spend some time preparing the pasta—cooking the fettuccine in a big pot of boiling water, slicing the chicken and browning it with sliced onions and mushrooms and a touch of garlic, and adding cream and parmesan to make a delicious sauce.

I don't have a dining table, but she won't mind eating on her lap. I put two wine glasses and the cold bottle of Sauvignon on the coffee table. I toss the green salad in a balsamic dressing and place half on each plate, stir the cooked pasta into the creamy sauce, and by the time I've dished it up, Liz is stirring and stretching, looking better for her rest.

"Goodness," she says, joining me on the sofa, "I crashed out. I didn't hear you cooking at all."

"I thought the smell might wake you. It does tend to linger here when I cook." I've put the fan on, and now I open the window to get the air circulating.

"This looks amazing." She picks up her plate and twirls her fork in the fettuccine before eating a mouthful. "Mmm, and it tastes so good. You always were the better cook."

My throat tightens, and I have a sip of wine to cover it. While I stayed with her, I did a lot of cooking as I found it comforting. Keith used to like the different pasta dishes I made.

"I'm so sorry about Keith," I murmur.

She stares at her food, inhales deeply, then lets out a big sigh. "Me too." She digs her fork into a piece of chicken with a bit more force than is necessary.

"Was it really the lamp that hit you?" I ask. I know Nick thinks she lied.

But to my surprise, she nods and swipes her fingers over her chest. "Cross my heart. He even said sorry. But he was so drunk he almost immediately lay down and passed out."

"How are you feeling about it all now?"

"Oddly distant." She lowers her plate to her knees and has a big mouthful of wine, sighing again as she swallows. "Like it's happened to someone else. I can't quite believe it. He's been horrid for a long time, but he's never done anything like this."

"When did it happen?"

"Last night. He'd been simmering all day. He knew he'd done wrong when he took the Christmas money I'd saved. He could see how upset I was about it, and he was really defensive and aggressive. Then I told him you were coming up, and he got angry and said you were poking your nose into things that didn't concern you."

That stings, because if it wasn't for me they'd be in a lot of financial trouble, but I don't react. "What did you say to that?"

"I told him he was being an idiot, of course. He didn't like that. He swore at me. I swore back. You know what it's like when you argue—things escalate, and you say stuff you don't mean. Well, I did mean most of them. I told him I'd had enough of his nasty behavior. He knocked a plate of biscuits off the table on purpose and they went all over the floor. I said he was being a pig because he knew I'd have to pick them up, and I wasn't his slave. When I bent down, he threw the bottle and it hit the lamp and fell on me. I was so shocked I burst into tears. He said sorry, but it was begrudging, and he immediately closed his eyes and went to sleep. That hurt more than the actual blow. I walked out, went into the spare room, and put the chair under the door handle. He didn't try to get in, though. Later, when I went out, he was comatose in front of the TV."

"Oh, Liz."

"I hate him," she says fiercely. Then she bursts into tears. "But I don't," she says through sobs. "I still love him. Why do I still love him?"

I know there's no point in telling her she's crazy to have feelings for him, even though part of me thinks that. I remember Nick's words, *I don't believe he's evil, and I do think he's obviously been driven to it out of misfortune and pain and misery*. He tried to explain that he understands how a man can get to that point, even if, as he said, there are no excuses that can condone what he did.

I stroke her back and soothe her. "You love him because he's your husband, and he wasn't always like this. You know he's been forced to be this way because of what happened to him. And we both sympathize with him for having his liberty taken away. He's the old-fashioned type of Kiwi guy who thinks he should be the one to pay the bills, and he feels emasculated because he's no longer able to do that. It all makes sense. But Liz... you know that doesn't excuse what he did."

"I know."

"You can't keep letting him treat you like this. He's suffered a terrible misfortune, but that doesn't give him the right to take it out on you. You deserve to be happy, to feel loved, the same way we all do."

Even as I say it, I wonder if I, also, deserve the same. Am I happy? I'm content, I suppose. I like my job, the people I work with. I have friends, and a roof over my head, even if it is a small one. I have food to eat and nice clothes.

Not everyone has that perfect person beside them all their life, I know that. Some people never meet Mr. or Mrs. Right. Or they meet them and their partner leaves them, or dies. A third to half of all marriages end in divorce—a statistic I find very sad. I'm hardly the only person in the world who's alone, and I know many others who would say they're very happy with their lot.

But I'm not. I'm lonely. I miss having a partner to talk to and share things with. And I miss sex. I miss being wanted, and having someone else give me pleasure. I try not to think about it, but it's true.

Liz sniffs, blows her nose, and has a large mouthful of wine. "I need time," she says. "To think about everything and decide what I'm going to do."

"Well, you're welcome to stay here as long as you want."

She reaches out and holds my hand. "Thank you."

"It's the least I can do after the way you looked after me."

"I don't know what I'd do without you," she says simply.

"You'd manage. You're stronger than you think."

She sighs. Then she gives me a mischievous look. "So… what about Nick?"

"What about him?"

"Oh, come on, Ellie. He offered to take us on a cruise for two weeks! Is he for real?"

"Oh yes," I say without hesitation. I know without doubt that he's offered the gift because he has a huge heart, and he genuinely wants to help.

"I can't believe it," she says. "I didn't think real people existed who were like that. Imagine having enough money to offer to send two people away on a cruise! It's the stuff of fairytales!"

She's right, of course, and that's without taking into account the money he's put into my account. Twenty thousand dollars. I'm still not certain I can accept it. Doesn't it make me beholden to him? But instantly I know that's not the case. He's a generous man, who gives frequently to numerous charities, and just like he did with the toys today, he often helps out with other tasks like fundraising. It stings a bit to think he sees me in the same vein—as giving to someone in need—but it's pointless to be offended by the truth. I am in need. Liz is in need. And because of that, I don't think I can turn the money down.

But what about the cruise? That would be a luxury we don't need.

I look at Liz, though, and see the glimmer of hope in her eyes. When was the last time she took a vacation? Not since Keith was injured, that's for sure. At first, she tried to get him out every week, take him on a drive to the coast or down to Whangarei to look at the shops. But he hates the palaver of going in the car, of watching her trying to get the wheelchair in and out of the back, and now they only go out if they have an appointment. She does all the shopping. As far as I know, he hasn't been out of the house for months.

I know what's going through her mind, because I'm thinking the same thing. How amazing would it be to spend two whole weeks on the ocean? Not having to worry about bills, food, drinks, or entertainment? Eating and drinking whatever we wanted. It would give her time to think about her marriage, and it would also mean Keith wouldn't be able to come and get her. I can imagine how that would take all the stress and anxiety away.

It would be the holiday of a lifetime, something neither of us would be able to afford ourselves. We'd be like two Cinderellas, and Nick would enjoy playing the Prince with the glass slippers.

"I don't know," I murmur. "It sounds fantastic. But how can I accept such a gift? Wouldn't he expect something in return?"

Her expression turns mischievous. "That would be an added bonus."

"Liz!"

"What? Don't tell me you haven't thought about it. The guy's a Silver Fox—he's gorgeous and sexy and loaded. Even if you're not interested in forever, why not have a fling?"

My jaw drops. "I couldn't!"

Now she looks impatient. "If he was interested in me, I'd snap him up."

"And you a married woman?"

"If I was you, I mean. I've never been unfaithful to Keith."

"I know. I'm sorry."

"No, it's okay." She has another mouthful of wine. "There was someone, once," she admits after a long pause.

My eyebrows rise. "Really? Who?"

"His name was Martin. He was quite a bit older than me. I met him at the library not long after Keith's accident. I used to go on Tuesdays, after I finished cleaning, and he was often there. He told me his wife had dementia, and he'd read in the evenings when he put her to bed. There was never anything… you know… about it. We talked, that's all. We went and had coffee a couple of times. I'd tell him a bit about Keith. He was very gentle and quiet. It helped a lot when things were hard at home."

"What happened?" I ask, conscious that she's speaking in the past tense.

"He just stopped coming. That was a few months ago. I don't know. Maybe he moved away. Or died." She looks sad.

Tears prick my eyes. It was such an innocent relationship, such a small thing to have brought her comfort. It makes my heart ache.

"Let's do it," I say.

She blinks. "Do what?"

"Go on the cruise with Nick. Screw it. We deserve a break, don't we?"

I'm pretty sure Liz will eventually go back to Keith. I've already quit my job, and in the New Year, I'll be moving up to the bay to support her. Life will be very different, and it's possible I'll never see Nick again. I'll make it clear when I talk to him that if we go with him, it doesn't change anything. But let's face it, I'd be crazy to turn down an opportunity like this.

Her face lights up with wonder. "You mean it?"

"Yeah, why not? He's a lovely guy, and he wouldn't have offered if he didn't mean it. He wants to help both of us. He told me that Emily Brontë said 'proud people breed sad sorrows for themselves.' I think that's very true."

Her bottom lip trembles. "I didn't think you'd agree."

"I wasn't going to. But you're right. He's lovely, and it would be nice to spend some time with him, just like you did with Martin."

She swallows hard. "I've never been on a cruise. Aren't they quite posh? I don't have many clothes with me, and nothing smart. And obviously, I don't have any money at all."

"It's okay, I got a Christmas bonus. We'll treat ourselves to a couple of nice bits we can mix and match. And we won't need money on the ship. It's fully inclusive, so we won't need to pay for food or anything."

She presses her fingers to her lips, her eyes shining. "I can't believe it."

"It's going to be great. And now we have things to do over the next day or two. I need to think about what I need to do at work if I'm taking some time off. I guess you'll have to let your cleaning firm know you'll be away? And speak to Carl?" I wonder what her son will say about what's happened?

She nods. "I might ring Stu as well. He can call in and keep an eye on Keith. That will make me feel better."

"Okay. First, though, I have to call Nick and let him know the answer's yes…"

Chapter Eleven

Nick

After dropping Elena and Liz off, I consider going back to the office. Lucas will still be there, and probably Ben as well. But I'd told them I wouldn't be in today, and anyway, I'm not in the mood. Work normally distracts and comforts me, but it's been an odd day, and I feel unsettled and a bit low, which is unusual for me.

I go home and take a swim in the pool for half an hour, enjoying stretching my muscles and the flow of the cool water over my warm limbs. After doing some lengths, I lean on the tiles that look over the view of Wellington Harbor, and rest my chin on my hands.

It's so quiet up here. There's barely a breath of air, and the evening sun is hot on my skin, hinting at the gorgeous summer to come. I like the peace, but right now I miss the constant chatter of my kids. They used to make such noise in the pool, dive-bombing each other, yelling and splashing. Olivia wasn't a great swimmer, but she would bring out jugs of lemonade and plates of muffins for when they got out, and fuss around making sure everyone had sun lotion on so they wouldn't get burned.

My life was so different back then. Packed full with a wife, kids, the house, my work, and friends, like a jar stuffed with pebbles and then with sand poured between the gaps. Now it feels as if there's one large, rather boring stone in there, rattling around on its own.

It's not all my fault. Obviously I couldn't do anything about the death of my wife, or the fact that my kids have all got their own lives now. There's not much to do to the house, and I've never been much of a gardener. I still see friends occasionally, but it's not the same when you're single, and I have to admit I've drifted away from the couples we used to meet up with. And work doesn't fulfil me the way it used to.

But I should have told Elena how I felt. I've lost her, and I can't blame anyone else for the fact that I waited too long. She'll call later and say she couldn't possibly accept either the money or the trip away, and that will be that.

I haul myself out of the pool, towel myself dry, and go inside to get changed. Then I walk through to the kitchen. I can't be bothered to cook myself a meal, but I have plenty in the freezer, and I take out a portion of Spaghetti Bolognese, heat it up in the microwave, then pour a glass of red wine.

I could sit on the sofa and watch TV while I eat, but I'm not in the mood. Instead, I carry the plate and glass through to the dining room. It's a beautiful room that also overlooks the harbor, and this evening it's filled with a gorgeous warm light the color of mandarins from the setting sun. I put the plate and glass on the table, walk through to my study to collect my folder and a pen, return, and place them next to my plate.

I eat the Bolognese and sip the wine while I read through the notes I've been making over the past few weeks.

Ever since I was a kid, I've written poetry and short stories. I have dozens of notebooks in a box in my study, all filled with jotted lines, words, and imagery that have sprung into my mind through the years.

I've never had much time to think about writing anything more than that, or to consider doing anything with them. I've never been published. I wouldn't know where to start, although it would be relatively easy to find out with all the resources on the Internet.

Just lately, though, I've been thinking about writing something longer. A book, maybe, although the notion of penning eighty thousand words or more is a tad daunting. But I have an idea in my head that won't go away. A love story of sorts, set here in New Zealand, in the South Island during the Otago gold rush of the 1860s. I like Nicholas Sparks's writing, and I could see it turning out something like one of his. I don't know if anyone would ever be interested in reading it, but it's itching inside me to get out.

I haven't told anyone of my plans because, deep down, I'm afraid they'll laugh at me. Nick Prince, CEO of the biggest toy company in New Zealand, writing his first book at the age of sixty! It sounds ridiculous, even to my own ears. Olivia knew I scribbled poetry, but she always thought it was one of my amusing little foibles, and she never took it seriously. Friends of my age go fishing on their boats in their spare time, or they play golf. They don't write stories.

Well, I might be sixty, but I have this burning inside me to do it, and I don't have to tell anyone else.

I'm halfway through the Bolognese and have added another page of notes when my phone buzzes where it sits on the table. I look at the screen, feel a flip inside me as I see Elena's name, and then my heart sinks as I know this is probably going to be a line drawn under our relationship.

"Hello?" I stand, pick up my wine, and open the sliding glass door so I can wander onto the deck.

"Nick?" Her soft, slightly husky voice sends a shiver down my spine. "It's Elena."

"Hey." I sip the wine, feeling the early summer breeze blowing across my skin. It smells of lavender and the roses Olivia planted years ago around the deck. "How's Liz?"

"She's okay. She had a sleep when we got in, and she's had a couple of glasses of wine. She's having a shower now. I think she's feeling better."

"I'm glad. Has she decided what she's going to do?"

"Not really. She's going to take some time to think about it." I hear her take a deep breath. "Nick… about your offer for the cruise…"

"Yes?"

"Well, we'd like to accept."

My eyes widen and my heart shudders to a stop. "Seriously?"

"Yes… if you're still offering?"

"Of course I'm still offering. I just assumed you'd say no!"

"I was going to. I do need to discuss something with you. I need you to know that it wouldn't change anything. I'm pretty sure Liz will go back to Keith in the New Year. She still loves him, and I can't imagine she'll make the break permanently. So I'll still be leaving work, and moving up there in January."

I look up at the eggplant-colored sky, watching a flock of geese flying overhead in their V-shaped formation. "I understand."

"I… I don't know how to say this, but…"

"Elena, I told you the offer has no strings attached. I'm not expecting anything in return. I know you have to go, and anyway, I left it too late to tell you how I feel. And it's okay. Well, it's not, but I mean I understand. There's no price I'm expecting you to pay. Who knows, maybe we'll get to have a dance together one evening or something. That will be nice. But otherwise it'll make my day to know you both had a good time and enjoyed yourselves."

She's silent for a moment. Then she says, "I suppose I'm finding it difficult to believe anyone could be so nice. But I've been with you a long time, so I know you are. It's just hard to accept such a generous offer."

"I know."

"Especially with the gift of the money, too."

I look into my glass, feeling a touch of guilt. I probably made the 'bonus' far too big, but I wanted to take away any worries she might have about looking after her sister over the Christmas period. What's the point in all that money sitting in my bank account when I could help so many people with it? I've been giving lots of it away lately, making numerous donations to charities, to hospitals, and to schools. I don't consider Elena a charity case, but it's true that I want to help.

"Sorry about that," I say.

"God, Nick, don't apologize. It was a wonderful gesture, and although part of me wishes I could be the bigger person and refuse it, I'm afraid to say I'm grabbing it with both hands."

I chuckle. "I'm glad to hear it."

"I'm taking Liz shopping tomorrow—she's worried she doesn't have the right clothes for the ship."

"Most of the time everyone is in shorts and tees, but in the evenings everyone's a bit more formal, especially in the restaurants."

"Yes, I thought that would be the case, so we're going to treat ourselves to a few slinky dresses."

My lips curve up. "I look forward to seeing them."

"Now, now," she scolds, but I can hear the laughter in her voice.

"Aw," I say, "if you're expecting me not to notice how gorgeous you are in your sexy high heels, and not to comment on it, you're going to be disappointed."

"I don't mind you commenting," she murmurs. "And thank you."

"What for?"

"For everything. I don't know what I would have done without you."

That cheers me up immensely. "Well, you're very welcome."

I hesitate, and she says, "What?"

"I'm writing a book," I reply. I blink with some surprise at the way I blurted it out, and I immediately regret it, hoping she doesn't laugh.

To my delight, though, she says, "Oh my God, Nick, really? What about?"

"It's a novel, set during the gold rush in the 1860s. I've only just started plotting it, but I thought I might use the time on vacation to get the first couple of chapters done."

"What a great idea. Oh you must tell me all about it when we're on the ship. Will I get to read it?"

"I don't know about that. I'll probably write two pages and change my mind. I'm not even sure why I told you."

"I'm glad you did," she says softly. "Well, Liz has finished her shower, so I'd better go. Will you let me know when and where you want us to meet you?"

"Yes of course—I'll email you all the details, along with the itinerary."

"Thank you. From the bottom of my heart."

"You're very welcome." I smile. "Speak soon."

We hang up, and I lean on the rail of the deck, watching the ferry making the crossing over the Cook Straight to the Marlborough Sounds.

A seed of excitement springs into life inside me, and Brock's words filter into my mind, that when lightning strikes twice, you have to grab the opportunity with both hands. *If you want her, you might have to make some sacrifices*, he said.

I told her this was no strings attached, and I meant it. I don't expect anything in return. But that doesn't mean it isn't a huge opportunity. I'll have two weeks to convince her that she doesn't want to be apart from me. Two weeks to persuade her we have a future together.

And I'm not going to waste a single minute of it.

*

At eleven a.m. on the twenty-third of December, I meet Elena and Liz at Wellington airport.

The two women have wide eyes and talk non-stop all the way to the plane.

"What are you nervous about?" I tease as we buckle ourselves in for the flight to Auckland.

They exchange a glance. "Everything," Elena says.

I do understand, sort of. Cruises have a reputation of being the vacation of choice for old, rich people, and to some extent that assumption is true. They're expensive when compared to a vacation in a five-star resort in Fiji or Rarotonga, which would probably cost about half what the suite costs on the ship. There's also a dress code, as I explained to Elena—no shorts in the restaurants, and three of the nights are formal evenings, which means dinner jackets for the men and cocktail dresses for the ladies. And there's not a lot for young people to do. Sometimes they have programs for the kids on board, and there's always the pool for them to splash about in. But mostly it's a time for folk of a certain age to relax and be waited on hand and foot, the ultimate luxury for most people.

There's also nothing nicer than waking up in the morning to a view different from the one of the night before. It's much better than staying in a hotel.

"Were the kids okay with you going away?" Elena asks.

"Yeah. They grumbled a bit at the beginning, something about the head of the family not being there to carve the turkey, blah blah, but Mum will be there. They won't even miss me when it comes to it."

"I doubt that very much," she says softly. "You have a big presence, and they all look up to you. But I'm sure it will do them good to be without you for once—and it'll do you good too to have some time to yourself."

Her words warm me through. "I hope so." I smile at Liz. "And how are you doing?" She's had her hair trimmed and styled, and she's wearing what looks like a new sundress. She's covered most of her bruises with makeup. She's uneasy, though, and she fiddles with the strap of her bag in her lap.

"I'm good, thank you," she replies. "I feel much better."

"She spoke to her son, Carl," Elena tells me. "He was very supportive, and he said he was surprised she hadn't walked out ages ago. He's going to fly home on Christmas Eve to spend some time with his dad. I think that'll be good for Keith."

"He felt guilty, I think, after saying he didn't want to come home for Christmas," Liz says. "I think he guessed that's what started it all off."

"Have you heard from Keith?" I ask.

"No. But Carl has spoken to his mate, Stu, who's been around there. Carl says he'll keep an eye on him. He told me to go away and enjoy myself, and not to worry."

"So we're all set," Elena says. She smiles, but she looks a little tense. I imagine it's been a difficult few days. She's obviously done her best to help Liz feel good about herself, but I'm sure Liz has been emotional and upset, and unsure about what will happen when they get back.

Now's not the time to worry about that, though. After the plane takes off and Tim comes over to ask if we'd like any refreshments, I tell him to pop the cork on a bottle of champagne. The two women's eyes light up, and they both give a brief, easily deflected protestation before accepting a glass and sipping it with delight.

"Get used to it," I tell them. "We'll be having Mimosas for breakfast, Irish coffees all day, and cocktails in the evening. Expect to sleep very well!"

They both giggle like schoolgirls, and I grin. I'm looking forward to introducing them to the Cerulean Blue, the beautiful ship that will be our home for the next two weeks.

Cruise vacations always feel like magical mystery tours, but this one is extra special. I study Elena's profile as she looks out of the window, and then meet her eyes when she brings her gaze back to me. With the sun slanting across her, they look like two sparkling emeralds today, glittering with excitement. At the prospect of the vacation? Or at the notion of spending time with me? I hope it's the latter, and my pulse picks up speed at the thought of the unknown adventures ahead of us as we sail off into the wild blue yonder.

Chapter Twelve

Elena

I don't think I've ever been so excited or so nervous.

Part of it, I know, is being with Liz. At any moment, I expect her to say she doesn't want to leave, and that she's going back to Keith. She's spent a good portion of the last couple of days wrangling with herself and feeling guilty for abandoning him. Deep down, she knows she's in the right, and she can't allow herself to be treated like that. But love makes no sense, and she's worried about him.

As we approach the gangplank onto the ship, I know it's her last chance to turn around and run back to the shore. But to my surprise, she doesn't. She shoulders her bag and strides along, and when we get onto the ship, she takes a big breath and lets it out slowly.

I hold out a hand, and she smiles and slides hers into it. Then she turns and slips her hand through Nick's elbow. "Thank you so much for this. I know I'll never be able to repay you."

"Obviously, that's not an issue," Nick states firmly. "Elena has been invaluable, and helping out her family is the least I can do."

It's a throwaway comment, but it warms me through and makes me sad at the same time. We've worked well together over the years. It's a PA's job to anticipate her boss's needs before they know them, and I like to think I've achieved that. I'm going to miss him a lot.

But I'm not going to think about that now. We follow the line of passengers into the ship, and Nick checks our tickets, then leads us down a flight of stairs to the Dolphin deck. Everything looks pristine—the plush carpets are a deep burgundy, the wooden handrails are gleaming, and the mirrors on the walls are polished and glitter in the afternoon sun.

At the bottom of the stairs, he follows the numbers on the doors and eventually stops by D630. "This is yours," he states. "I'm next door in 632."

All the doors are open, and as I walk in, with Liz following, I see our two suitcases waiting just inside.

It's a family suite, with two bedrooms adjoining a shared living area. Both bedrooms have a bathroom with a shower, and one has a bath. The living area has a two-seater sofa and an armchair, and a round dining table with four chairs. There's even a balcony, big enough for two loungers as well as a table and chairs. The decor is blue and white, with light wood polished to a high shine. A tiny Christmas tree sits on the table, the tinsel sparkling in the sun. The place is bigger and nicer than my apartment.

Emotion overwhelms me, and I burst into tears.

"Aw," Liz says. "Don't, Ellie, or I'll start."

"Jeez," Nick says, coming into the room, "what are you two like? Come here." He puts his arms around me and holds me tightly.

I sniffle and snuffle into his shirt, comforted by the feel of his arms around me. Liz smiles, opens the sliding doors, and goes out onto the balcony, leaning on the balustrade and looking down at the ocean, giving us some privacy.

"What's this about?" he murmurs in my ear, rubbing my back. "I don't think I've ever seen you cry."

"Sorry," I whisper, fumbling for a tissue. I move back a bit and blow my nose, but he doesn't lower his arms. "It's lovely, Nick. You're so incredibly generous. I just feel overwhelmed."

"It's only what you both deserve," he says simply. "I'm glad you like it."

I look up at him, into his bright blue eyes. They're the color of the summer sky outside, with golden flecks in the middle. I've never noticed them before, but then I've never stood this close to him.

His gaze drops to my mouth, and he studies it for a moment. Suddenly there's no air in the room. I want him to kiss me more than anything else in the world.

He lowers his lips… and gently kisses me on the forehead.

Then he lets his arms drop and moves back. "Why don't you take some time to settle in and explore the ship? And then maybe we could meet for dinner?"

"That would be lovely," Liz says as she comes back in.

"I'll book somewhere. Six o'clock okay for you both?"

"Perfect," I reply happily, and he smiles and goes out, closing the door behind him.

I look at Liz, and the two of us burst out laughing and throw our arms around each other. "Am I dreaming?" She hugs me tightly. "I feel as if I'm in a fairytale."

"Me too." I might earn more money than she does, but I've never been on a vacation like this. "Which bedroom do you want?"

She moves back and we go over to the doorway. "I'll take the one with two single beds," she says. Then she gives me an impish look. "You never know; you might need the double bed."

My jaw drops. "Liz!"

"What happens on the cruise ship stays on the cruise ship," she tells me, and I hear her laughing as she wheels her suitcase into her room.

A small smile plays on my lips as I do the same with my case, heave it up onto the bed, and start unpacking. It's never going to happen, of course—the last thing I need right now is to fall even further in love with Nick Prince. But it's like window shopping, I guess. Nobody has to know what goes on in the privacy of your own mind.

I sing as I take out several unworn summer dresses and hang them up in the wardrobe, then put my freshly ironed T-shirts and shorts in the cubby holes. I can't remember the last time I treated myself to new clothes. In the first few years of working for Prince's Toy Store, I bought several expensive suits, and I'm still wearing those, pleased the quality fabric has lasted so well. But it was great fun to try on new things. I'm looking forward to wearing them, and I know Liz is, too.

The bathroom contains some complementary products, but I lay out my makeup and the things I can't do without like my favorite moisturizer and deodorant. Then, taking the daily newsletter that's been left on my bed with me, I go back into the living room and out onto the balcony.

Apparently there's a party to celebrate when we leave port at three p.m., which should be fun. The newsletter includes the full itinerary. I read it all on the email Nick sent me, but I look through it again to see if anything's changed. Today is the twenty-third, and now we have three whole days at sea before we arrive at Brisbane on the east coast of Australia on the twenty-seventh. That means we'll be at sea for Christmas Eve, Christmas Day, and Boxing Day. They've planned a lot of activities, from lectures on art, moviemaking, and history, to fun games in the Atrium, to lessons on sketching and painting, to dance and yoga classes.

I'm stunned at how much is available on the ship—there's a theater, a cinema, an art gallery, a library, an Internet Café, a spa and beauty salon, several swimming pools, and umpteen restaurants. Numerous bars boast varying themes focusing on cocktails or whiskies or the type of music they play like jazz or blues. It really is like a small city where they've made the most of every inch of space.

I look up at the sky. By the angle of the sun, I'm facing north-east, which means if we traveled in this direction in a straight line, we'd probably hit Mexico or Peru. It always surprises me when I look at Google Maps how far New Zealand is from everywhere. It's over fourteen hundred miles from Auckland to Brisbane. New Zealand is like a jewel that glimmers in the midst of the vast South Pacific Ocean. We'll be visiting the breathtaking Fiordland National Park on the west coast, and towns including Dunedin, Christchurch, Napier, and Tauranga. I can't wait!

Footsteps sound behind me, and then Liz joins me on the balcony. "How are you doing?"

"All unpacked," I say. "You?"

"Yep. Ready to go and explore."

"Come on then."

"Do we need to take money?" she asks. I've given her some for spending.

"I don't think so. Nick said we can put everything on our rooms and settle it at the end, and anyway all the food and drink is included."

She giggles like a schoolgirl. "Come on!"

We hang our key cards on their lanyards around our necks, leave the rooms, and set out to explore.

The ship is busy, with last-minute passengers still making their way to their rooms. We go to the Promenade, accept a glass of wine from the waiters by the door, and follow everyone out onto the deck as the ship finally leaves port. Christmas music has everyone dancing as they wave at those on shore, and Liz and I join in, sipping our wine and laughing as we bop along to the songs.

Afterward, we hand our glasses back and start exploring the ship. We soon get hopelessly lost, but have a fantastic time wandering up and down the decks, oohing and aahing at everything we see. We find the Explorers' Lounge with its gray-and-gold decor and a Christmas tree in the corner that glitters under the overhead lights, and discover that its menu offers specialty liqueurs and spirits that can't be found anywhere else on board. From there we discover the huge theater with its amphitheater-style seating, and take one of the leaflets that detail all the entertainment available throughout the trip, which includes an old-fashioned Christmas pantomime.

Next to the theater is the art gallery, and we spend a pleasant half hour looking at the paintings and sculptures that are going to be available for sale at an auction to be held halfway through the voyage. Then we go all the way up to the Lido deck, where we're stunned to see the three pools complete with hot tubs—a quiet adult-only pool, an indoor pool, and a huge outdoor family pool. Here there's also a pizzeria, a fish-and-chip café, a burger bar, and an ice-cream parlor, serving food to the families who are already splashing in the water or stretched out under the shade of umbrellas.

At the end of the deck is the spa and beauty salon, and we investigate the options, promising each other we'll be brave and treat ourselves to a massage and maybe a manicure at some point. We have a quick look around the gym and sauna—Liz laughs and says she won't be spending much time there, but I decide to join one of the yoga classes for their early morning sessions, and make a note on my phone of the times.

There's plenty more to explore, but we decide to go down to the Crooners Lounge, attracted by the decor of highly polished dark wood, cream and gray furniture, and subtle white fairy lights twinkling around the bar. It's quiet there, and a pianist is playing an old Sinatra song, his smooth voice a gentle accompaniment to the cocktails the patrons are sipping. We order two martinis and take them over to plush cream chairs by the window, overlooking the ocean.

"Are we really here?" Liz sips her martini. She's wearing one of her new sundresses, with pretty orange-and-yellow flowers that lend a bit of color to her pale cheeks. I know she feels out of place because I do, too, but the alcohol will help us relax, and I'm sure that after a few days we'll begin to feel more at home here.

"It is like a dream." I wonder what Nick is up to. I feel a bit guilty at leaving him. The man has paid for both of us to be here and we go and abandon him! Equally, though, I'm sure he's looking forward to some time alone. Not for the first time, I wonder how his book is coming along. Apart from the few lines of poetry I saw on his bedside table, I wasn't aware he wrote.

"I wonder where we'll eat this evening." Liz looks out to sea, and a shadow crosses her face.

"Are you thinking about Keith?" I ask, already knowing the answer.

She nods and stirs her drink with the olive on the cocktail stick. "It's funny to think of him at home, on his own. I hope he's okay."

"He'll be fine," I say firmly. "He's not completely helpless." When they first discovered he would be confined to a wheelchair, his mate Stu, who's a builder, widened some of their doorways, and put supportive bars in the bathroom and moved the hand basin so Keith could maneuver easily in there. He's gone to the shops and stocked Keith up with food, and he's calling in a couple of times a day to check on him. Carl will also be arriving tomorrow.

She takes the olive off the stick and chews it thoughtfully. "I still feel sad. He deserves it, I know. And it would serve him right if I never went back."

"It would." I decide it's time for some honesty. "I've done my best to see things from your side, and to understand why you've stayed with him. But he's been a right bastard to you. He's unpleasant and rude, and he never says thank you for all the things you do for him. I wouldn't mind half as much if he'd rung you as soon as you left, apologized profusely, declared his love, promised to change, and begged you to come home. But he hasn't even called!"

Her eyes glisten. "I know."

"He doesn't deserve your loyalty. A relationship has to go both ways, otherwise you're just being a doormat."

She swallows hard and bites her bottom lip.

Immediately, I feel guilty. "I'm sorry, that was too harsh."

"No, you're absolutely right. Of course you are. I've put up with his bad moods and abuse for far too long. I thought I was being a good, supportive wife, but you're right, I've become a doormat, and he walks all over me. Well, I'm done with that." She lifts her chin. "I'm not going to let him treat me like that anymore. I deserve to be happy, and to be loved, don't I?"

"Absolutely you do."

"And so do you." She gives me a direct look. "You've been amazing, Ellie. Don't think I'm not aware of what you've given up for me. But you can't spend the rest of your life putting me first."

"You mean the world to me," I say simply. "When I was falling apart, you picked up the pieces and held them together with both hands. I couldn't have gone on without you. And being there for you is the least I can do."

"I'm so lucky to have you," she says, her eyes glistening again.

I lean forward and take her hand in mine. "And I you."

We tighten our fingers, then both laugh and lean back. "To us," I say, lifting my glass in a toast.

"To us," she repeats, "and to the marvelous adventure to come."

I sip my drink, thinking about what she said: *You can't spend the rest of your life putting me first.* My family will always be the most important thing in my life. But it warms me through that she's so appreciative of what I've done for her.

We finish our drinks, then decide to retire and rest until six, when we're due to go to dinner with Nick. We return to our rooms, and I stretch out on the bed and set my phone to go off at five thirty. Then I close my eyes, tired out from all the excitement, as well as the wine and the martini.

I dream of glittering lights, romantic music, and Nick's lips pressing on my forehead, his arms warm around me.

Chapter Thirteen

Nick

When I knock on the girls' door five minutes before six, it's Liz who opens it.

"Well," I say, smiling, "don't you look like the bees' knees!"

She brushes down her new dress, which is an attractive cerise color and flows over her curves without clinging. She's tied her hair back in a neat ponytail and slotted a clip with a small pale pink flower behind her ear, and she's wearing lipstick that matches it. "It's been nice having time to spend on myself," she admits. "As well as a reason for dressing up."

"I know what you mean." I follow her into the room, then stop at the sight of Elena standing in the middle, slotting in an earring. She's wearing a white gown that sparkles in the late afternoon sun, and her hair is bright blonde and shiny. For a moment, I can see her in a white veil, clutching a posy of flowers and holding out a hand for the ring to be slipped onto her finger. Then the image fades and it's just a pretty summery dress, fresh and alluring.

"Hey," I say softly.

"Hi." Her gaze brushes down me like a feather, making the hairs rise all over my skin. "You look nice. Like you should be in Egypt in the nineteenth century shooting lions and tigers."

That makes me laugh. I'm wearing a short-sleeved white shirt, no tie, light trousers, and a linen jacket. "At least I don't have a pith helmet."

She giggles, picks up her keycard, and hangs it around her neck. "Shall we?"

I lead the way out, heading down to the Promenade deck and past the theater to Romano's Restaurant.

"Ooh," Elena says as we approach, "Italian."

I stand aside at the door to let them precede me. "I hope that's okay?"

"Lovely." They give the waiter our room numbers, and he leads the way inside.

I asked for a table by the window because I wanted this to be a special first night, and I'm pleased when he takes us to a quiet table in the corner. The decor is understated and elegant with black furniture, gray cushions, white pillars, and white crockery. The table bears a Christmas decoration and a lit candle.

I hold Elena's chair for her, and the waiter holds Liz's, and then I take my seat. He hands us a menu, and I nod when he asks whether we'd like bread and olive oil to start.

"And a drink to begin with?" he asks, handing me the wine list.

"Would you like champagne?" I ask the two women. "Or would you prefer something different?"

They exchange a glance and I can see them trying not to laugh. "Champagne would be lovely," Elena says in her best I-drink-it-all-the-time voice. I give her a wry look, glance at the menu, and order a bottle of the Veuve Clicquot, and the waiter goes off to get it.

"Nick," she scolds. "You really don't have to do this."

"It's what I'd have if you weren't here," I say honestly.

"Oh. Okay. Well, you know what I mean." She looks at her menu, her cheeks turning a light rose-pink.

Liz smiles at me and looks at her own menu. I grin and study mine.

The waiter returns with sliced bread in a basket and a dish containing olive oil and salt, shows me the champagne and opens it, and pours us all a glass. Then he takes our orders. We decide to opt for a shared meat and olives platter to begin with. Liz chooses the seafood linguine for a main, Elena has the lemon and rosemary chicken *scaloppine*, and I go for the prosciutto-wrapped pork tenderloin. The waiter retreats, and we all sip our champagne.

"I think I'm dreaming," Liz says.

I chuckle. "So come on then, what have you been up to today?"

They tell me how they've been exploring the ship, and all the things they've found. "Did you go to the party?" Elena asks.

I shake my head. "I had a bit of work I wanted to catch up on."

"Work!" She looks alarmed. "Oh Nick, seriously?"

"Just a few emails," I say, amused. "Nothing too heavy. Afterward, I had a walk around the promenade and then a whisky in the Hemingway Lounge."

"With a cigar?" she teases. "You're such an old-fashioned gentleman."

"Never smoked in my life," I reply. "But I'll take the compliment, thank you. So… what do you think of the ship?"

"It's amazing," Liz says immediately. "I didn't know what to expect, to be honest, but it's far surpassed all my expectations."

"I love the way all the bars are so individual," Elena adds. "One was playing jazz music, and then when we walked around the corner, the next had a pianist playing Sinatra songs, but they were completely separate. It's very cleverly done."

"I could live on board," Liz says. "Everything I could ever want is here." She lowers her gaze to her champagne then and lifts the glass to her lips. I'm guessing she's thinking about Keith.

"So what do you have planned for tomorrow?" I ask, hoping to distract her.

"We're thinking about going to the pantomime tomorrow afternoon," Elena states. "I haven't been to one since I was a kid. That should be fun."

"Are you going to visit the beauty spa?"

"Maybe later in the week. Tomorrow we'll do some more exploring. We didn't quite get around all the decks today. Perhaps we'll do a bit of shopping."

"I can't believe it's Christmas Eve," Liz says.

"There's a party in the evening," I tell them. "If you're into dancing."

Elena's eyes light up, but Liz laughs and shakes her head. "I've got two left feet."

"You have not," Elena scolds.

"Yes I have, and you're just being polite. No, I don't think I'm quite ready for a party, but you two should go."

I see the two of them exchange a look, and Elena gives her sister a warning glance. "I'm not going without you," she states.

I concentrate on dipping the bread into the olive oil and the salt. Has Liz been trying to persuade Elena to spend some time with me alone? If so, I understand why Elena's reluctant. She won't want Liz to feel like a fifth wheel, and besides, I'm sure she's not going to want to risk our relationship developing into anything deeper. She's obviously determined to keep her distance.

Well, I'm just as determined to convince we're meant to be together. We have a whole two weeks at sea. Surely that's enough time to convince her?

The meat and olives platter arrives, with slices of *mortadella* and salami, *mostarda di frutta* and glistening olives. While we eat, I try to keep the conversation light. We talk about the places we're going and whether we've been before. Neither of the women has been to Brisbane, Fiordland, Dunedin, or Tauranga. Elena has visited Napier and Christchurch a few times. Wellington is the only place they've both been.

Liz clearly hasn't traveled much at all. Elena has been to Sydney and Melbourne—I suspect it was with her late husband, although she doesn't clarify.

"Have you traveled a lot?" Liz asks me.

"A bit."

"A bit," Elena scoffs. "He's always going away on business," she tells her sister. "London, Paris, Berlin, Tokyo, New York."

I nod. "Mostly alone though. Olivia didn't like traveling." She disliked the disruption to her routine, the food, and the crowds, and much preferred staying at home.

"I should have said," Liz comments, "I'm very sorry to hear that she passed away. She must have been very young."

"Fifty-seven. Yes, it was a bit of a shock."

"How did she die?"

"A brain aneurysm. Very sudden. At least she didn't suffer." I sip my champagne. I don't like thinking about that night.

"Tell Liz about the time you got lost in Amsterdam," Elena says.

"No, Ms. Hunter, I don't think I will, thank you very much." I smile though, aware she's trying to lighten the mood.

"Or how about when you fell off the boat in Rarotonga?"

"I wasn't aware you knew that story." It happened on one of the few times Olivia and I went away with the kids.

"Oh, I know plenty more," she says, her eyes gleaming.

I smile, but I feel a twinge of resentment. Olivia was quick to pass on my secrets, while all the time keeping plenty of her own.

"Sorry," Elena murmurs. "I didn't mean to embarrass you."

I suppose I shouldn't be surprised she picks up on my mood so easily. We have worked together for a long time. "Oh, I've done many, many stupid things over the years. I'm not surprised a few of them have leaked out."

Liz giggles, then nods as the waiter approaches and offers her another glass of champagne. She presses her lips together as she watches him fill her glass, then sips the bubbles. Her cheeks have taken on a rosy glow that I don't think has anything to do with the late summer sun coming through the window.

He takes our plates away and soon places our mains before us. The pork comes with crispy rosemary potatoes. Liz's linguine contains prawns and clams, while Elena's chicken is accompanied by grilled asparagus and creamy mashed potatoes.

Liz comes out of her shell after a few glasses of bubbles, and proves to have a teasing sense of humor much like Elena's. Despite the fact that neither of them have gone to university, they're both well-read and interesting to talk to, and time passes pleasantly as we discuss everything under the sun.

For dessert, Liz chooses roasted almond and espresso cannoli, while Elena has a ricotta and cinnamon trifle with salted amaretto. I can just about manage a slice of pear and hazelnut torta Caprese, rich and fudge-like.

"I'm so stuffed," Liz states at the end of the meal. "I couldn't eat another thing!"

"Can you manage a coffee?"

She blows out a breath. "I don't think so."

"Maybe we should take a short walk," Elena suggests, "let our dinner go down, and then perhaps we'll be able to fit one in afterward."

I'm happy with that, so we leave the restaurant and walk the short distance to the large double doors that lead outside. Liz has brought a jacket and Elena a wrap that she places around her shoulders. The sun is low on the horizon, turning the sea into a jewel box of carnelian, sapphire, amethyst, and amber colors.

"What a lovely way to travel," Elena says, tucking her hand through my elbow as I offer it to her. Liz does the same on the other side, and we walk slowly along the length of the ship, passing the occasional couple out to get some fresh air, and one or two individuals using the circular area to jog around and get some exercise.

"There's something nice about the time it takes," I agree. "On a plane you don't always get the same sense of distance."

The breeze tugs at Elena's hair and lifts the floaty fabric of her dress, making her laugh. She has long, slender, shapely legs I've often admired from a distance when she walks away from my desk in her high heels. Tonight she's wearing a pair of strappy silver sandals I haven't seen before, and her toenails are a cherry-red. I'd like to kiss them. The thought takes me by surprise. Where did that come from? The lust is sudden, and somewhat delicious.

Since Olivia died, I've been careful to steer my thoughts away from sex. I'd honestly thought it was something I wouldn't experience again. Although I had a few partners in my youth, I was faithful to my wife all the time she was alive, and I couldn't imagine sharing myself with someone like that again. I liked Elena, but I've ignored my feelings because I've had to.

But now... I let my mind stray to thoughts of sliding the zipper of her new dress down her back, exposing her slender shoulders, her no-doubt soft, pale skin. Of discovering what kind of underwear she likes—lacy and sexy? Simple white cotton? Either is appealing right now. I imagine exploring the peaks and valleys of her body, with my fingers and my mouth. It would be an exotic adventure into unfamiliar territory.

Maybe I should get myself a pith helmet after all.

She looks up at me as I give a short laugh, and her eyes meet mine. "What's so funny?" she murmurs.

I shake my head, not daring to tell her. "Nothing." But I can't stop thinking about her naked now, and I know it's showing in my eyes, because her cheeks pinken, and she drops her gaze.

Liz shivers next to me as the cool breeze blows across us, and I suggest we take the next door back inside and find ourselves a bar. We've walked all the way around the ship, and we enter near the Crooners Bar. We find ourselves an empty table not far from the pianist, who's playing old-style melodies like Nat King Cole's *The Christmas Song*, and a waiter comes over to take our order. The two of them decide to finish off the evening with a cocktail, while I choose an Islay malt whisky over ice.

The waiter has just walked away when I see a man walking toward us from across the room. He's wearing a navy-blue uniform with a white shirt. His insignia—four gold stripes with a wide bottom stripe and a top loop—mark him out as the captain of the ship.

"Daniel!" I get to my feet and greet him as he comes over and gives me a bearhug.

"Nick!" He's about the same age as me and the same height. I'm sure women find the contrast between his curly silver hair and brown skin very attractive. "Good to see you. It's been a while."

"You're looking well."

"You too. Being CEO clearly suits you."

I grin and gesture to the two women who have now got to their feet. "This is Elena Hunter and Elizabeth Rice, my companions this vacation. Ladies, this is the captain and my good friend, Daniel Erueti."

"I understand we have to thank you for finding us a last-minute suite," Elena says as she shakes his hand. "Thank you so much. We really appreciate it."

"Not a problem at all. I'd do anything for this good man here." He turns to Liz and shakes her hand, too. "Nice to meet you, Elizabeth."

"Oh, it's Liz," she says shyly.

"Liz. How are you enjoying your stay on the ship so far?"

"I'm having a wonderful time. It's the best vacation I've ever had."

"I'm pleased to hear it." He smiles at her, and I notice he's holding her hand a little longer than is strictly necessary. Oh… does he find her attractive? He gives her a long look before he finally releases her, and Liz blushes furiously.

Elena meets my gaze, her lips curving up.

"You must excuse me," he says, "I'm about to go on duty. But tomorrow night, would you all like to join me for dinner at the Pukeko Restaurant?" He says 'all', but he's looking at Liz.

She and Elena appear alarmed at the thought of eating with the captain. "We'd love to," I reply, amused.

"I'll send an invitation," he says. "Seven o'clock. See you then!" He gives a parting wave and strides off out of the room.

"Oh. My. God." Liz's legs give way and she sinks into her chair. "Are we really going to dine with the captain?"

"It'll be a lovely meal," I reply. "The restaurant has a Michelin-star chef who specializes in fusion cuisine with a Kiwi twist."

"What do we wear?" Elena asks faintly.

"What you have on will be fine," I tell her. "It's really nothing to worry about."

She looks at her sister, and her lips twitch. "He liked you."

Liz goes scarlet again. "Ellie!"

"Is he married?" Elena asks me.

"Divorced," I reply.

"There," she says. "He's available."

Liz's glow is positively radioactive.

I just smile. Daniel is married to the ocean, which is the main reason his marriage failed a few years ago. I don't think he was devastated. I'm sure he has more than his fair share of onboard romances, and I wouldn't want vulnerable Liz to get swept up in his wake, but I'm sure a little light flirtation will do her the world of good.

Our drinks arrive, and they sip their cocktails, exchanging them so they can each try the other's. I have a mouthful of whisky, conscious of feeling unusually comfortable and content. If I'd come alone, although I could have mixed with the other passengers, I would probably have ended up eating on my own most of the time, which isn't half as much fun. It's been nice to have company, and twice as nice to be with Elena.

She's leaning her head on a hand now, obviously beginning to feel the effects of the busy day and the alcohol. Her gaze is resting on me, and this time, when I meet her eyes, she doesn't look away. Instead, with her legs crossed, she reaches out a toe and pushes my knee. I'm not sure if it's the whisky or her smile that heats me from the inside out.

Chapter Fourteen

Elena

The next day, I open my eyes, and for a moment I'm confused. The light is different, and the door isn't where it should be.

Then I hear the ever-present rumble of the ship's engines and feel the very gentle motion, and I remember where I am. Immediately, a wave of excitement washes over me.

Not in my wildest dreams would I ever have imagined spending Christmas on the ocean. I've had friends who've had boats, and even been invited out once or twice, but there's a big difference between chugging around the coast on a small boat that smells of fish, and living a life of luxury on an ocean liner.

Today we're on our way to Australia, and when I rise and go out into the living room and onto the balcony, I can see nothing but sea. The Tasman stretches out before me, a rich blue under the early morning sky, tinged with gold. They've put the ship's time back by an hour as Australia is three hours behind New Zealand, so it's only six a.m. at the moment, and the day is all shiny and new.

I lean on the balustrade and look to my left. I'm separated from Nick's balcony by a barrier, carefully constructed to preserve guests' privacy. I wonder if he's up yet, maybe having a coffee, or even out for a walk. I know he doesn't sleep well, and that he's an early riser.

Well, it's none of my business. It's nearly time for my yoga class. I visit the bathroom, pull on my smartest pair of yoga pants and a new white T-shirt, slide my feet into my sneakers, smooth my hair into a ponytail, and leave the cabin, pulling the door closed quietly behind me. I know Liz won't wake until later, and we've planned to take a late breakfast at nine.

SANTA, THE BILLIONAIRE

I make my way up in the elevator to the Lido deck, emerge about halfway along by the indoor pool, and walk through the spa area to the fitness center.

I'm just about to turn into the center when I glance to my left at the gym. I stop and stare. Nick is in there, dressed in shorts and a vest, running on the treadmill. He's wearing earpods and looking at an iPad attached to the front of it, and he's facing a little away, so he hasn't seen me.

I watch him running, noting the dark patch marking his back, and the way his thigh muscles bunch and stretch.

If he saw me, this hot, sweaty man might walk toward me with those blue eyes fixed on me, pin me up against the wall, and crush his lips to mine.

Ooh. Now there's a fantasy I haven't had before.

I moisten my lips with the tip of my tongue, turn away, and mutter to myself as I walk into the fitness center. I really must get a grip on my imagination. It's not only running away with me, it's sprinting like Usain Bolt.

The yoga class is an absolute delight. The glass walls look out onto the shining ocean, and the early morning sun slants through and falls across the yoga mats in golden bars. Somewhat shyly, I choose a mat at the back, and it's only minutes later that the instructor begins a warm-up routine that has me bending and stretching all my muscles. She takes us through a variety of asanas, and by the time the session is over, I feel loose, warm, and more than ready for a shower.

I thank the instructor and head out, and walk straight into Nick.

"Well," he says. "Good morning."

I stare at him, unable to remove the image of my fantasy from my mind. He has a deep V of sweat marking the front of his vest, and his hair is damp at the temples. "Mm," I reply. "Yes, it is."

His lips curve up. "Did you access your third eye in there or something? You look zoned out."

I give myself a mental slap. "Sorry, yes, it was quite the experience. Are you off to shower?"

"I thought I might have a dip in the hot tub, actually. Care to join me?"

My jaw drops at the thought of a semi-naked, glistening Nick. "Um… I don't have my swimming costume." I brought one, but it's in my cabin.

"Just strip off," he says. Then he bursts out laughing at the look on my face. "Elena, I'm joking." He takes my hand and leads me into the beauty salon. To one side, a range of costumes hangs on a rail. "Choose one," he says. "Put the cost on your room."

Nick told me that the trip was fully inclusive, but I've spotted the additional costs that could quickly add up if I'm not careful. However, I can't refuse because of money after he generously gave me that huge bonus.

And anyway, it's not the cost of the costume that's the problem.

But the temptation to be close to him overrides my doubt, and I nod and pick up a couple of costumes to try on. "I'll meet you in the hot tub," I tell him, and he grins and heads out of the spa.

I blow out a long breath and go into the changing rooms. This will be the first time he'll have seen me wearing next to nothing. I'm not twenty-one anymore, and I'm neither as slim nor as firm as I used to be.

But neither is he, and anyway he's just a friend, and I don't have to impress him.

Yeah, yeah. You keep telling yourself that, Elena.

I'm tempted to choose the plain black costume as I know they're usually the most slimming, but I've never been one to wear much black as it depresses me, so in the end I opt for a pretty navy one with light- and dark-blue flowers all over it. It's ruched at the front and is a flattering fit. I leave my clothes in the changing rooms, come out and ask them to put the cost on my room, and head out of the beauty spa.

This pool is adults-only, and as it's early there are only two other people in there, swimming lengths. Nick's the only person in the hot tub, which is bubbling away merrily. He's sitting facing the pool, his arms outstretched along the back of the tub, and he watches me as I rinse myself under the shower, then climb the steps, sit on the side, and swing my legs over the edge.

"Good choice," he says as I lower myself in.

"Thank you." I sit on the seat next to his, in touching distance, but far enough away so I don't have a coronary.

The crystal-clear water is hot, and the jets massage my back and legs. It's blissful, and I lean back, close my eyes, and let out a long sigh.

When I finally open them, he's still watching me. His hair is damp—I think he might have had a quick swim before I came out—and smoothed back off his forehead. His beard glistens. His light-brown skin shines in the overhead lights. Saint Nick looks rather sexy when he's wet.

"Having a good time?" he asks softly.

"I'm having a fantastic time, Nick. Thank you so much."

"You don't have to keep thanking me," he scolds. "So what's next on the agenda for you and Liz today?"

"Breakfast at nine," I reply. "We're going to try the buffet. Then we're hitting the shops this morning."

"They have a great range of jewelry here. Lots of Kiwi-made bits."

"I'll definitely check that out. We want to treat ourselves to a few mementoes of the trip too—a cruise T-shirt, or some coasters, that kind of thing."

"And you're going to the pantomime this afternoon?"

"Yes—would you like to come?"

He smiles. "No, thank you. I'm going to work on my book today."

"Oh, yes, I was going to ask you about that. How is it coming along?"

"Good. I did some research yesterday. Today I want to try to work out a rough plot. I might even start the first chapter, if I'm brave enough."

"I'd love to read it when you're done," I tell him honestly. "I'm sure it's going to be amazing."

"I'm not expecting miracles. It'll just be nice to get it out of my head and onto paper. Well, onto the keyboard."

"So we'll see you at dinner tonight?" I ask, trying to hide my disappointment.

"Oh yes." His expression turns mischievous. "I get the feeling Daniel's offer surprised you both."

"Eating at the Captain's table was not something either of us envisaged."

"It'll be great," he says. "Dan is a good guy, and we've been friends for a long time."

"He knew Olivia?"

He nods. "He came to her funeral." He looks away, out to sea.

Olivia's ghost hovers, a shadow in the corner of my eye. It's strange—I've spent all the time since she died worrying that she would be angry with me for having feelings for her husband. But Nick said she wanted him to promise, if and when something happened to her, we would get together. That must have been so hard for him, and he told me it still plays on his mind that if he now gives in to his feelings, it'll mean he lied to her when he said he wasn't interested in me. Will she always stand between us? Or will it be possible for us to finally put her ghost to rest?

I sigh. It's irrelevant really, because it wouldn't solve the problem of Liz and her complicated life. I wonder now, though, what would happen if she decided not to return to her husband? Where would she live? What if she chose to stay in Wellington? How would that change things?

It all seems so up in the air, and it makes me uneasy to think about it.

"How's Liz?" Nick asks, bringing his gaze back to me, and I have the feeling his thoughts are following a similar pattern to mine.

"She's okay. She had a lovely time yesterday. But Keith's mate, Stu, had to go away for the night to visit his in-laws. Her son, Carl, doesn't get there until this afternoon, and she still hasn't heard from Keith, so she's a bit worried as to how he's coping. I told her it's not her responsibility to ensure his safety, but she's still concerned."

"Of course."

I like that he doesn't mock her for being worried about her husband, even though he obviously dislikes the way Keith's treated her.

"At least she doesn't have long to wait," Nick says. "I presume her son will call her when he finally gets there?"

"Yes, and that should put her mind at rest."

He nods, and we sit companionably in silence for a while. He closes his eyes and tips his head back, obviously enjoying the heat of the water.

I take the opportunity to study him, letting my gaze roam over his glistening body. Broad shoulders, toned biceps, and that intriguing dip at the base of his throat. I want to lean forward and touch my tongue to it. I want to kiss up his throat and jaw, to nuzzle his ear, and slide my hand into his hair. I want to kiss his mouth again, to have him claim me the way he did at Liz's house, hard and passionate.

He opens his eyes, catching me looking at him. Our gazes lock, and I can't look away. His eyes are so blue, and those gold flecks are mesmerizing.

He doesn't say anything, and neither do I. There's nothing to say, really. We both know we find each other attractive. We both know we're floating in an ocean of possibility. But there's a dangerous riptide below us. I can't afford to give in to my feelings. Leaving him is already going to break my heart—how would it feel if we'd slept together, if I'd fallen even more in love with him?

But as my gaze lingers on his mouth, I feel such yearning that it makes me ache.

"You shouldn't look at me like that," he murmurs, a frown flickering on his brow.

"Sorry." I finally look down into the bubbling water. My pulse is racing, and my mouth has gone dry.

"I don't mind," he says, and he reaches out and tucks a wet strand of hair behind my ear. "It just means I'm not going to be able to get out of the hot tub for a minute or two."

His voice is teasing, and it's only as my gaze drops automatically below the water line that I realize what he's referring to.

I look back up at him, and now I can barely breathe.

His eyes are hot, filled with desire. "I want you," he states simply. "I have for a long time. I want to kiss you. I want to make love to you. But more than that, I want you in my life, Elena. I need you to know that. I'm done with denying it, and with ignoring my feelings. I know things are hard for you at the moment, and your sister comes first. So I want to say, I'll do whatever it takes. If Liz goes back to Keith, and you decide you're still going to move to the Bay of Islands, I'll fly up every weekend and see you. Or, if I have to, I'll move up to be with you."

I stare at him. "You'd leave your family, your job?"

"Well, I can still do most of my job online. Of course I'd miss the kids, but I'd be flying down frequently."

My jaw drops. "I couldn't ask you to do that for me."

"You're not asking; I'm offering."

"Yes, but…" How do I explain it? "We've not even been on a date! You couldn't throw away your whole life on a whim."

"Well, for a start we've worked together for ten years, so I'd hardly call my feelings for you a whim." His direct look is amused and a touch scolding, and I suddenly remember he's the CEO of a multinational company. "But you're right. I could fly up at weekends for a while, until we decided it's what we both wanted. You should know, though, that I've been thinking about putting the house up for sale for a while."

"Your family home?" I press a hand over my heart.

"Don't you start. Ben's bottom lip trembled when I mentioned it. But it's far too big for me on my own. And it holds too many memories." He frowns. "I know I'm sixty, but I'm *only* sixty. I could, God willing, have another twenty or thirty years." He gives me an earnest, almost desperate look. "I miss Olivia, and I've spent two years grieving for her. But I can't spend the rest of my life doing it. I don't know if that makes me a bad person, but I just can't. Life is for living, and if I'm going to stay in that house and mourn for her every minute of every day, I might as well just end it all now."

"Don't say that," I whisper, tears pricking my eyes.

"I told her I didn't feel anything for you," he whispers furiously, "but I do. Do you think if I give in to my feelings now, it means I'm being unfaithful to her memory?"

"I don't know," I say honestly. "I'm not a philosopher. All I know is that you're a good man, and when she was alive you were faithful to her. And I'm not sure if I believe in soul mates either. I think we choose a mate, and if we're lucky we get on very well and stay together for the rest of our lives. But do I believe it means we're destined to be with one person? No, not at all. It's human nature to search for the attractive features in another person. In my mind, it doesn't make you unfaithful. Thoughts matter, but actions matter more."

We fall quiet, and I can see he's thinking about what I've said. My mind is whirling. He's willing to give up his family and his home and come up to the Bay with me? I can't process that right now. I need time to think about the implications of it.

All I can process is him saying he wants me. It's my Christmas wish come true—but I don't know what to do with that information. How can I celebrate that and decide what happens now when my sister's life is falling apart in such a terrible way?

And I can't ask Nick to sell his home, move away from his family, and come up to the Bay with me when we haven't even kissed properly yet! We haven't been on a single date. We might discover when we've been together a while that we're incompatible for some reason, and how will I feel then if he's made such huge changes in his life for me?

I don't know what to say, or how to deal with the information. But still, the fact that he likes me, that he wants me in his life, makes a warm glow begin in my belly that I know will stay there for the rest of the day.

Chapter Fifteen

Nick

I spend a pleasant day on my own, something I haven't done for a long time. Usually at home, even when I'm not working, one of the kids is calling in, or a friend stops by to see how I'm doing, which is lovely, don't get me wrong. But for once it's a treat to have some peace and quiet.

After leaving Elena outside her room, I go into mine, dress in comfortable track pants and a T-shirt, then go for a walk to give the staff time to clean and tidy the suite. I check out the ship's library, discover a Nicholas Sparks book I haven't read before, and take it to the Patisserie. I'm not a great breakfast person, but I'm getting peckish, so I order a Danish pastry and a latte, and eat and drink while I read.

It's not long before my attention wanders, though, and I find myself looking out of the window at the waves, which are gold-topped in the morning sunshine. I feel as if I unzipped my fly this morning when I declared my feelings for Elena. I don't know what I expected—some sign of pleasure or excitement from her, for sure. Instead, though, she merely looked uncertain and worried, although her cheeks did flush, and she did say thank you quietly before declaring it was time for her to get out of the hot pool and return to her room.

Should I have kept quiet? I don't think Brock would have approved of that course of action. He'd have said to make my position clear. I suppose it makes sense that she'd be wary, considering how up-in-the-air Liz's life is at the moment. Elena had her future planned out—she was convinced I had no feelings for her, and she was ready to move on. Now I've thrown it all into disarray. It's no wonder she's confused.

I close my eyes and think about the moment she came walking out in her new swimming costume. She's tall and slender, and she'd tied her hair back, exposing the delicate, pale skin of her neck. As she slid into the water beside me, it had taken every ounce of willpower I possessed not to drag her into my arms and kiss her senseless.

It's been over two years since I had sex. I've tried to train my mind not to think about it. But all of sudden it's like I'm sixteen again, plagued with constant images of undressing a woman and discovering what she looks like without her clothes. Not just any woman, though. I've admired Elena for a long time, noting her shapely, slender legs, her elegant mannerisms, the interesting curve of the Cupid's bow of her lips, but it seems that once I let go of the dog inside me that has been straining at his leash, there's no holding him back. Now I can't stop picturing her breasts, the curve of her waist, and how it would feel to slide inside her.

Jeez, Nick, get a grip. I remind myself of how she told me she's waited too long for me, and that I've killed any feelings she had for me. I think it was a knee-jerk reaction, and I don't think she meant it. But I can't dismiss her words just because I don't like them, even if they stab me in the gut every time I recall the moment they left her mouth.

I'll have to wait and see what happens, and try to rein in my mind every time it attempts to stray from its path.

Determinedly, I make myself read a couple of chapters of the book until I've finished my breakfast, and then I take a walk around the deck to stretch my legs. As I wander back through the ship, I spot Liz and Elena in one of the shops, but I duck into a corridor before they see me. I don't want them to feel as if they have to spend every waking minute with me. And besides, I have work to do.

I go back to my room, and the first thing I do is call Kora.

"Dad!" she says, sounding delighted, which brings gladness to my heart. "Where are you? On the ship?"

"Yep. In my room. I just wanted to check up on you and your new family."

"We're marvelous, thank you. Well, knackered, obviously. Absolutely shattered, actually. Callum's eyeballs are hanging on his cheeks. But I'm happy, Dad. Really happy."

"I'm so glad," I say, swallowing hard against a lump that forms in my throat. "Are you at Buck House?"

"No, we're leaving soon. Ben and Heloise stayed last night, but the rest of us are going up for the afternoon, and we're all staying the night tonight."

"I just wanted to say I hope you have a great time. I miss you all." It's true—I feel a sudden wave of homesickness for the familiar setting and my kids.

"You didn't have to go sailing the ocean waves and leaving your family behind," she teases.

"I know. Part of me wishes I'd stayed at home now."

"Aw. You don't mean that. I'm sure you're having a fantastic rest—just what you need. And how is Elena, by the way?"

My lips curve up. I told the kids about my offer to take Elena and her sister with me. They all teased me about our relationship until I told them about her sister, and then they were suitably horrified. "She's well, thank you. Enjoying her vacation."

"And Liz?"

"She's okay. It's hard for her not to think about her husband and what happened, but she's enjoying the change, I think."

"I'm glad to hear it. I keep thinking about her."

"Well, I won't keep you, I'm sure you've got lots to do. How are Jamie and Rachel?"

"Gorgeous monkeys. Rachel has a little cold so no doubt Jamie will get one too, and probably me and Callum!" She sounds deliciously happy. "Will you call us tomorrow?"

"Definitely. Take care of yourselves."

"Love you."

"Love you too." I hang up.

Contented that they seem to be doing all right, I make myself a coffee and take it outside onto the balcony with my laptop. I came here to work on my book, and it's time I stopped screwing around. I've made copious notes, and I need to plot the damn thing out so I know where I'm going.

I put Elena and my family firmly out of my mind and get to work.

*

Elena

Liz and I spend a pleasant enough morning looking around the shops and touring the remainder of the ship. Under my urging, she treats herself to a new sunhat and a pretty wrap for when we go to the pool, but afterward she falls quiet, and I can tell she has something on her mind.

We've decided to skip lunch as we ate quite a big breakfast, but around two p.m. we stop at the Patisserie in the Atrium and order ourselves a coffee and a muffin to share.

"Okay, out with it," I say as we sit at a table by the window. The Atrium is busy, with people strolling through the shops, stopping to ask questions at the main desk, or booking excursions. Liz watches the couples walking by, some of them hand in hand, with a look of longing on her face.

"I can't stop thinking about him," she says simply. "I can't believe he hasn't rung." Her jaw knots as she clenches her teeth. "I really thought he'd miss me."

"Of course he misses you. But it's a game of chicken now. He's angry because you stood up for yourself and walked out. If he calls, he's admitting he was in the wrong."

"Does he really think he's in the right?" Her eyes glisten. "When we married, I never envisaged we'd end up like this."

"I doubt any divorced couples do."

"We're not divorced," she says, and her voice is a touch sharp. "We're having difficulties, but I'm not ready to sever the tie to him yet."

"You're right. I'm sorry."

The waiter brings our coffees over, and she stirs a spoonful of sugar into hers. "I know you think I'm crazy for not telling him I want out."

"Of course I don't…"

"You do, and I understand why. But it's as if for the last thirty years I've been building this house, and I've invested all this time in making the bricks and laying the floorboards and putting the windows in. The thought of walking away just makes me so sad."

I reach out and take her hand. "I understand, I really do. But the thing is, people change. He's not the man you married."

"I know. But it's hard. I've seen how much pain he's in. And I know how much it tortures him that he can't work. It's struck at the very heart of his masculinity, and I know women mock that nowadays and say it doesn't mean anything, but it does. We're animals at heart, aren't we? And the males are supposed to provide for the females and look after them."

I refrain from telling her it's the twenty-first century and women don't need a man to look after them now, because I know what she's trying to say. Most men would struggle if they discovered they could no longer work. Women somehow find it easier to pass the time at home, and it's a well-known fact that they cope better with retirement.

It makes me think of Nick, probably currently in his room, writing. He took over as CEO when his father could no longer work, but I know it's not a job he's comfortable doing. He's smart and resourceful, but in another lifetime, I think he'd have worked in marketing or advertising. It's only now that I wonder whether he ever had a choice of career. He's hardly going to complain, bearing in mind the toy company is so successful and his family is so well-off, but it's never entered my head that it might not be what he wanted to do.

We go back to our room for an afternoon rest before the pantomime that starts at four. I'm lying on my bed, reading, when I hear Liz talking to someone in her room. Keith? I don't want to eavesdrop, but I try to discern her tone. She's not angry or pleading.

I get up, go into the living room, and put the kettle on for a cup of tea. I'm just making it when she comes out. Her cheeks are red, and her eyes are wet. She shakes her head when I indicate the cup, and sinks onto the sofa.

"What's happened?" I ask gently, coming to sit beside her.

"Carl rang." Her voice is dull, like a piece of tarnished silver. "He finally got home. He said the place is a mess, and Keith's furious and won't stop yelling. He's calling me all the names under the sun." Tears run down her cheeks. I don't think she even notices. "Carl was really upset."

"Oh, Liz…"

"I said I'd come home, and he begged me not to. He told me to keep away, and said his dad needed some time. I don't know what to do…"

My heart breaks, and I take her in my arms and hold her while she dissolves into tears.

We sit like that for a while, the early afternoon sunlight streaming across us. Suddenly, I think it was a terrible mistake coming away. I thought it would be good to remove the option for her to return, but now the ship feels like a prison. Not that I want her to go back, especially if my nephew is telling her not to, but I can't help but think she's going to be so miserable for the rest of the vacation knowing she's stuck here.

Eventually, exhausted, she says she's going to lie down. I watch her go into her room and close the door, knowing she'll probably cry herself to sleep.

I wrap my arms around myself, feeling alone and adrift. Outside, the ocean slides by in a gleam of blue, but I can find no pleasure in it. I don't know what to do, or how to help.

And suddenly, there's only one person I want to talk to.

I text Nick, *Hey, it's me. Do you have time for a chat?*

He comes back immediately, *Of course! I'm in my room.*

I scribble a quick note to Liz and leave it on the coffee table, then take my key card and slip out of the room. It's only a couple of paces to Nick's door. I knock on it, and he opens it and steps back to let me pass.

"Everything okay?" he asks as I go in.

"Not really." His room is similar to mine, with just the one bedroom and a slightly bigger lounge. It's neat and tidy. His laptop sits on the coffee table, with a notepad and pen next to it. His sweater hangs over the chair. I feel the urge to pick it up, press my nose to it, and sniff it.

"What's happened?" He gestures to the sofa and sits in the chair. I sink down. He's wearing cargo shorts and an old, faded, blue T-shirt, and his feet are bare. His hair is a bit ruffled. You'd never guess the guy was a billionaire.

I tell him about Carl's phone call. "She wants to go home, but Carl told her not to," I finish. "I think that upset her more than anything." I give a long, heartfelt sigh and lean back. "I don't know what to do."

He sits forward, his elbows on his knees, fingers linked. "Maybe you don't have to do anything. What she's going through is a process. It was never going to be straightforward. Marriage isn't linear like that. She's like a yacht, tacking from side to side to get to the next piece of land. Not every day is going to be good. And not every day will be bad."

I consider his words, seeing the wisdom in them like pearls at the bottom of the ocean. "You're right. I suppose it's natural that she's going to be upset."

"Of course it is."

"I feel as if it's my job to stop that, to remove any unhappiness from her life."

"Well, you're her sister and she's helped you out in the past, so you're going to want to solve her problems for her. But you can't. All you can do is provide her with the tools to make her own decision." He gives me a direct look. "She may well end up going back to him. Are you prepared for that?"

"I don't know. That's going to be hard."

"But it's a possibility. And if that's what she's chooses, you're going to have to accept it."

I swallow hard. "I don't want her to go back to him."

"I know. If she does, I hope she has the courage at least to wait until he recognizes the error of his ways. I don't think she should go rushing off home yet. But I understand why she's worried about her son."

"I feel so impotent. There must be something I can do."

He purses his lips. "You could ring… Carl, is his name?" I nod. "Yes, you could ring Carl and just make sure he's coping okay. Say you're here for support if he needs you."

"That's not a bad idea," I say slowly. "I could double check he doesn't want Liz to go home."

"I'm sure he's worried about his mum, but you could reassure him she's okay here, and that you're hoping she continues her vacation, to give his dad time to think about what he's done."

"You're right."

"Why don't you ring him here? I'll make us a coffee."

"Okay." I take out my phone, go out onto the balcony, and ring Carl. I leave the door open, though.

He answers after a few rings. "Hello?"

"Hey, sweetie, it's Auntie Ellie here."

"Hi. Oh, it's nice to hear from you." He sounds relieved.

"I just wanted to make sure you're okay," I tell him. "Mum said things are a bit tricky there."

"We're okay," he admits. "Dad was really angry when I got here. I didn't tell Mum, but he's smashed up a couple of plates and ripped up some of her magazines."

"Oh dear."

"I've cleaned it all up. He's calmed down a bit now. He couldn't remember how to turn the oven on, and he couldn't reach the microwave, so he's been eating baked beans cold from the can."

I sigh. "Ah."

"It's only what he deserves," Carl says fiercely. "It's my fault. I shouldn't have told Mum I wasn't coming home for Christmas."

"Darling, you're not to blame at all."

"It's nice of you to say so, but I am. I couldn't face another Christmas with him. But I didn't think about what might happen when I said that. I should have been there to support Mum."

"Honey, their marriage has been in trouble for a while, and it's absolutely nothing to do with you. Actually, I think it's good that it's finally come to a head. Now it'll be sorted, one way or another."

"Do you think they'll get divorced?" he asks in a small voice. I guess it never gets any easier to hear your parents' marriage is breaking down.

There's no point in lying to him. "I don't know. I do know your mum still loves him. She wants to come home."

"You mustn't let her," he states firmly. "I told her not to. He doesn't deserve her. At the moment he's just angry that she's gone, but he needs to think about what it would be like if she doesn't come back. I'm not going to let him treat her like that again. You've got to keep her there, Aunt Ellie."

"I'll do my best. I agree that it'll do them good to have some time apart. Now, I just want to check that you're coping okay there."

"Yeah, I'm okay."

"I know it's not going to be a great Christmas for you, and I'm sorry about that. What I've done is put some money into your bank account."

"Aw, Ellie…"

"It's okay, my boss gave me a big bonus! Now, do you have your Mum's car?"

"Yeah, it's on the drive."

"Why don't you call into town and pick up some groceries for you and your dad? We just need to get them both through the next few weeks."

"I don't think I can cook a Christmas dinner," he says, and I chuckle.

"I wouldn't worry about that. Get some basic things like bread and milk, and then whatever you need to rustle up some meals." I know he's a pretty good cook—that's something Liz did teach him before he left. "Maybe some nice steaks, and some chicken. And some meals for the freezer for when you don't feel like cooking. And get some chocolate."

"Okay."

"You're in touch with Stu, right?"

"Yeah. He's been coming around every day, apparently."

"Good. Make sure you ring him if you're worried about anything. I'll look after your mum, and hopefully by the time we come back, they'll both have had a break, and cooler heads will prevail. Their emotion will have died down a bit, and they'll be able to talk about what's happened."

"Okay. Thanks for ringing, Auntie… and thank you for the money."

"No worries, love. You take care of yourself, okay?"

"Okay." He hangs up.

I stand there for a moment, looking out to sea. A pod of dolphins is swimming alongside the ship. It's the first time I've seen them, and I can't help but smile as I watch one after the other jump out of the water, while below me those watching from the Promenade deck cheer and clap.

I'm glad I rang. Nick was right—what Liz and Keith are going through is a process. It's not up to me to make decisions and decide the outcome of their marriage. It's her life, and it's her choice. I can only be there to help.

Chapter Sixteen

Nick

"Okay?" I ask Elena when she comes back in.

She nods. "He's a good boy. He's determined to make sure that his dad doesn't treat her badly again. He's asked me to make sure that she doesn't go home. I hope she won't want to get off the ship."

"Do you want to go and check on her?"

"I'll let her sleep for a bit."

"All right. What would you like to do? Do you want to stay here and have a cup of coffee? Or go out for a walk?"

"I'm happy to stay here," she says. "And I'd love a coffee."

Pleased, I get up and begin making it.

"How's your plotting coming along?" she asks, gesturing at the notebook on the table.

"Not bad, actually. I think I have a loose plot drafted out. And I've written the first couple of pages." I press the button on the coffee machine, and the hot espresso descends into the first cup.

"Can I read them?"

"Ah…" I put the second cup under and change the capsule. "I'm not sure I'm ready for that!"

"You don't trust me?"

"Aw, it's not that. Nobody's ever read my stuff."

"Not even Olivia?"

I add some milk to the cup and pass it to her. "When I was younger, I showed her some of my poetry a couple of times, she either laughed or teased me that the only rhyming I could do was moon, June, and spoon. She wasn't greatly encouraging."

I pick up my cup, then pause and look at Elena. "Sorry, I shouldn't have said that. I feel bad now."

"I know what she was like," she replies. "She was very vocal with her opinions where art was concerned. Sometimes I agreed with them, sometimes I didn't, but I rarely argued with her. I liked that she was willing to voice her thoughts. It didn't mean we had to agree all the time."

"No, I suppose not." I sink into the chair and stretch out my legs. I don't want to talk about Olivia. "Well, the first couple of pages are on the laptop, if you want a look."

She puts down her coffee, pulls the computer onto her lap, and presses the button. "Is your password still BuckHouse61?"

I chuckle. "Yeah." The house and the year I was born. It's the same on all my PCs, and she often uses my work one.

It occurs to me as she types it in that Olivia didn't know my password. She never asked, and I never told her. Strange how sometimes your PA knows more about you than your wife.

Elena sits back with her cup and spends a couple of minutes reading the first few pages. I sip my coffee, nervous at her reaction. If she laughs or is dismissive, I think I might give up. I don't know why I have so little confidence where my writing is concerned, when I'm self-assured in the real world.

Eventually, she puts the laptop down and lifts her gaze to mine. Her eyes are filled with wonder. "Oh, Nick. It's amazing."

My heart lifts, but I try to act casual. "You like it?"

"What a fantastic opening—the two men fighting over the gold in that creek bed. It was brutal but honest and heartbreaking, too."

"It's a true story," I admit. "Jacob and Edward were real, and they were enemies before the gold rush began because Edward had had an affair with Jacob's wife. When they met in that creek bed, it was destined to end badly."

"Maybe there are accounts of it," she says, "but the way you brought it to life gave me goosebumps. Oh, I can't wait to read the rest of it. You've got to let me read it when you're done!"

"Definitely," I say, and smile. I wonder, though, where we'll be when I write The End. Will she be living in the Bay? Will I be with her?

She checks her phone, noting the time. "I don't think Liz will want to go to the pantomime, somehow." She sighs.

"Do you want me to go with you?"

She laughs. "No, it's okay. I'm sure it's not your thing. It's not my thing really, I just thought it would be different. I'd rather stay with Liz and make sure she's okay. I just hope she wants to go to dinner tonight." She finishes off her coffee, then chews her bottom lip. "I don't suppose you'd come and try to persuade her?"

"Me? I'm sure the last thing she wants is a man telling her what to do."

"No, you're wrong, she looks up to you. I know she'd listen to what you have to say."

"I'm happy to talk to her if you'd like me to."

"Come on, then."

We leave the cups by the coffee maker and head out to their room. Elena lets us in, and we enter quietly. "Wait here," she says, and she slips into Liz's room.

I go out onto the balcony and look out at the ocean for a few minutes until I hear footsteps behind me. Elena is walking out with Liz behind her. Liz looks white-faced, and her eyes are red and puffy. She attempts a smile.

"Hey," I say gently. "How are you doing?"

Her bottom lip trembles, and then she bursts into tears.

"Oh dear." I put my arms around her and give her a hug. "Come on, everything's going to be all right."

Elena stands to one side, pressing the fingers of one hand to her lips. "Don't cry," she whispers.

"I'm sorry." Liz dabs at her eyes, struggling to regain her composure. "I just keep thinking of what Carl said. It's not fair to leave him to cope with Keith. I really should go home."

Elena gives me a desperate look.

I rub Liz's back. "Come and sit down," I say in as soothing a voice as I can manage. "Look, I know this is none of my business. But would you like to hear my advice?"

She nods and blows her nose as we sink into the sofa."

"I don't know your husband, but I'm sure you wouldn't have married him unless he was a good man. I know you hope he's still that man inside. But I don't think you're going to find him if you go back now. Sometimes, when you're down, you can't start going back up again until you hit rock bottom. I'm sure that at the moment he's expecting you to rush home when you discover he's in trouble. But he needs to get to that point where he truly thinks you're not going back.

Only then will he have to face up to what he's done and decide what he wants in the future."

She swallows hard. "I just feel so bad leaving it all on Carl's shoulders."

"I understand that. But Carl is… what… twenty-one now?"

"Twenty-two."

"He's a man who's been coping on his own since he went to university. He obviously feels guilty that he instigated this event by saying he wasn't coming home."

"It wasn't his fault." She defends him immediately.

"He's not to blame," I reply, "but he should have understood what actions his decision might provoke in Keith. He told Elena that he's not going to let his dad treat you like that again. He wants to take responsibility, to help you, and to help his dad see the error of his ways. Personally, I think you should let him. Keith's behavior and the decisions he makes aren't your responsibility. A husband and wife choose to share their lives with each other, but they should always respect one another. Unfortunately, respect is often the first thing to go when you've been with someone for a long time, and occasionally the relationship needs a nudge to get you both back on track."

Liz studies the tissue in her hands, thinking it through. I glance at Elena, who smiles.

"Okay," Liz says in a small voice. "I'll wait a bit longer."

"Good." I get to my feet. "Now the best thing I think you can do is make the most of your time on vacation. Starting with tonight. Why don't you spend some time relaxing and getting ready, and I'll knock on the door at ten to seven to pick you both up?"

"All right."

"I'll see you both later."

Elena accompanies me to the door and holds it as I go out. "Thank you," she whispers. Her eyes are alight and full of an emotion I can't decipher—admiration, maybe?

"You're welcome. I hope I made sense. See you tonight?"

She nods, and closes the door behind me.

*

True to my words, at 6:50 p.m. I knock on their door. After ten seconds or so it opens. They come out into the hallway, hesitant and obviously a bit nervous.

Liz is wearing a long blue summer dress and she's carefully applied her makeup to hide any sign that she's been crying today. She looks much brighter, and quite pretty with her dark-blonde hair that tumbles around her shoulders. But I only have eyes for Elena.

She looks stunning tonight in a floor-length, pale-green, sleeveless summer dress. Man, she has a great figure. Her blonde hair gleams in the light, and she's made up her eyes with a green sparkly eyeshadow that makes them glitter.

"Wow," I say, "I'm the luckiest man on earth being able to take not one but two such gorgeous women to dinner."

Liz giggles like a fourteen-year-old. Elena gives me a wry look, but she slips her hand into mine as we walk along the corridor. "Thank you," she mouths, although I'm not sure if she's referring to the cheesy compliment or the help I gave her with her sister earlier.

It's the first time we've ever held hands, and it feels curiously intimate as we walk through the Atrium. I'm wearing smart navy trousers, a white shirt without a tie, and a smart-casual light blue jacket, but I know everyone's not looking at me. I hadn't realized just how beautiful Elena is. Or maybe I have, but I've spent the last twelve years trying not to notice. It's like I've been pointedly staring in the opposite direction all this time, and at last I'm finally allowing myself to look directly at her.

I squeeze her fingers a little, and she glances up at me and squeezes back. Not long after, we have to part to get past a group of people, and she walks ahead with Liz, but the memory of touching her lingers, and I hope it's not the last time it'll happen.

We arrive at the restaurant and are shown through to the large circular table that's already half full. Daniel stands as we approach and says our names, then introduces everyone who's seated. He shows Liz to the seat next to his, and I take a chair between her and Elena. Within ten minutes everyone has arrived, and the waiters hand out our menus.

I know the girls are nervous, and I half expect them to remain silent, but to my surprise they both chatter away through the evening. Daniel and Liz spend ages talking about the places he's visited during his time on board various ships. Liz hasn't traveled much, but she has read a lot of travel books, and I can see he's taken with how much she knows about the countries he's been to.

Elena talks occasionally to the elderly gentleman on her right, who it turns out ran his own furniture business until he retired a few years ago, and she brings me into the conversation by saying I'm also the director of my own company, and soon we're exchanging experiences and enjoying finding common ground.

The meal is magnificent, and I can see both Liz and Elena are wowed by the quality of the dishes. The Christmas music and the twinkling tree in the corner give everything a festive twist.

My fears that Liz wouldn't be able to get past her worries are unfounded. Daniel turns on the charm, and I can only imagine how it must feel to have someone pay her such attention after being ignored for so long.

Several hours pass without us noticing, but eventually one of the couples announces they're going to join the party in the Milky Way Lounge, and people start rising and saying their goodbyes, promising to keep in touch. Daniel says his goodbyes, and I note that he lifts Liz's hand to his lips and kisses her fingertips before he departs.

"I think I'm going to go to bed," Liz says as we get to our feet.

"Aw." Elena looks disappointed. "Come on, you promised me we'd do some dancing."

"I've had a wonderful time," Liz says. She's had a few glasses of wine, and her cheeks are flushed. "But I'm really tired."

"Okay. Come on, then."

"No, you stay with Nick," Liz protests. "Go and have a drink or something. I'll be fine."

Elena glances at me. "Are you heading back?"

I was going to, but I'm not going to pass up this chance to spend some time with Elena alone. "I'm happy to go and have a drink, or a walk on the deck."

"Okay." She kisses her sister on the cheek. "I'll see you in the morning."

Liz smiles at me. "Thank you for a lovely time."

"You're welcome, I'm glad you enjoyed it."

She gives us a last wave and heads off to the elevators.

Elena watches her go, then turns back to me. The fairy lights make her eyes twinkle. "So… shall we go for a walk on the deck?"

"Sounds great."

We push open the large double doors and head outside. It's not cold, but the ocean breeze brings a touch of coolness to the warm evening. Elena's brought a dark-green pashmina, and she places it around her shoulders.

Feeling brave, I hold out a hand. Part of me expects her to explain that earlier was a one-off and I mustn't overstep the mark, but to my pleasure she slides her hand into mine, and we begin to walk along the length of the ship.

It's quiet out here, with just the rush of the waves and the occasional Christmas tune filtering out from the restaurants and bars. Sometimes we pass other people out for a late-night stroll, who nod and smile. It occurs to me that it must look as if we're a couple. If only that were the case.

Toward the front of the ship, Elena pauses and leans on the railing. I lean beside her, our arms just touching. Behind us, a man who sounds like Michael Bublé is singing *Have Yourself a Merry Little Christmas*.

"Oh, look!" Elena points up to the night sky. The moon hangs above us like a silver Christmas bauble, almost full. A small cloud is moving across it, and it looks for all the world as if it's Santa in his sleigh, off to deliver presents to the children in the southern hemisphere. The stars are like the Earth's own fairy lights.

"It's a wonderful night when you've got small children," I say. "That time when you leave a mince pie for Santa and a carrot out for Rudolph is so precious."

"I wish I'd experienced that," she says softly. "I feel as if I've missed out on so much. I try not to think about it, but Christmas is a time for kids, isn't it? It makes me sad."

"I'm so sorry." I put my arm around her shoulder, and to my surprise she turns toward me and slides her arms around my waist.

I rest my lips on her hair, and we stand there like that for a while.

Eventually, she moves back and looks up at me. Her eyes glisten in the moonlight, and she smiles. "Sorry. I didn't mean to be maudlin. It's the champagne!"

"It's okay." The festive song weaves around us, and I take her hand. "Dance with me."

She gives a small laugh. "Really?"

"There's no one around." I begin to move to the music, and automatically she moves with me. Smiling, she lifts her other hand to my shoulder, and steps a little closer.

We dance to the rest of the song, and then to the next one, which turns out to be *White Christmas*.

"I'm having such a lovely time," she murmurs.

"I'm glad. It's only what you deserve."

"You've been so kind, to me and to Liz. I can't explain what a difference you've made."

"I haven't done anything."

"You say that, but you have, Nick. You've given her the opportunity for a taste of freedom. What you said today about Keith and her son really touched her. I don't think she'd thought of it from Carl's point of view—that she should give him the chance to help his dad. It really made her think."

"Well, if I helped even a little, I'm glad."

"You've helped a lot." Her green eyelids glitter as she looks at my mouth. "Will you kiss me?"

My heart skips a beat. "You don't have to repay me." The absolute last thing I want is for her to feel she owes me.

But she gives a little shake of her head. "I know. That's not why I said it."

"It's the champagne, is it?" I tease.

"Maybe a little. It's just… it's Christmas Eve. And it seems the night for wishes to come true. I'll understand if you'd rather not. I can't promise anything." She lifts her gaze to mine. "So will you? Kiss me, I mean?"

"Yes, Elena. I'll kiss you." I don't need any further prompting, and I lower my lips to hers.

Chapter Seventeen

Elena

Part of me had expected Nick to continue to protest that he couldn't possibly kiss me, not if I wasn't prepared to commit to anything more. So when he immediately agrees and lowers his mouth to mine, it takes me by surprise.

His lips are cool and firm, but the kiss is tender, gentle. His beard and mustache are surprisingly soft on my skin. He kisses me once, twice, a longer third time, then lifts his head to look at me.

I don't know whether it's the fact that it's Christmas Eve, whether it's because I've eaten the best meal of my life, or if it's the champagne—possibly all three, with the champagne in the lead—but I feel as if I have tweety birds circling around my head. I feel dizzy, deliciously so, drunk on the smell and taste and feel of the man before me.

He tips his head to the side, looking at me as if he's waiting for me to end the kiss, maybe even run away. I don't. The last thing I want is to end this magical moment.

I don't know what it means. I have no idea what comes next, or where the future will lead us. All I know is that I want him to kiss me again, and I don't want to analyze why.

The small smile that touches his lips seems to suggest he understands this. He places his hands on my shoulders and turns me so I'm leaning against the railing. He moves a little closer, so he's pressed against me, and my heart races at the contact. We're in public! It feels shocking, even though there's nobody around. He's looking down at me, because he's taller than me even though my sandals have heels. Oh God, he's so incredibly handsome.

He cups my face in his hands, his skin warm against mine. His thumbs brush my cheeks, and he studies my mouth as if he's thinking about all the ways he could kiss me, going through them, choosing which one he fancies. My pulse races as I wonder what options he's considering. Gentle? Firm? Passionate? Demanding? I want him to kiss me the way he did at Liz's house. I want him to *want* me, as if he can't bear to leave me alone. I've never been wanted like that in all my life.

His head still tilted a little to the side, he lowers his lips to mine again.

This time, the kiss is ardent, hotter. He touches his tongue against my bottom lip, requesting permission, and I'm more than happy to open my mouth and give him access. He brushes his tongue inside, and my whole body heats at the welcome invasion. Ooh, that's erotic, the slick, sensual slide of it against mine, the taste of the whisky he had at the table, the feeling of him inside me, even in such a small way. It's an intimate foray into territory I haven't entered for a long, long time. Ricky never, ever kissed me like this, with such tenderness, such yearning, as if he'd die if his lips were parted from mine.

Nick's hands slide into my hair, and ever-so-subtly the temperature rises between us. My hands rest on his chest, and I splay them out, feeling him through the soft cotton shirt. Then I slip my hands around his ribs, under his jacket, and onto his back. I want to be closer to him. I rest against him, leaning into the kiss, and he lowers his arms around me. He's warm and reassuringly solid. I feel protected, safe in his embrace.

Ooh, he's taking his time, drawing out the moment. The sea breeze lifts my hair around my face, tugs at my wrap, but he just tightens his arms and continues to kiss me. He presses his lips to my cheekbones, my eyebrows, the spot between them, down my nose, and back to my mouth. He nibbles my bottom lip, dips his tongue inside, and, basically, kisses the living daylights out of me, until my lipstick has vanished, my hair is mussed, and I'm breathing so heavily I sound as if I've just finished a marathon.

When we finally come up for air, I'm glad he's still holding me, because my legs have turned to jelly and I don't think they'd hold me up.

"I feel a bit faint," I tell him.

"Me too. I don't think either of us has breathed for the last five minutes."

We both laugh, and he moves back a little. He slides his hands into the pockets of his trousers, and suddenly I can see how he would have looked as a young man in his early twenties, lean and handsome, a little bashful.

He offers me his elbow. "Come on. I don't want you to get cold."

I slide my hand into the crook of his arm, and slowly we walk back along the length of the ship.

"Christmas Day tomorrow," I murmur.

"Yeah. Crazy, eh?"

"Are you calling the family?"

"Yeah, probably in the afternoon."

"Send them all my love, won't you?"

"Will do." He stops by the doors into the ship and pauses with one hand on the handle. "Elena…"

I look up at him. His blue eyes look black, twinkling with the reflection of the stars above us.

"I don't know what to say," he says eventually, with a little laugh.

"How about Merry Christmas?" I whisper.

He smiles. "Yeah. Merry Christmas."

I reach up and press my lips to his cheek, and then we go inside.

The ship is busy, with people going to and from restaurants, drinking in the bars, and dancing at the parties, but I'm exhausted from the day and more than ready for bed. As we walk to our rooms, though, I start to get nervous. I kissed him, when I promised myself I was going to keep my distance. He's a man, and a full-blooded one at that. What's he going to think?

Is he going to ask me back to his room?

And what will I say if he does?

Instantly, I know I'm not ready. Not after one kiss. My heart races, and my mouth goes dry.

But as we approach the rooms, he pauses by mine and bends to kiss my cheek. "Thank you for a lovely evening," he says.

"I had a wonderful time."

"I'm glad. I hope Liz is okay. You know where I am if you need me." He backs away.

"Goodnight," I call after him.

He waves and goes into his room, and the door slowly closes behind him.

I let myself into my room. It's quiet, and as I approach the bedrooms I can see Liz's door is closed.

I go out onto the balcony and lean on the balustrade. The water is relatively calm and looks like a sheet of metal in the moonlight.

Nick obviously isn't going to take anything for granted. I should have been more trusting. He knows I need to help Liz first before I make any decisions about my own life.

But he also knew I needed that kiss more than anything in the world.

I press my fingers to my lips, remembering how passionately he kissed me. Even now, it makes my skin tingle and my heart race.

I shouldn't have let him do it, though. Because now I know what it's like, I want him to do it again.

*

On Christmas morning, I skip the yoga class and have a very rare lie-in. The clocks have gone back another hour during the night. Liz and I decided yesterday we'd have breakfast delivered to our room, and just before eight there's a knock at the door. The room attendant brings in a tray with our choice of cereal, fresh fruit, croissants, and preserves, and Liz comes out yawning as I start making us both a cup of coffee.

We take the tray out onto the balcony along with the few Christmas presents we've brought with us, and we sit and eat as we watch the sun bouncing off the waves.

"I fell asleep the moment my head hit the pillow," Liz states. "I think it was nervous exhaustion. But I had a lovely time yesterday."

"I'm so glad."

"What did you get up to when I left?" she asks.

I spread raspberry jam on a piece of croissant. "We had a walk around the ship. It was lovely, very Christmassy."

"How nice." She sighs and picks up one of her parcels. "It's funny to think it's Christmas Day. I wonder if Keith will open the presents I bought him."

"I expect so." I watch her peel the paper off the parcel, revealing a scarf she said she liked on her first day on the ship.

"Oh, it's so pretty. Thank you."

"You're welcome. I'm glad you like it."

She begins to open the next one, then stops halfway through. "I'm going to call him today."

I put my coffee cup down on the saucer. "Are you sure that's a good idea? I thought you were going to wait for him to call you."

"I was. I have been. But he's obviously not going to. I need to talk to him," she says earnestly. "I can't wait any longer." She looks calm and in control.

I nod. "All right. What time?"

"I'll have a shower and get ready. I've texted Carl that I'll ring him on FaceTime at ten o'clock." She doesn't say, but I wonder whether it crosses her mind that hopefully Keith won't be drunk that early in the day.

"Okay."

We finish our breakfast, shower, and dress. "Do you want me to go for a walk?" I ask.

"No, please stay," she begs. "Moral support and all that."

"All right. I'll sit out here." I take my book and go out onto the balcony.

My stomach churns. I don't really want to listen to their conversation, but she sits on the sofa, so I can't help but overhear. I wish she wasn't calling. I can't imagine this is going to go any way but tits up, as Nick would say.

The Wi-Fi isn't great on board so far from shore, but she manages to get a connection.

"Hey, can you see me?" she asks.

I hear Carl's voice. "Yeah, there you are. Oh is that your cabin? It's bigger than I thought."

"It's lovely. I'm very lucky."

"Are you having a good time?"

"It's not the same as spending Christmas with my family," she says tactfully.

"Yeah," he says, and his voice sounds wry. "You're really missing out."

"How's he doing?"

"You don't want to know."

"Carl…"

"He's shit, Mum, 'scuse my French, but he is. He's miserable and angry, and he hasn't stopped drinking since I turned up."

I glance over my shoulder. Liz's shoulders have slumped, and her fake jollity has evaporated. "Can I talk to him?"

"He's asleep, crashed out after drinking vodka until three a.m. And to be honest, Mum, I don't think he'd talk to you."

"He's still angry with me?" she asks in a small voice.

He hesitates. "To be honest, I think beneath it all, he's ashamed, but he won't admit it, to me or you, or even to himself. I think he's dug himself this hole and he doesn't know how he's going to get out of it. He's furious with the world, with God, for putting him in that wheelchair, when you and I and everyone else get to walk around and be normal."

Liz sniffs, and I know she's crying. "I'm so sorry…"

"None of this is your fault, Mum. All you've done is be supportive. Nobody could have asked for more. No, this is all him, and he needs to think about the choices he's making."

"Has he asked for me to come home?"

"Mum, he's hardly strung two coherent sentences together."

"Please can I talk to him?"

"Why?" Carl's getting angry now. "Ever since I got home, all he's done is rant and rail against you. Even if he was awake, I wouldn't let him within a mile of you. You did the right thing by going away. Just enjoy your vacation and put him out of your mind. He doesn't deserve you. Look, I can hear him getting up, I've got to go. I'll speak to you soon."

Silence falls. I look over my shoulder. Her phone is resting on the table. Liz is sitting with her face in her hands.

Sighing, I go into the room and put my arms around her, and she bursts into tears.

*

After a while, I run her a bath, and she has a long soak. When she comes out, she's wearing the toweling robe and her hair is wrapped up in a towel. Her eyes are bright, and as she sits down, she lifts her chin.

"I've decided," she says. "Fuck him."

I raise my eyebrows. "I see!"

"I was lying in the bath, and I suddenly thought, Keith has ruined Christmas for me, and I'm not going to let him ruin this vacation."

I smile. "Good for you."

"I mean it! Carl said all Keith has done is rant and rail against me. It's not my fault!"

"No, it's not."

"And I'm not going to feel guilty for not hanging around to be his punching bag." I can see the indignant burning inside her. "He's my husband, and I know it's my duty to help him as much as I can, but not at the expense of my own happiness."

"Or your own safety."

"Exactly. If he's determined to ruin his life, he can damn well do it without me. Nick said that when you marry someone, you choose to share your life with them, but that you should always respect one another. Well, Keith doesn't respect me. He hasn't for a long time. And I deserve respect."

"You do."

"You know who does respect me? Daniel."

I feel the first flicker of wariness. "I guess."

"He treats me like a woman, Ellie. As if I'm interesting and important." Her expression softens as she sees the look on my face. "Don't worry, I'm not going all doe-eyed over him. I know he probably has a different fling on every trip. He's a charmer. I'm not blind. But while I'm here, why shouldn't I enjoy spending time with him if he makes me feel good?"

"I can't think of a reason," I reply, smiling.

"I'm not going to spend another minute worrying about Keith," she says fiercely. "I'm not going to do it. I'm going to have an amazing time, and when I get back, if he doesn't get on his knees and beg me to come back, well, he can go fuck himself."

That makes me laugh. Liz so rarely swears. "You go, girl!"

"I'm serious!"

"I know. Come here." I pull her into my arms and give her a big hug. "I'm glad to see you're feeling better. It's so horrible watching you go through this."

"I'll never stop loving him," she whispers, her voice catching. "Deep down. But I'm not going to let him treat me like this. I do deserve better."

"Yes, you do."

"Thank you for being there for me."

"You're very welcome. Shall we get ready for dinner now? I get the feeling it's going to be an amazing meal."

"Yes, come on. I'm starving, and I'm going to drink a whole bottle of champagne by myself." She grins.

I chuckle. "All right. Nick's going to knock on the door at midday, and he's taking us for pre-dinner drinks, so we don't have that long."

She goes off to her room, singing *Santa Baby* as she goes. I smile as I walk into my bathroom, and I start sorting out the makeup I want to wear today. I'm so glad she's feeling better. It saddens me that Keith is obviously in such a bad way, and I do feel for Carl—what a miserable Christmas he's going to have. But there's not much I can do about it now. Liz is right—we need to make the most of our time here, and have ourselves a merry little Christmas.

Chapter Eighteen

Nick

The Christmas meal proves to be a lot of fun. Daniel has invited us to dine with him, and at the Captain's table the champagne is flowing, crackers are exploding, and the Christmas music is almost drowned out by the chatter and laughter.

It's not the same as being with my kids, and ultimately Christmas is about family, but I enjoy being with Elena, and everyone's spirits are so high that it's impossible not to have a great time.

Liz sits next to Daniel, and although he plays the gracious host and keeps the party rolling, most of the time he and Liz are engaged in a private conversation that brings a flush to her cheeks and a girlish flutter to her eyelashes.

Elena told me quietly when we were first seated what happened in this morning's Skype call, so I can't say I blame Liz for making the most of the attention Daniel pays her.

I'm returning from a visit to the Gents' to let out some of the champagne when I turn a corner, dodge to avoid a passing party of people, and almost walk into the two of them lip-locked in a steamy clinch, half-hidden behind a pot plant.

"Whoa!" I stop as they break apart. "I'm so sorry."

Daniel laughs. "No worries."

"Excuse me." Liz's face turns bright scarlet, and she runs around the corner, back to the restaurant.

Daniel grins at me. I give him a wry smile back.

"Be careful," I say mildly.

"About what? She has a shit of a husband, and she's been having a crap time. If she wants to cheer herself up, I'm not going to turn her down."

"I doubt she was the one to initiate that kiss," I point out.

His lips twist. "Yeah, maybe not. But she's a grown woman. If it made her feel better, what's wrong with that?"

I surprise myself with feeling a surge of irritation at his cavalier manner. "What's wrong with it is that she's not in a good position to make decisions about her life right now. You're taking advantage of her vulnerability."

"I'm not forcing her to do anything she doesn't want to do. And I don't think you should be the one to judge her choices. I think she's had enough of other people making decisions for her, don't you?" He lifts an eyebrow, then turns and walks back to the restaurant.

I follow him slowly, frowning. Maybe he has a point. If Liz wants to have a fling while she's away, why shouldn't she? I know that today women are struggling to fight against slut-shaming—the criticizing of women who go against society's expectations of their sexual behavior and appearance.

But that's not what's making me feel uneasy. I wouldn't give a damn if Liz were to have an affair—that would be her business and nothing to do with me. But it's easy to make bold decisions as a knee-jerk reaction when you're angry. She's been starved of love and affection and respect for a long time, and her husband has hurt her terribly. But it doesn't mean her marriage is over. She might regret it big time if she sleeps with Daniel and then Keith finally turns his life around and wants her back.

Or maybe she won't—what do I know about the hearts and minds of women, really?

I enter the restaurant to see Elena and Liz getting to their feet and saying their goodbyes. My heart sinks. It's only four p.m. Is that it for the night?

"We're heading off," Elena tells me as I approach the table. "It's been a lovely day."

"Will I see you this evening?"

She hesitates. "Probably not. I think we'll have a quiet night in."

"On Christmas Day?" I ask, unable to stop a note of disappointment creeping into my voice.

"I'm sorry." She looks down, not meeting my gaze. This is about last night. She's afraid to be alone with me in case she gives in again.

"It's okay." I put my arms around her and give her a hug. "Merry Christmas, honey. Have a nice evening with your sister."

She buries her face in my shirt for a moment. Then she moves back and gives me a bright smile. "See you later."

"Yeah." I turn and kiss Liz on the cheek.

"Thank you for a lovely day," she says, her face still red. She can't meet my eyes either.

"You're welcome. See you tomorrow."

The two of them walk away and disappear around the corner.

The mood at the table changes subtly after that. A lot of alcohol has gone down, and the volume has gone up. Two of the men are making loud, unfunny jokes, and some of the women are screeching with laughter, making my head hurt. Daniel has left, and people are talking around me rather than to me.

I make my excuses and return to my room. Picking up my iPad, I go out onto the balcony. The sky is blue above me, but the horizon is thick with clouds; it's going to rain tonight.

I ring the kids, because I promised them I would, and pin a smile on my face as they all come to Ben's laptop to wave and cheer. Kora and Callum lift the twins' hands to wave at me, and baby Estella laughs and swats the screen as she sees my face.

Gradually they drift away, and eventually I'm left looking at my eldest son, who picks up a glass of wine before taking the laptop out onto the deck.

"Everything all right?" he asks.

Behind him, I can see the familiar view of Wellington Harbour, with the ferry making its way across the Cook Strait. I miss my home, and I miss my family, but I could see they were doing just fine without me. I feel an odd sense of displacement, of being no longer needed. The house isn't the same without Olivia and all the kids. And I never wanted to run a company.

"I'm thinking of stepping down," I say.

His eyebrows rise. "What?"

I look away, across the ocean. Far in the distance, a black-and-white orca's fluke lifts gracefully out of the sea before disappearing again, then a smaller one appears next to it—it's a pod of killer whales.

I look back at him. His face shows complete surprise. I thought the kids might have discussed this happening, but apparently not.

"Dad... what the fuck? Where did that come from?"

"I'm not cut out to do the job. I never was. I don't have the brain for it."

His brow darkens. "That's utter bullshit. You're the smartest man I know."

I feel a wave of affection for him. "No, I'm not, but thank you for saying it. I'm many things, but brainy ain't one of them. I'm not saying I don't have other skills. I can handle people. And I'm not afraid to take chances. I bring other things to the table. But I'm not dynamic anymore. I don't have the energy. The company needs a younger man behind the wheel, someone with ideas and drive."

"You're only sixty, Dad, and you're a young sixty at that. You've got a lot of working years left in you yet."

"Years I don't particularly want to spend behind a desk." As soon as I say it, I realize it's true.

"What do you want to do? Go fishing? Play golf?" His tone is a tad sarcastic, even aggressive, but I know him well enough to see that he's upset.

"Maybe," I say mildly. The truth is, I don't know what I want to do. Write my book. Travel, perhaps. Despite the ups and downs of this vacation, I'm enjoying being on the ship, and I'm looking forward to calling in at different ports, seeing the changing scenery.

He glances behind him, inside the house, then looks back at me. "I don't know what to say."

"Would you take up the role?"

"Of CEO?" He runs a hand through his hair and leans back in the chair. He's quiet for a long time, thinking about it.

Angling the laptop so he can see me, I rise and go into the cabin, make myself a coffee, and bring it back out onto the balcony. I sit and sip it, enjoying the hot, strong flavor after the sweetness of the champagne I had at dinner.

"Well?" I ask.

He looks down at his wine. "Would I really be your first choice?"

"You're my eldest, and the most capable, so yes, that's why I'm asking you."

I can see the compliment has pleased him. He sits with his elbow on the arm of the chair, his fingers resting on his lips, thinking again. He's been through so much, and I've just had to sit and watch all the shit roll over him. His ex, Rebecca, was a complete bitch, and I'm happy to say that, even though you're not supposed to speak ill of the dead. I'd never have said so to his face, and I felt a bit guilty thinking it, but I was relieved when he was finally free of her.

I'm so pleased he's found Heloise. She's like a lighthouse in his life, keeping him away from the rocks.

"I'm flattered you asked me," he says eventually. "But I don't think I'm the right choice."

I'm not surprised by his answer, but I don't reply and sip my coffee, letting him explain.

"I don't have the family head for business either," he admits. "We're cut from the same cloth. We're ideas men, creatives. But to be honest, I don't have the drive or the energy to do the job either."

"Well, I don't agree with that. The effort you put into the theme park has proven that to be untrue."

"Because it was a project I enjoyed. But to be responsible for the day-to-day running of the whole company? I don't think it's for me. I think we both know Lucas would be far better at it than I." He smiles. "But I appreciate you asking me."

"You're my boy," I reply, my voice turning husky with sudden emotion. "And you'll always be my firstborn. Do me a favor—take some time to think about it. Talk it over with Heloise. And we'll discuss it more when I get back."

"All right. How's it going there? Are you having a good time?"

"Maybe Christmas wasn't the best time to go away." I clear my throat. "But it's very restful."

"Good." His gaze appraises me. "How's Elena?"

"She's fine."

He tips his head to the side. "Is it working out?"

"I might have to get back to you on that."

"That surprises me. Heloise said she thought it was just a matter of time. She said the first day she met both of you, she was convinced Elena had feelings for you."

"Really?" I sigh. "Maybe that's true. But she has other, bigger priorities right now."

"Well, I hope it works out."

"Yeah. I miss your mum."

He smiles. "Me too. But Elena's lovely. Don't give up, eh? Turn on the old Prince charm, and I'm sure she'll come around."

I chuckle. "All right, off you go then. Give my love to Heloise, and kiss your bib-bab for me."

"Will do. Take care."

We hang up.

I close the laptop and finish my coffee, watching the clouds darkening on the horizon. I'm not surprised that Ben is reluctant to take the role. He's right—we're cut from the same cloth. Lucas was in the front of the queue when all the business acumen was given out. He's young enough to have the drive and ambition the company needs, but old enough to make the sensible choices. He would be fantastic behind the wheel, if Ben ends up deciding it's not for him, and I suspect he's not going to change his mind.

I hadn't planned this. It wasn't until the words left my mouth that I realized I was going to say them. But now I have, I feel a sense of peace settle over me. I'll be free to do whatever I want, go wherever I want.

Be with whomever I want.

I don't know if it will make a difference to Elena. But just the way she's putting herself and her family first at the moment, I need to do the same and do what's best for me. I haven't made the decision to step down for her. I hope it means there might be a future for us, but even if it doesn't, it's still the right decision for me.

Freedom. It's an odd word for a billionaire to use. You'd think being rich would be the very definition of it. But money brings its own responsibilities, its own chains. I'm not saying my life has been hard by any means. I know I'm privileged, and I have no idea of the suffering some people have to go through. But it doesn't mean my life is without struggle, without pain. Having money doesn't make you immune to emotion and grief.

I do miss my wife, but I'm only sixty, and I'm lucky enough to have my health. I feel as if I'm about to board a plane to a faraway land. There's all this promise stretching out before me, all this unchartered territory. The world really is my oyster, and probably all the other shellfish too.

So what do I want?

I slink down in the chair, resting my head on the back, my eyes half closed, and let my mind drift to the cabin next door, as I think about the elegant woman with the sleek blonde hair who lit me up from the inside out when I kissed her last night.

That's what I want.

*

I'm not going to get her anytime soon, though. I see very little of either her or Liz over the next four or five days. We meet up for dinner, but our days are spent apart—me mostly staying in my cabin, working on my book, and the girls doing various activities on the ship—attending art classes, going to the theater and the cinema, and treating themselves at the spa.

On the twenty-seventh, we arrive at Brisbane, and the two of them are very excited to do some Australian shopping. I've been to Brisbane several times on business, and I'm not bothered about shopping. I also have no intention of trying out the skydiving excursion or scaling the Story Bridge. Instead, I take a stroll down the Brisbane Riverwalk, then have a cold beer and a Ploughman's lunch while I jot down some of the things I've seen this morning in my notebook. I haven't written any poetry for a while, and I take the time to compose a few verses, enjoying the cool beer and the Brisbane heat.

When we depart the city, everyone on board gradually settles back into life at sea. The girls spend their days swimming, getting their hair done, going to the open-air cinema on the top deck, or just sipping lattes in one of the cafés. As far as I know, Liz still hasn't spoken to Keith, and most evenings when we dine at Daniel's table she and Daniel are locked in close conversation, looking for all the world like lovers as they hold hands and whisper in each other's ears. Determined that it's none of my business, I look away and talk to Elena and the other guests.

As time wears on and Liz and Daniel get more caught up in one another, Elena and I find ourselves talking more to each other at dinner than to anyone else. Gradually, we explore each other, discovering our tastes in music, film, food, and travel, and even our opinions on religion and politics, finding most of our views matching. Sometimes we talk about Olivia, and I like that we can discuss her without either of us feeling awkward or guilty, but most of the time we talk about the world and the people in it.

I don't tell her about my conversation with Ben, though, because I don't want her to think I've made the decision for her.

And at the end of each evening, we all walk back to our rooms together, and she and Liz go into their suite, and I go into mine.

*

New Year's Eve dawns brilliant and bright, perfect for the ship's slow progression through Fiordland. This is the most popular tourist destination in New Zealand, and it's easy to see why, as the ship makes its way through towering cliffs streaked with waterfalls, past the mountain shaped like a bishop's hat called Mitre Peak, and into the triumphant beauty of Milford Sound.

The clocks have gone back to New Zealand time over the past three days and it feels a bit more normal. Everyone spends time taking photographs, sketching, peering through binoculars, or having a drink with friends while watching the spectacular views. I continue to write on my balcony, although I'm constantly distracted by pods of bottlenose dolphins, New Zealand fur seals, little blue penguins, and humpback whales.

That evening, at dinner, as the cliffs gradually turn orange and purple in the setting sun, Elena and Liz are full of enthusiasm as they talk about all the photos they've taken. After we've eaten, Elena shows me her phone, and I enjoy the opportunity to lean close to her as she flicks through all the pictures.

It's only when we look up that we see Liz and Daniel's seats vacant. Elena frowns, and she gathers her bag and walks out into the corridor. She stops there, looking down into the lounge next door. I rise and walk over to her, and follow her gaze.

The Milky Way Lounge is hosting a New Year's Eve party. Music is playing, and colored lights flash patterns on the dance floor. At the edge, in semi-darkness, Daniel has his arms around Liz, and they're turning slowly, gazing into each other's eyes.

I look at Elena. "Are you worried about her?"

"She's a big girl. She can make her own decisions." Her lips are thin with disapproval, though.

"You've counseled her against seeing him?"

"I said she should sort things out with Keith first before she started looking around. But she's hurting, and she's enjoying all the attention. And who am I to judge?" She turns her green eyes back to me. "I don't like infidelity, though. Maybe I'm old-fashioned."

I smile. If I hadn't been convinced that I was in love with her by now, then that comment would have cemented it.

I glance at the clock on the wall. It's nearly nine p.m. "Still three hours to go," I point out. "You're not done for the night, surely?"

She hesitates, turning her bag in her hands.

"Would you like to dance?" I ask.

She glances at Liz and Daniel again, then looks back at me. "Not really."

"Want to go for a walk?"

"I think I just want to go somewhere quiet."

"There aren't going to be many quiet places on the ship tonight."

She brushes her hair back from her face. "Maybe we could go to your room and have a drink?" Her face is innocent; she means exactly what she says. I think she just wants to get away from the responsibility of having to look after her sister for a while.

"Of course." I offer her my arm, she slides her hand into it, and together we walk slowly through the ship and down the stairs to our floor.

Chapter Nineteen

Elena

Nick lets us into his room, and we take off our jackets. He toes off his shoes—something he does at work beneath the desk, making me think of him as a small boy, running around shoeless at school.

"What would you like to drink?" he asks, going over to the bar. Most rooms stock a small minibar, but the suites have half bottles of most spirits and a range of wines, which can be easily replaced with a simple phone call. "Champagne?"

For most of this vacation, I've drunk champagne. I'd hardly touched it before, and everyone knows it's classy and expensive, and I wasn't going to turn it down when it was flowing like water.

But now I look along the line of colorful bottles, and think about what I really fancy. "No thanks. I'll have a Glenfiddich, please," I reply.

"Yeah, I'll join you." He takes out two tumblers, retrieves some ice cubes from the box in the top of the fridge, and pours a generous amount of the amber liquid over them. "I didn't know you liked whisky."

"Ricky got me onto it," I admit. "It's one of the few positive things I took away from that relationship." Immediately I regret saying it. I sound bitter, and I don't want Nick to think I'm a bitch.

He doesn't reply, and he brings the glasses over to the sofa.

Elsewhere in the ship, I'm sure parties are kicking off as we slowly move toward midnight, but here it's quiet. He's switched on the small wall lights but left the overhead light off, and it feels cozy and warm. He gets his phone, props it up on the table, chooses a jazz playlist, and presses play, keeping the volume down. Then he picks up his drink and sips it, looking at me.

He's wearing beige trousers and a short-sleeved white shirt without a tie. His wrist bears his classy Patek Philippe Nautilus watch that cost a cool thirty-five grand—I know, because I looked it up one day. He wears his wealth casually—he's not ostentatious, and I like that.

We both sip our drinks, the jazz music spiraling around us. It's nice to have him all to myself for once, but suddenly I feel self-conscious and a little awestruck, the way I always do when we're alone. He makes me tongue-tied, I don't know why. I think it's his eyes. They always look… interested. It wouldn't surprise me if he had x-ray vision and he could see through my clothes. The guy is sixty, and he's still the sexiest man I've ever met. I bet he's amazing in bed. Oh God. I mustn't think about sex, not now we're alone.

"I want to apologize," I say softly.

His eyebrows rise. "For what?"

"We haven't seen much of each other over the past few days. That doesn't seem fair after…"

He turns to face me, propping an elbow on the back of the sofa and his head on his hand. "After we kissed? That was a free gift, Elena. There was no obligation to purchase the product."

That makes me laugh. "You know what I mean. I just want to say, it wasn't a conscious decision—to keep my distance I mean. Liz and I have been talking, a lot. It's been good for her, although I don't know that it's actually got us anywhere. She's a bit… distracted."

"You mean with Daniel?"

I nod, feeling the familiar frustration and worry rising within me. "I've tried talking to her about him, but she won't listen. The thing is, Keith still hasn't rung her, and the more time that's passed, the more indignant and rebellious she's got. And I can't blame her, you know? But I don't want her to do something she's going to regret."

He sighs. "I tried talking to Daniel, too. I told him she was vulnerable and said he shouldn't take advantage of that, but he just told me he wasn't forcing her to do anything she didn't want to do, and that she'd had enough of other people making decisions for her. And I thought, well, maybe he's right."

"Yeah. That's sort of the conclusion I came to tonight." I blow out a long breath. "Enough about Liz. I don't want to talk about her all evening." I give him a bright smile. "So did you call the kids today? How are they?"

"They're good." He clears his throat. "Actually… I told Ben I was thinking of stepping down."

I stare at him. "What?"

"I didn't plan it. It just sort of came out."

My jaw drops. "What did he say?"

"He was shocked. I offered him the role of CEO and told him to think about it, but I don't think he's going to take it. I didn't think he would, but he's my eldest, and I wanted to give him the option. I think he'll pass it on to Lucas, though."

"But… what about you?" I'm genuinely stunned.

"Well, first, I did it for myself, not for anyone else." He means he hasn't done it for me. "I'm ready for something new," he adds.

"Like what?" I ask softly.

"I don't know yet. I'm going to sell the house, get somewhere smaller, cozier. Maybe I'll travel for a while. Do some charity work, possibly. And writing, of course. I'm really enjoying writing the book, and I'd like to do more."

We're sitting close enough that our knees are touching. It feels intimate, private. I feel honored that he's chosen to share his thoughts with me.

"Like I said," he continues, "I haven't done this for you. But it does mean I'm free. And if, in time, you are interested in starting something… well, maybe we can talk about where to go from here."

My head spins. Ever since he declared his feelings after our kiss under the mistletoe, I've been convinced it wasn't going to work. There were too many hurdles to overcome, too many problems standing in the way.

But now? Is it really possible we could have a future together, regardless of what happens with Liz?

His blue eyes are watching me, and there's a small smile on his lips. "We don't have to make any decisions now," he says. "Don't panic."

"I'm not panicking. I'm just struggling to accept it's a real possibility."

"Why?"

"The future is like the ocean spread out before me, vast and endless, ready to be explored. I'm sitting in a boat, waiting to push off from the shore, but I just don't have the courage to let go of the rope."

I can see he's struggling to understand why I'm so reticent.

"Do you not want to be with me?" he asks. "Because if that's the case, please, just tell me. I'm a big boy. I can take it."

"It's not that, Nick." God knows, it's nothing like that.

It'll be midnight in a few hours. Tomorrow is my birthday; I'll be fifty. It's been feeling like an ending, but for the first time I realize it could also be a beginning.

I look at the gorgeous, sexy man before me, and fear lies in my belly like a coiled snake. I thought I'd laid my past to rest, but it's only now, looking into his blue eyes, I realize that's not true.

"I need to tell you something," I admit. "About Ricky."

"Okay." He has a sip of whisky, and I do the same, needing the Dutch courage.

I drop my gaze to my glass. "I met Ricky through work. At the time, I was PA to the manager of a small office supplies company. Ricky was in charge of quality assurance. We used to chat in the breakroom during lunch, and we discovered we shared a love of theater and movies, and started going together. The relationship developed from there.

"Looking back, I can see now there were signs from the beginning that things weren't right, but I didn't spot them at the time. He was affectionate and loving. But he was never very interested in sex."

I glance up at Nick briefly, then look back at my glass. "I didn't have a lot of experience. I'd had a couple of partners when I was younger, but you know what that's like, all fumbling around, and nobody has any clue what they're doing. Everyone jokes that men think about sex every seven seconds, but I just assumed it was an exaggeration. It certainly wasn't high on Ricky's agenda, and even though I sometimes wished it was, I told myself not everyone's libido is the same, and I learned to live with it.

"We married, and the years went by. And we had sex less and less. First it was once every couple of weeks, then once a month. By the time I was thirty, it was once every few months, and then only when I instigated it. And I always felt as if he went along with it to keep me quiet, you know?

"We had a busy social life, and apart from that, we got along relatively well. I tried not to think about it too much. But I suppose deep down, I knew something was... awry. We started to grow apart. I've always been a lark, and he was always a night owl. He'd stay up later and later, and end up sleeping in the spare room, saying he didn't want to disturb me, until eventually we just slept in separate rooms. I knew that wasn't right. And it wasn't what I wanted. But he refused to talk about it."

I have a large mouthful of whisky, finishing off the glass. "Could I have another?" I whisper.

"Of course." Nick finishes off his own, then rises. I try to calm my breathing, gaining courage from the alcohol threading through my veins. This is hard. But I have to tell him everything, or this is never going to work.

He comes back and takes his seat, sliding my glass over to me. "Are you okay?" he asks gently as I have another big mouthful.

I nod. "I need to get it off my chest."

"Okay. So you were sleeping apart. What happened next?"

"We were thirty-three. I was at work. I had a migraine, and I came home early one day. I went into the bedroom, and..." I swallow hard. "I found Ricky in front of the mirror, dressed in my clothing."

Nick stares at me, his jaw dropping. "Shit. I thought you were going to say he was in bed with someone else." He leans back and runs a hand through his hair.

I bite my bottom lip hard as it trembles. "Are you going to laugh?"

He frowns. "There's nothing funny about it."

My eyes sting, and I've never loved him more than I do at that moment. "No, there isn't."

A silence falls between us as I fight against tears. He gives a long sigh, then puts his arm around me and pulls me close. "What happened?" he asks gently.

"He ran into the bathroom and locked the door." I tremble as I remember. "I was shocked, but I was okay about it. I mean, there are a lot worse things he could have done—as you said, he could have been with someone else. It was only clothing, after all. I tried to talk to him about it. Then and in the days and months after. I read up a lot about it. Most crossdressers are straight, and they're often married. It doesn't mean they're gay or bisexual. I just wanted him to talk to me."

"And did he?"

I can feel the warmth of Nick's body against my arm, and smell his body spray. I like being this close to him. "One day, after a couple of drinks, he opened up a little. He said his mother caught him trying on some of her lacy underwear when he was twelve. She beat him for it with a belt."

"Jesus."

"Yeah. He said he hadn't done it since. I did everything I could to help. I tried to get him to go to a counselor. I told him I didn't mind, and I was happy to talk about it. But he was excruciatingly embarrassed. I asked him whether he could only get turned on when he was dressing up. He refused to reply, but I think the answer was yes. I told him maybe we could try having sex while he was dressed up, but he nearly died of embarrassment."

"Not every woman would have been so understanding," Nick states.

I shrug tiredly. "I just wanted my marriage to work. But over the next few months it was like he couldn't bear to be in the same room. He was ashamed, I think. And then I turned thirty-four, and it suddenly occurred to me that we'd never talked about children, not properly. When I had raised the question, he'd always said later, when he was ready. So I asked him one day, and he told me there and then that he didn't want kids."

"Ah, Elena…"

"I got angry, then. I said he'd misled me, and wasted my time. I wanted children, and I knew my most productive years were slipping away. He wouldn't argue with me, though, he just sat there while I yelled at him. I don't know how he felt deep down, whether he was gay and trying to pretend he wasn't. He wouldn't open up. And in the end I walked away. I went to Liz and Keith's house. I thought that if I gave him some time on his own, he might realize he missed me and that he would rather work it out with me. And then just a few weeks later, a friend of his found him in the garage. He'd put a hosepipe on the exhaust of his car, and killed himself."

Nick kisses my temple, resting his lips there. "I'm so sorry."

I lean against him, letting him lend me his strength. "It was awful. I felt I was to blame because I hadn't tried hard enough in the marriage. I know I should have seen a therapist, but I couldn't bring myself to talk to anyone about it. I felt… ashamed, too. I don't know why. Maybe I thought I should have known what he was into when I met him. I should have realized he wasn't interested in me in that way. But I was so inexperienced. I just didn't understand."

"I'm really sorry you had to go through that."

"Me, too."

I have a big mouthful of whisky and let it burn down to my stomach. I feel lighter now I've finally told him.

"And what about after Ricky?" Nick asks, moving back a little. "There hasn't been anyone else?"

I shake my head. "It took me a couple of years to get over his death. Eventually, I went on a couple of first dates with guys that friends fixed me up with, but I didn't click with any of them. Then I moved to Wellington, and I met you." I give him a small smile. "And after that, no man I met lived up to you, Nick. I've never felt about anybody the way I felt about you. But you were married to my best friend. And although Olivia had her quirks, it was always very clear that she was crazy about you."

I lift his hand in mine and study his wide palm, his strong fingers. "I know you say you're ready to move on, but I have one more thing to admit to you. You might not like it, and I want to start by apologizing profusely. I didn't mean to read it. It was sitting on your bedside table the night Kora's twins were born and you sent me to pick up some clothes. But it was a poem, and it said, 'You haunt me in the dark hours. I paint pictures of you on the canvas of my mind, To fill the lonely hollow inside me. I hunger. I ache. I yearn for you.' And now every time you tell me how you want to be with me, I can't rid myself of those words, because they seem so filled with longing for her. Tell me honestly… do you really think you're ready to say goodbye to her?"

He studies my face, and for a moment I wonder whether he's angry. It was a huge invasion of his privacy, after all.

But then, to my surprise, he gives a mischievous smile. He leans forward and looks into my eyes.

"Elena," he explains patiently, "the poem was about you."

Chapter Twenty

Nick

"Me?" Elena blinks.

"Yes. I have to say, I'm flattered you've learned it off by heart."

She looks completely dumbfounded. "But..." Her voice trails off.

"It wasn't a very good poem," I admit, "but it was heartfelt. I was lying in bed, thinking about you, missing you. And it just sprung into my mind."

"But... I saw the poem back in October. Before we kissed."

"Uh, yeah."

"You were thinking about me back then?"

"I told you, I've been thinking about you for a long time." I can see, though, that she obviously doesn't believe me. Even though I tried to explain why I didn't make a move on her after the kiss on Halloween, she assumed it was because my grief vastly outweighed any affection I felt for her. She doesn't understand the internal battle I've been fighting all this time.

And she really doesn't comprehend the depth of my feelings for her.

"I'm glad you confided in me," I tell her, taking her hand. "It means a lot to me."

She clears her throat. "I just wanted you to know that... well... sex hasn't been an important part of my life."

What's she trying to say? "Do... you want it to be?"

She moistens her lips with the tip of her tongue. "Well, it's just... I thought I should be clear... I'm not... you know..." She trails off and bites her bottom lip.

"Sweetheart, I'm confused. Are you trying to say you're not interested in sex?"

"God, no." Her reply is vehement enough to make me laugh. "I'm very interested. In sex. With you." She blushes. "It's just that I wasn't sure what you wanted, you know, if you were just looking for companionship…"

"Companionship?" I'm not sure whether to be amused or insulted. "I'm sixty, not ninety. Everything's in good working order, if that's what you're trying to ask. I'm not at the Viagra stage yet."

"No!" Her blush deepens until she's the color of a cherry tomato. "I'm sorry, I didn't mean to insult you."

"I'm not insulted—"

"I'm so bad at all this. I was trying to explain that I'm not very… experienced. It hasn't been a big part of my life, and I wasn't sure if you were expecting it to be a part of ours, if we got together."

I turn fully to face her. "Honestly? I would never make a move if I thought a woman wasn't interested. But, hand on my heart, I have to say that where you're concerned, I'm very interested in getting my leg over."

She stares at me for a moment, and then giggles rise up inside her and spill over. I watch her, amused, as she struggles to contain them, pressing her fingers to her mouth as if she can physically force them back in.

"Sorry," she says when it becomes clear there's no stopping them. "It's the whisky, and the nerves."

"Jeez, Elena, don't be nervous. How long have you known me?"

"Yes, but that's the point." Her laughter fades away, and she looks at me earnestly, shyly. "I've watched you for so long, observed how other people behave around you and react to you. You don't realize how popular you are, Nick. How affable you are, how relaxed you make people. You're so confident, so at ease in your own skin. Women react to you because you're so damned sexy. I feel like I'm going on a date with George Clooney."

It's only then that I really understand how she's feeling. She told me that for the past twelve years she's been on a couple of dates, but no other man matched up to me. Obviously, that's bullshit, because I'm the first person to admit I'm far from perfect, but she's put me on a pedestal, and now she's terrified of disappointing me.

"I'm just a man. And I'm hardly a stud, Elena. I don't have a lot of experience with women, and it's been an ice age since I went on a first date. I'm nervous, too."

She stares at me. "Seriously?"

"Yeah, especially now you have all these expectations." It's not a complete lie.

Her gaze drops to my mouth for a moment. She's thinking about kissing me. "So… you are interested… in a sexual relationship…"

And to think I was concerned she'd think I only wanted her for sex. "Yes," I tell her. "Please." We both laugh.

Briefly, I think of Olivia. For over thirty years, she was the only woman in my life. It's strange to think about being with someone else. I am a little nervous. But I'm excited, too. Elena is gorgeous and elegant and, I have to admit, I find her naïvety oddly sexy. I like that she's not had lots of lovers, and that she's uncertain. She deserves to have someone show her how amazing it can be when they really want you.

I move a bit closer to her, my arm still around her shoulder. Her cheek is only inches from my lips.

"I'm sorry if this all sounds a bit pathetic," she murmurs. "It's just that it's not been a big part of my life for so long, and I don't know what to expect. I don't know what's normal."

"Honestly, I don't think there's any such thing, only what a couple in a relationship wants. It's a private thing, and it doesn't matter how many times the couple next door is doing it, or in what positions. It doesn't matter if you do it once a day or once a week or once a month or never, if you're both happy. The issue comes, as you've found, when one person isn't happy."

I kiss her cheek. "But we shouldn't be thinking of any of that right now. We just need to relax and enjoy this. Maybe it'll work out, and I hope and think it will, but maybe it won't. Perhaps life will take us in different directions, and that's okay. The past has gone, and tomorrow is another day. All we have is right here, right now. Today is all that matters."

She lifts her gaze to mine. "It's my birthday tomorrow."

"I know."

"I'm fifty."

I smile. "I know."

"I want to make sure Liz is okay. I owe her, Nick, so much. But… I'm beginning to think that what I need is important, too."

I nod slowly. "And what do you need?"

She looks back at my mouth. "You. And… I want… to be wanted. More than anything in the world."

I've not pushed getting physical because I didn't think she was ready, but it's time I took the lead. It occurs to me that she's probably never been seduced. Never had a guy try to get her into bed. Not in a tacky way because he wants to get laid and she's the first port in a storm, but because he really, really wants her, and he's determined to show her the depth of his desire. She's probably never had a guy talk dirty to her. Or get her all hot and bothered and embarrassed and blushing by his description of what he wants to do to her.

Well, we'll have to see what we can do about that.

Chapter Twenty-One

Elena

Sex. The word is flying around in my head like a bird trapped in a room.

I'd convinced myself Nick wasn't interested in a physical relationship. I have no idea why. He has five kids, so clearly he likes sex. Olivia dropped a few hints, too, that their love life was very active. One day, she had dark shadows under her eyes, and I said she looked tired. She replied, "That's Nick's fault. I swear the man would keep me up all night, every night, if he had his way." So he obviously has a high sex drive.

Maybe it's because he hasn't dated anyone since she died, and I assumed he'd learned to live without it, the way I have.

Or maybe it's just that my self-esteem is so low, I couldn't believe this gorgeous, rich, sexy guy who could have any woman in the world would be interested in me.

He's studying my face, and that look in his eye is back, the one that suggests he's using his x-ray vision. "All right," he says. "It's time I explained a bit about that poem you read that you weren't supposed to."

"I am sorry," I say again. "I feel terrible."

"So you should. It was private. I should put you over my knee for that."

"I…" I stop as the words sink in. Wait, what? He raises his eyebrows at me. I stare at him, trying to discern if he's serious. Now he looks as if he's trying not to laugh, but he covers it with a sip of his whisky. Ooh, those eyes. They make me tingle all over.

"I don't sleep well," he continues. "Never have. I often wake in the early hours and can't get back to sleep. Sometimes I get up, but most times I lie in bed and just let my mind wander."

His left arm is still around me. Now he lifts the hand holding the glass and brushes my cheek with the back of his knuckles. He's looking at my mouth, and I know he's thinking about kissing me again. I remember the kiss we had out under the stars, and my pulse doubles its pace.

"Quite often now," he continues, "when I wake, I think of you. I picture you—from your blonde hair to your slim figure, to your green eyes, and your lips with this beautiful Cupid's bow." He touches his thumb to it, and a frisson runs down my spine. "You do haunt me in the dark hours," he murmurs. "And I do paint pictures of you in my mind. I lie there, missing you, aching for you. Imagining what it would be like if you were there with me."

He tightens his arm around me, bringing me closer to him. Then he bends his head and touches his lips to mine, his mustache tickling my top lip. Just lightly—a butterfly kiss. "I picture kissing you," he whispers. "Your mouth, your breasts, down your body. And I imagine moving inside you."

A tiny moan escapes my lips. I don't have any control over it.

"Sometimes," he murmurs, kissing up my cheek to my ear, "I'm so hard for you, I have to invest in a little DIY to take the pressure off." He takes my earlobe between his teeth and tugs it.

The thought of him taking himself in hand and stroking himself until he… oh God… while he's thinking of me… I feel faint.

"What about you, Elena?" He sucks my earlobe gently. "Do you ever think about me when you touch yourself?" He nuzzles my neck.

I close my eyes. I've died. I've left this life and I've gone to heaven without realizing it. No man has ever talked to me like this. I'm turning to caramel inside.

"Do you?" he prompts, kissing back up my cheekbone to my mouth. "And don't tell me you don't do that. You're far too sexy not to."

I can't bring myself to open my eyes. "Yes," I whisper. "I think about you." For years, I've dreamed about him, and pictured him when I'm alone in bed at night.

"Maybe one day you can show me." His voice is husky with desire.

"Oh God…" My eyelids flutter open. Those sexy blue eyes are full of heat.

"First, though," he says, quite firmly, "I'm going to make love to you tonight. I can't wait any longer." Then he kisses my cheek. "Will that be okay?"

I moisten my lips with the tip of my tongue. Am I really going to do this? "Yes."

"I'm going to start by taking off your clothes and kissing every inch of your skin. From here…" and he runs a finger down my neck, "all the way down here," with his other hand, he brushes down my spine, "to your toes. Is that okay?"

"Yes…" I squeak.

"Then," he says, "I'm going to kiss back up to your thighs. And I'm going to make you come with my mouth, because when I finally slide inside you, I want you to be relaxed and comfortable and ready for me. Is that okay?"

I stare at him, speechless, unable to form any words. His eyes hold a touch of amusement. He knows perfectly well what he's doing to me. He's seducing me, slowly removing all my inhibitions one by one, unravelling me like a woolen sweater, and he's enjoying every minute of it.

"Are you trying to give me a coronary?" I whisper. "Are you trying to kill me?"

He gives a short laugh, takes my glass from me, and puts both of them on the table. Then he turns and pulls me into his arms. "Come here, my little firecracker."

He crushes his lips to mine, and I give in, throw my arms around his neck, and kiss him back.

Ohhh… the bliss of a proper kiss… his hand holding the back of my head so I can't move away, his head angled so his lips slant across mine, his tongue delving into my mouth, hungry, demanding I give in to my passion. And I do, because I can't do anything else; I can't hold back, and I can't pretend I don't feel anything for him. I'm lava-hot, molten inside, burning up for him. Ten years of longing, yearning, waiting, and it all comes down to this—his mouth on mine, hard with need.

He slides his arms around me, and then he's tipping back onto the sofa cushions, pulling me with him so I'm half-lying on him. His fingers tug at my waist, where my top is tucked into my skirt and then, after he frees it, he slips his hands beneath the silky fabric onto my skin.

We both exhale with an "Aaahhh…" I lift my head a little to look at him. His bright blue eyes are hot with desire. Keeping them on mine, he slides his hands up my ribcage, then forward to cup my breasts, still encased in my bra. "Oh yeah," he says, with such boyish enthusiasm that it makes me laugh.

I kiss him again, feeling him move one hand to my bra catch, and then with a flick of his fingers it's undone. Oh, that was flash… He slides his hands up under the lacy cups, and then he's brushing his thumbs across my nipples.

I feel as if I'm dreaming, being carried away on a cloud of pleasure. I'm making love with Nick! I almost giggle. I could not have foreseen this a year ago. Who'd have thought I'd be lying here, on the sofa, making out with a billionaire?

His hands are warm on my skin, his fingers teasing me, continuing to turn up the heat. I hook the leg that's lying on top of him up a bit more, and I catch my breath as I brush against the front of his trousers. He has an erection. Nick Prince has an erection because he's kissing me. Oh, holy shit… I run a hand up his leg and cup him, then stroke him gently. He rests his head back on the cushion and looks at me, then closes his eyes. Encouraged, I undo his belt, slide down his zipper, then wrap my hand around him in his silky boxer shorts. He groans and swells, pushing up a little, so I stroke harder, thrilled to touch him. Oh that's so hot, maybe if I slide my hand inside his boxers he'll let me take him all the way…

At that moment, he grabs my hand and opens his eyes. They're a tad exasperated. He puts his arms around me and then, I don't know how, he manages to twist expertly and suddenly I'm pinned against the back of the sofa, half underneath him, my arm trapped, our legs a tangle.

"My rules," he states in his firm billionaire CEO's voice. "My pace." He catches my hand as it strays toward his crotch, pulls it up so it's imprisoned between us, and kisses me again, hard.

Not to be outdone, I fumble at his shirt buttons, wanting to feel his skin. Moving too quickly, I pull too hard and one of them pings off. I giggle against his lips, feeling them curve up in response. I move the sides of his shirt apart to expose his tanned chest with its scattering of light-brown hair, and spread my hands across it, moving them under his shirt to his back. Ooh, all that warm skin. I skate my fingers around his ribs to the front and feel his flat nipples. He twitches and mumbles something incoherent.

While he continues to kiss me, he pushes up my top, his hands hot on my skin. There's no way I can get my bra off while I'm pinned down, but it doesn't seem to bother him, and he just moves the lace up with the top before bending his head and taking a nipple in his mouth. I close my eyes at the sensation of his tongue stroking me, and then I shudder as he sucks. Pleasure washes over me like an ocean wave warmed by the sun. My hands curl on his back, my nails lightly scoring against his skin, and he groans.

He kisses back up my neck to my mouth, his beard tickling my skin on the way, and I let my tongue dance with his, loving his need, his obvious passion. I hadn't expected this. I thought it might feel awkward and polite, and I'd be embarrassed and have to follow instructions. I'm completely unprepared for the heat that rose so suddenly between us, and the way instinct is driving us.

I'd like him naked; I'd like to see him, to hold him, feel him, but equally there's something incredibly sexy about this urgency, this need. My right leg is underneath him, and his erection is pressing against my hip, but that's not where I want it. I shift on the sofa, pulling him more on top of me, and he moves to the side, and ohhh… yeah… there he is, nestling between my legs, pressing right where I want him, with only the silky material of his boxers and my skirt and underwear between us.

I slip my hands down his back, under his trousers, then beneath the elastic of his boxers, and onto the muscles there. "Mmm…" I murmur against his lips, feeling the muscles move as he flexes his hips and gives a small thrust against me.

"Elena…" He exhales against my lips and moves again, arousing us both. "You're going to be the death of me…"

"Sorry," I whisper, then moan as he thrusts again.

"Don't apologize. It's… aaahhh… *sexy as*."

He likes me being forward. That gives me courage. I slide a hand between us and tug up my skirt. Something rips, the stitching on the hem, probably, but I'm past caring. He helps me, pushing it up my thighs, and then he rocks his hips, and it's just our underwear separating us.

He lifts his head and looks at me. "I had such plans," he states.

"Screw the plans." I move a hand beneath him and tug my underwear to one side.

He gives a short laugh and lowers a hand to his boxers, then stops. He looks up at me, and I can see something has occurred to him. "Shit," he says. "I've just realized, I don't have any condoms." For the first time maybe since I've known him, he looks embarrassed. "Some fucking Casanova I am."

I giggle. "I have a Mirena coil fitted. Don't worry about it."

"But—"

"Nick, for Christ's sake, I haven't been with anyone for fifteen years and you've only had one partner for a millennia. Do you really think we've got a problem with STDs?"

"Ah, no, I guess not." He looks over his shoulder. "I should at least make an attempt at being romantic and get you to the bedroom…" He looks back at me. I give a small shake of my head. His lips curve up.

He slides a hand beneath himself, tugs down the elastic of his boxers, and maneuvers the tip of his erection down through my folds. "I feel like I'm sixteen again," he murmurs, pushing his hips forward so he enters me a little. He brings his hand back up so he can brace himself on his elbows. "I'm all hot under the collar."

I look up into his eyes, take a deep breath, and exhale slowly, trying to relax as he slides inside me. "Ohhh…" I can't help but exclaim at the sensation of being stretched and filled. He's not a small guy, and it's a strange mixture of unusual and uncomfortable and exquisite.

He pauses, lowers his head, and kisses me, the softest, gentlest kiss I've ever had. "I'm just crazy about you," he whispers.

My eyes prick with tears. I've waited so long for this. "Don't make me cry."

He smiles. "Just relax." Carefully, he withdraws until he's almost out of me, then pushes forward again. This time, coated with my moisture, he slides right in.

He waits again, letting me adjust. "Just a bit more," he says.

I blink. More? Once again, he moves back, then forward. He stops, pushes my thighs to my chest, tilting my pelvis up, and sinks in even deeper. I gasp, automatically wrapping my legs around his waist. He smirks. "Balls deep," he says mischievously. A strand of his hair falls across his forehead. The suave, sophisticated businessman has vanished, and a sexy stud has taken his place. I hadn't expected this.

I brush my hands down his back, onto his hips, enjoying the movement of his muscles as he begins to move inside me. There's no room at all, and I can't do anything but lie there, pinned to the cushions, but I don't give a damn because it's wonderful, and anyway he seems to know what he's doing.

He kisses me while he moves, his tongue playing with mine, and we lie there like that for what seems like hours, him thrusting slowly, kissing me, stroking me, until I'm completely relaxed, and my body is beginning to stir. Nerve endings tingle, tiny muscles begin to tense all through me, and my breathing grows deeper as pleasure spirals inside.

My hips move against his, and he shifts up an inch and changes the angle somehow, and ohhh… now he's grinding right against me. That's clever… and he knows what he's doing, because he lifts his head to look at me, and his hot eyes hold mine captive.

He moves faster, sliding right inside me, long hard thrusts, and I dig my nails into his back, throbbing, aching. I'm turned on as much by his need as my own, and I have the sudden knowledge that my climax is inevitable. He's guiding me to the edge, and he's right with me, and we're going to tumble over together.

He lifts up a little, hooking an arm under my thigh to pin it there and changing the angle again, and all I can do is lie there and let him plunge into me, oh shit, and my orgasm hits suddenly and without warning, long, hard pulses that make me squeal and clench around him. He crushes his lips to mine, and then he stiffens, his muscles tightening, and he's coming inside me.

"Fuck," he says, loudly and with feeling. One hand clenches in my hair, pulling my head back, and his lips bruise mine a little as he kisses me. His hips jerk, and I dig my nails into his skin and hold him there, wanting to squeeze every drop from him. It feels like it goes on forever, the two of us locked together, hot, hard, and blissful, before it finally releases us, and we breathe with deep, ragged gasps.

Slowly, we descend back to earth. I can't move an inch. Although he's propped on his elbows, the rest of him is heavy, and I'm completely pinned beneath him. All our clothing is tangled, and so are our legs. He's still inside me. I don't ever want him to leave.

That was the hottest, most erotic thing that's ever happened to me. And I know with all certainty that it's not going to finish tonight. I'm never giving him up. I want this to be a part of my life until my dying days.

Finally, he lifts his head. We look into each other's eyes for a long time.

"Sorry about that," he says eventually, and we both laugh. "It's your fault," he adds, a touch accusatory. "I had all these plans to be slow and romantic."

"Foiled again." I smile. "You realize, though, that we're stuck here for eternity?"

"Uh, yeah. What's happened?"

"Your elbow is on my hair. Ow."

"I somehow managed to hook my watch on your bra strap. Hold on."

It takes us several minutes to disentangle ourselves. He's missing a shirt button, and the hem of my skirt is dangling down. Everything is twisted around and rucked up. I'm deliciously disheveled. He manages to get to his feet and extends a hand to help me up, and we stand facing each other, straightening clothes and doing up the remaining buttons. I feel like I've run a marathon—my muscles ache, my hips are stiff, and I can barely walk.

"Aw," he says, arching his spine, "my back. I forgot I wasn't a teenager." We both laugh, and he pulls me into his arms. "Are you okay?" he asks with concern.

"I'm wonderful."

"I didn't hurt you?"

"Nick, it was a-*ma*-zing. I feel like a million dollars."

"You didn't tell me," he says, with some amusement.

"Didn't tell you what?"

"That you're a total sex kitten."

"What?"

"There's you, acting all shy and 'I couldn't possibly,' and then you set the bed alight. Well, the sofa."

"Nick!"

"It's not a complaint. It's just that I thought I was the one doing the seducing, but I think in the end it turned out to be the other way around."

I chuckle and rest my cheek on his chest, and he tightens his arms around me. "No regrets?" he murmurs.

"God, no."

"I'm glad."

"You?" I move back and look up at him, wondering if he's thinking about Olivia.

But he just smiles and shakes his head. "I'm so glad you came away with me," he says, and he takes my face in his hands and kisses me before moving back again to look me in the eyes. "I think…" He gives me a hesitant smile. "I think I'm more than a little in love with you."

Emotion sweeps over me, sudden and brutal. "Oh…"

"I hope that's okay."

"Yes, Nick. It's okay. It's very okay."

"And you know that's not it, don't you?" He's suddenly the successful billionaire CEO again, his expression full of determination, brooking no argument. "I'm not letting you go."

"We'll see," I tell him, but inside I bubble with happiness.

Chapter Twenty-Two

Elena

He makes us both a coffee, and we curl up on the sofa together, me with my head resting on his shoulder, him with his arm around me. He stretches out his legs and rests his feet on the coffee table, crossing his ankles. The jazz music is still playing, and I watch his feet tap in time. Steam rises from our coffee cups. The second button of his shirt is missing where I pulled it off, and the parted cotton reveals his light-brown skin and a few manly hairs. He smells nice. I like every single thing about this guy.

Something very odd occurs to me. I feel happy. It comes as a shock. I sometimes feel content, after a workout or a run, or following a good meal, or an evening out with a friend. But I can't honestly recall the last time I felt happy.

I kiss his jaw, and he kisses the top of my head.

"How's the writing going?" I ask.

"Good, thanks. I finished the first chapter. I'm pretty happy with it."

"Can I read it?"

"If you like." He bends to lift his laptop from the table, pulls the file up on Google Docs, and hands it to me.

I sip my coffee as I read it, taking my time, enjoying the notion that these words came out of his head and flowed down his fingers onto the keys. It's like seeing an x-ray of his body, peering inside him, strangely intimate. I can tell he's a poet first and foremost; his language is poetic, the prose having a rhythm to it, full of assonance and alliteration.

But the story is powerful, too, and he manages to convey the desperation and fury of the two men who are fighting over the gold they've found in the riverbed, the competition over the nuggets of metal hiding a much deeper feud over the woman they both love. For a moment I get lost in their struggle, and I can almost feel the icy-cold water soaking into my clothes as they fall onto the rocks. They roll and thrash, and then the water runs red with blood as Jacob picks up a stone and smashes it onto Edward's skull. The details are just sketched with a few words, but the nature of it is horrific, and tears prick my eyes as Jacob stands and looks down in terror at the broken body of his once-friend.

"Oh Nick. It's amazing. I don't know how you managed to convey such emotion, but it's really shocking. Those poor men."

"Do you think I managed to convey how they felt? I've been thinking about them for so long."

"I do." I put the laptop down. "You really have a talent for it. You simply have to keep going."

"Thank you. I will. I'm determined to finish this." He looks pleased.

"You're very clever." I look at his mouth, thinking about how passionately he kissed me while he was sliding inside me. How he likes to hold me tightly, to make sure I don't get away. A touch of the CEO comes through, dominant and bossy. I like that.

"Don't look at me like that," he scolds. "You'll get me all riled up again."

"Maybe I want to."

"At my age? Are you trying to kill me off?"

I snort. "Don't make out like you're enfeebled. I'm betting you're as lusty as a man half your age."

He chuckles. "Is that a complaint?"

"God, no." We both laugh.

I finish off my coffee and put the cup on the table. Then, with an exclamation, I check my phone. "It's 11:48!"

"Nearly your birthday." He smiles.

"A new year." I think then of Liz, and wonder where she is. In bed with Daniel? Or is she on her own somewhere? I feel a stab of guilt; I haven't thought about her for a while.

"Thinking about Liz?" he asks, and I nod. "Do you want to check and see if she's in your room?"

If she is, I know she's going to be subdued and probably upset. "I'll go back after the clock ticks over," I reply. "I know it's selfish, but I want just a few more minutes to myself."

"That's fair enough." He takes my face in his hands. "Why don't we make out for a whole year?"

I laugh, then lift my arms around his neck and tilt my face up for his kiss. Mmm... that's blissful. His kisses are soft and luxurious. It's like wrapping myself in a cashmere sweater. He kisses my nose and eyebrows, my cheeks and back to my mouth, and I lose myself in just being loved until he lifts his head and says, "Happy birthday."

I glance at my phone—it's midnight.

"Happy New Year," I whisper, and we kiss again. "Best birthday ever," I tell him honestly.

He grins. "That's a nice thing to say. Now, hold on a minute. I've got something for you." He gets up, goes into his bedroom, and comes back out with a small parcel. He sits beside me again and hands it to me.

It's beautifully wrapped, probably by an assistant, I would think, as I've seen his attempts at wrapping presents and they're what you'd expect from a guy. I undo the bow and pry off the lid.

It's a pair of earrings—small studs with a glittering heart dangling from them. I know without having to ask that the stones are diamonds. There's no way he would have bought anything else.

And they're hearts. It's not a gift a boss buys for his PA. I feel warm from the roots of my hair to the tips of my toes.

"They're beautiful," I tell him, my voice husky with emotion. "Thank you so much."

He puts his arm around my shoulders. "Happy birthday, sweetheart."

"Sweetheart?" I tease. "Is that what I am, now?"

He looks surprised, then smiles. "I suppose so. Do you mind?"

"No."

He kisses my nose. "Look, there's no need to rush anything. I know you want to get Liz sorted, and although I think most of my kids are expecting us to get together, it's still a delicate matter."

I nod; I understand. They might expect it, and they might all be grown up, but the replacement of their mother is still something they could struggle with.

"But I want you to know," he continues, "that after what's happened tonight, we're going to be together. One way or another. So be aware and start thinking about what you want to do, because at some point in the not-too-distant future, we're going to have that conversation."

I stick my tongue out at him. "You're quite bossy."

"You don't become director of an international company without learning how to boss people about."

"So I see." I smile. "I understand, and I will start thinking about it. If it's really what you want?" A small part of me is still struggling to believe he's chosen me.

"You have to ask?" He feigns indignation. "After I put on my best performance?"

"Your best performance is banging me on the sofa like a sixteen-year-old? I've changed my mind."

"You cheeky..." He pushes me onto my back and gives me a long, hard kiss. "Next time," he promises. "I'll use all my best moves."

I look up into his eyes and give a happy sigh. "I can't wait."

*

Not long after, I blow him a kiss goodbye at the door and let myself into my cabin. The door closes slowly with a click behind me.

It's quiet, but as I walk in, I see a figure lying on the sofa. I duck into my room and place the box Nick gave me on the chest of drawers, take off my shoes, then come out again. Liz hears me and sits up. Her eyes are sleepy and red-rimmed, and her face is blotchy; she's obviously been crying.

"Sorry to disturb you," I murmur, walking up to her. "Are you okay?"

She nods, but her bottom lip trembles. I drop to my knees beside her and put my arms around her, and she hugs me as if she's clinging to a life raft.

"I'm so sorry I wasn't here," I say, guilt washing over me as I think what a wonderful time I've been having.

"It's okay. Have you been with Nick?" Her words are very slightly slurred. I think she's close to being drunk.

I nod as we move back. "Would you like a cup of coffee?"

She nods. "Please."

I start the coffee machine and watch the espresso begin to fill up one of the cups. Then I turn and rest on the worktop, folding my arms.

"Did you have a nice time?" Liz asks.

"Yes, thank you." I'm not ready to discuss what happened yet. "What about you? Last I saw you were dancing with Daniel."

She looks at the tissue in her fingers and fiddles with it. "He was lovely. We danced for ages. He's so…" Her face lights up briefly, and then she glances up at me, and her expression dulls again. "He asked me to go back to his room. And I said yes." She lifts her chin as if she's waiting for me to scold her. I don't say anything though, and after a moment her bottom lip trembles again. "I really like him," she whispers, tears glimmering in her eyes. "He makes me feel beautiful and clever and funny. I know a lot of it is just talk, I know he just wanted to get into my knickers."

"Aw, Liz…" I sigh and put another cup in the machine.

"No, I'm not stupid, but that's okay because he could have chosen anyone on board, and he chose me. Do you know how that makes me feel?"

"Kinda," I admit.

"Even if he did it because he thought I was vulnerable and an easy choice, I still found it flattering." She blushes then and presses the heel of her hand to the center of her forehead. "Jeez. I heard my own words then. I sound so pathetic."

"No, you don't."

"Yes, I do. But it meant so much. I haven't slept with Keith since his accident, did I tell you that? Two years without sex!"

Try fifteen and see how that feels, I want to say, but this isn't about me, and anyway it's not the same. I can't imagine how she must feel.

"We used to have such a good sex life," she says, and a tear trickles down her cheek. "And it all disappeared overnight because of that stupid fucking accident."

I add some milk to the cups and sugar for Liz, bring them over to the sofa, and sit beside her.

"I miss it," she says wistfully, sipping the hot coffee. "I miss being close to someone, and I miss being wanted."

"Yeah, I get that."

"I just needed someone to want to be with me." She looks sadly into her cup.

"Liz," I say gently, laying a hand on hers, "you don't have to explain yourself to me. You're a grown up, and you've been treated very badly. I understand why you tried to find yourself a few minutes of happiness. Who am I to criticize or judge you for that?"

More tears trickle down her cheeks. "You're so nice. I hope Nick appreciates how lovely you are."

"I think he does." I remember the box in my room, and his tender kisses, smile, then remember myself and wipe it away, but she's searching for another tissue and is too miserable to have caught it. "So what happened?" I ask.

"We started to… you know… make love, in his room. We took off our clothes, and he said I was beautiful." Tears are running freely down her face now. "We got into bed. But when it came to it, I couldn't do it. I froze up. I got up and pulled my clothes on and ran." She bursts into tears, puts down her mug, and covers her face with her hands.

I sigh and take her in my arms again. Part of me is relieved at the news, because I'm sure if she'd gone through with it, she'd have woken up tomorrow and felt twice as bad.

But then again, maybe she wouldn't; perhaps finally it would have convinced her to leave her bad marriage behind. What's the right course of action? I don't know, and I'm not sure I'm the right person to give her advice.

Well, she's not asking for any, I remind myself, only for comfort, and that I can give. I lean back with her in my arms and kiss the top of her head and rub her arm until her sniffs die down. She sags against me, obviously exhausted.

"Come on, let's get you into bed," I tell her, and I get up and pull her to her feet. "We'll talk more tomorrow."

She mutters something, but lets me lead her into her room. I help her take off her dress and shoes, then pull back the covers and help her into bed. I cover her over with the duvet like a child. She'll have mascara on the pillow in the morning, but she's too tired and drunk to take off her makeup now.

"Goodnight," I murmur, and she mumbles it back, but she's already almost asleep. I turn off the light, creep out, and close the door.

I blow out a long breath, pick up my coffee, and open the sliding door to the balcony. It's cool out here, but the breeze is pleasant on my warm face. Ahead of me, the cliffs of Fiordland slip by soundlessly in the darkness. In the distance I can hear singing from one of the parties going on above me. Way above, the moon is waning, but she still throws out some light, covering the table and chairs and balustrade in silver.

I feel for Liz, so much it hurts. All she wanted was some comfort and to feel wanted, but the trouble was that she wants that from the man she loves, not some stranger. Like me, she's never slept around, never had casual sex, and I think it's hard—especially at our age—to start now. I might have had sex tonight—and on the sofa, of all places, like a teenager—but Nick is hardly a stranger.

I want you to know… that after what's happened tonight, we're going to be together. One way or another. His words make me glow. Yes, I want to be there for Liz, but whatever happens with her marriage, I'd be foolish to turn my back on this relationship now, when I have a chance at happiness.

Is it really possible for Nick and me to be together, to have a proper relationship, where we live together, go to bed at night, wake up in the morning, share our lives? It's more than I ever thought possible.

I know there are things we need to sort out first—Liz, his kids, and his job. But suddenly the future holds such promise it's positively glittering, like the stars, or like the diamonds in the earrings he bought me.

Neither of us has said I love you yet, but it's very early days. He said he's *in* love with me. And tonight he said it with his body, even though his mouth didn't form the words. He told me, *I'm just crazy about you*, right as he was entering me. Mmm… my body heats at the memory.

I cup my hands around the coffee cup, and I stand there for a long time, a smile on my lips, replaying the evening like a video in my mind.

Chapter Twenty-Three

Nick

The next morning, I send Elena a text at eight a.m., when I think she and Liz might be close to getting up. *You two up for breakfast? I'd like to share a croissant with the birthday girl.*

She replies almost immediately, *Definitely! Give us ten?*

I text back, *Will do!* I'm already dressed, but I finish off a cup of coffee on the balcony while I wait, and re-read the email from Ben a second time.

He chats about Heloise and baby Estella. Then, at the end, he finishes with a couple of sentences. "By the way, I spoke to Lucas about you stepping down. I hope that was okay. He started the conversation by saying he was a bit worried about you and sensed your mind hadn't quite been on the work lately, so it felt the right time to share. I told him I didn't want the job, and that you asked me because I was the oldest, but that he was the right person for it. He was stunned and didn't say much. Just thought I'd pre-warn you!"

I put down my iPad and sit back, looking out at the view of Dunedin before me. The ship arrived at the port in the early hours, and I watched the sun come up over the view of the hills in the distance. Larnach Castle is over there somewhere. Brock's nephew, Leon, got married there around this time last year. I was invited, but it was still shy of the one-year anniversary of Olivia's passing, and I wasn't in the mood for celebration. I booked a shore excursion out there today, but I forgot to ask if Elena was going.

Part of me wishes Ben hadn't told Lucas. It's a delicate matter, and I wanted to be the one to raise it with him. But my boys are close, and I don't blame Ben for sharing.

So Lucas has picked up that I've been a bit distant? I thought I'd hidden it, but he's obviously spotted that my heart isn't in the work anymore.

I thought he might have emailed me, but I haven't had any messages. I expect he's thinking it over, and he'll probably want to talk about it when I get back.

I wonder what he thinks—whether he'll want the job. I'm sure he will. At times like this, I wish he had a partner to talk things over with. I know he has a lot of girlfriends, but I don't think there's anyone serious at the moment. I don't know why. He's a good-looking guy, he's intelligent, and he's loaded. He's more wary than my other kids, though, more cynical, more cautious, maybe because he had a bad breakup some time ago. It turned out she was interested in his money, and I'm sure that's on his mind now with future dates. It's not something I had to worry about, because Olivia had no idea I was rich when we first started dating.

For the first time, I wonder how Elena feels about the fact that I have money. I'm sure most people would laugh at that and say yeah, I'm sure she's really upset about it! But she's a very individual person, and because she's currently struggling for money, she's very proud. I know it took a lot for her to accept this trip, and the money I put into her account. How will she feel to be with me permanently? Maybe even to marry?

Wait. Huh? Marriage? I surprise myself by considering the word. We haven't even been on a proper date yet. Last night doesn't really count... I think I know her well enough to know the relationship is going to be very successful, but of course I could be wrong.

But if I'm not... and if we are still together in six months or a year... is marriage something I'd consider?

I lean back and let the morning breeze brush my face. After last night, I'm certainly not averse to being in a long-term relationship with her. I've always found her attractive, and over the past week that general attraction has bloomed into something deeper and sexier, but I still wasn't prepared for the level of heat that exploded between us last night. The way she wanted me right there, on the sofa, and her passionate reaction, her soft cries and the way she clawed at my back...

I shift on the chair. One step at a time. First we have to get ourselves into a position where we can date properly and get to know one another on a more intimate level. Then I can think about the M word.

The ten minutes is nearly up, so I take my cup in, pull on my sneakers, pick up my jacket, and head out. The coach leaves at nine for Larnach Castle, so there's plenty of time to eat.

Elena opens her door, and I feel a boyish lift of my heart at the sight of her. She's wearing jeans today, with a white blouse and white sneakers, and a plum-colored jacket. She looks young and chic. And now all I can think about is kissing her and undoing the buttons of her blouse. What am I, fourteen?

"Morning." I smile.

"Morning." She gives me a breezy smile back. "Sleep well?"

"Nope. You?"

"I got a few hours." She looks over her shoulder as Liz comes out. Her sister is pale, and she's not wearing any makeup today.

"Happy New Year," I say to Liz, and I bend and kiss her on the cheek.

"Thank you, Happy New Year to you, too," she says.

"Come on," Elena says briskly in her best this-is-how-I-get-the-secretaries-organized voice. "You need to get some breakfast down you, then you'll feel better."

We head off, Liz in front of us. I glance at Elena and raise my eyebrows, and she pulls an *eek* face and shakes her head. Clearly, something happened last night.

We go to the Pantry, which is a buffet-style restaurant, and help ourselves to whatever we fancy for breakfast. Elena chooses a fresh fruit salad with yoghurt, while I opt for a McDonald's-style breakfast burger with a sausage patty, bacon, egg, and hash brown.

"Hungry?" she asks, amused, as we pour ourselves a coffee.

"I worked up an appetite," I reply, and grin as she nudges me.

"Shh," she scolds, but her eyes sparkle.

I bend closer, my mouth to her ear. "What happened with Liz last night?"

She glances around, sees Liz heading back to the table with just a cup of coffee, and sighs. "She went back to Daniel's room but couldn't go through with it. I wonder how he's feeling about it this morning. Do you think he'll be angry?"

I frown. "He's pretty placid. And he's a nice guy, even if he is a bit of a womanizer. I'm sure he'll be fine."

"I hope so. She's pretty cut up about it."

I inhale, enjoying the smell of her perfume. "You smell nice."

Her lips curve up. "Thank you."

"And you look terrific. You have a... glow."

"I wonder why?" She gives me an impish smile. She reaches across to pick up a couple of slices of toast, and I can't help but notice the movement of her breasts.

"Are you wearing a bra?" I ask suspiciously.

She laughs. "No. I can't believe you noticed that."

"Of course I noticed. And now I'm going to be thinking about it all day." I blow out a breath.

"Are you on an excursion?" she asks, amused.

"Yes, to Larnach Castle."

"Aw, we're off to the city for shopping."

I sigh. "Oh well. I guess I'll see you for dinner tonight."

"I hope so." She picks up her tray, and we make our way back to the table. "Here." She puts the plate of toast and butter in front of Liz, who's nursing her coffee cup. "Eat this."

"I'm not hungry."

"I'm not going out with you until you eat something," Elena says firmly.

Liz glares mutely at her, then picks up a slice and starts buttering it.

"Is there anything I can do?" I ask gently.

She shakes her head. "No, thank you. It's my own fault. I got myself into this situation; it's up to me to get out of it."

I nod, but I make a mental note to find Daniel and talk to him. I'm sure he's fine, but the last thing she needs is for him to give her the cold shoulder.

My heart goes out to Liz as I watch her crunch her toast and look out of the window, her gaze distant. Then she sighs and looks back at me and smiles.

"You look nice today," she says. "Your shirt is the same color as your eyes."

"I was going to wear my white shirt," I reply, "but it appears to be missing a button."

Elena coughs and glares at me. I just grin.

"I half wish I'd decided to go to Larnach," Liz states. "You'll have to take some photos to show us."

"Brock's nephew got married there," I tell them, "but I couldn't make it at the time, so I'm looking forward to seeing it."

"What a lovely place to tie the knot," she says. "Where did you and your wife marry?"

"Uh… down in Christchurch, because that's where her parents lived." I glance at Elena. She's concentrating on gathering a few blueberries on her spoon. I've never felt odd talking about Olivia with her before, but now, all of a sudden, I feel awkward.

"I had a lovely wedding," Liz says wistfully. "On the beach in Paihia. It was so romantic. Keith looked gorgeous in his suit." She bites her toast absently, looking out at the boats sailing by.

Elena glances at me, and she gives me a small smile. I return it, wishing I could take her hand, but I know she wants to keep this quiet for now. I feel for her. It can't be easy dating a guy who's had a whole lifetime with another woman, including having a large family. When I get home, the first thing I'm going to do is put the house up for sale. Even if we were to stay in Wellington, I don't think Elena would want to live in it. It's Olivia's home, and I want a fresh start.

It's not long before it's time to go. I say goodbye to the girls and watch them head off to their assembly point before I go to the room where I'm meeting my party. Within thirty minutes we're walking to the coach, and then we're off to Larnach.

I spend a pleasant couple of hours having a tour of the late-nineteenth-century castle, then go off on my own for a walk through the grounds, where I take some photos to show Elena later. Finally I rejoin my party at the café and have a coffee before we all head back to the coach.

There are other excursions planned for the afternoon, but I'm pleased I chose to stay on the ship as I have a few tasks to carry out. First, I text Daniel and ask whether he has five minutes to catch up. He agrees to meet me at one p.m. for some lunch, and he's already there when I walk into the Patisserie a few minutes before.

"I've only got half an hour," he states.

"No worries." We order some club sandwiches and a couple of slices of cake and take a seat by the window.

"No trips this afternoon?" he asks.

"No, I've got a few jobs to do," I reply. "So… I hear last night didn't go well."

He gives me a wry look. "What did she tell you?"

"Not much. Elena mentioned that Liz went back to your room but couldn't go through with it."

"Yeah. Got my motor running then ran for the door." He sighs.

"Sorry to hear that. If it's any consolation, she looked pretty upset today. I don't think she's slept much."

He leans back as the waiter brings over our coffees and thanks him, then adds a spoonful of sugar and stirs it. "I guess it's nice to know she didn't just walk away and forget about me, but to be honest it doesn't make me feel good to know she's suffering." He lifts an eyebrow at me as he sips his coffee. "That surprises you? You don't have a very high opinion of me, do you?"

"Honestly? Your track record isn't great, Dan. A different woman in every port? On every ship? It's none of my business—you're single so why shouldn't you make the most of it? And as you said, Liz is a big girl and able to make her own decisions. But I'm a big fan of Elena, and she's worried about her sister, so..."

"Fair enough."

"It's just... go easy on her, eh? I think she really likes you, and it sounds as if you gave her a much-needed boost. It's going to be tough for her to deal with what happened."

"You think I'm angry with her?" This time Daniel does look offended. "Jesus, give me some credit. I like her, Nick. She's smart, and she's brave, and she's funny. We clicked, and last night just happened—I didn't plan it, whatever you might think. I was enjoying spending time with her. If you must know, *she* suggested we go back to my room. I asked her if she was sure and she said she was. I could see she was trying to prove to herself she was ready to move on. I don't want to break up a happy marriage, but if a woman I like wants to sleep with me, I'm not going to say no. I was actually hopeful she might leave the bastard. I'd have been interested in furthering the relationship if she did. It's the first time I've thought that about any woman since Cynthia and I divorced."

The waiter turns up with our sandwiches and places them before us. I spend a moment extracting a few from the stack and have a big bite. Daniel is an old friend, and I'm conscious I've offended him.

"I'm sorry," I tell him. "I had no idea, and it's my fault for jumping to conclusions. I'm over-sensitive because I happen to have a stake in all this." I tell him how I'm hoping that Elena and I will be able to develop a relationship.

His stiff spine relaxes, and he nods and tucks into his sandwiches. "I could see you were into her," he states. "And from the way she looked at you, she likes you, too." He smiles and says hello to a couple who pass by, then turns his attention back to me. "You're doing okay then, after Olivia?" I haven't seen him since the funeral.

I look out of the window. The sky has turned cloudy, and the first drops of rain are starting to fall. I hope Elena has thought to take an umbrella. "It was tough for the first eighteen months."

"Elena's your PA, right?"

"Yeah. She was also Olivia's best friend."

"Ah."

"Olivia told me once that if something were to happen to her, she wanted us two to get together." My lips twist. "It's been tough getting that out of my mind."

"Ouch, yeah, I can imagine."

He sighs. "I didn't think it would be so complicated at our age, but it is, somehow."

"Yeah. I wish I could wave a wand and make everything right for Liz," he says. "But she still loves her husband. I know I've got to let her go."

He changes the subject then, and we finish the sandwiches and cake, and before long he says he has to leave. We shake hands, and he says to join him for dinner tonight, and the girls are welcome too, despite everything that's happened.

I wander back to my room, thinking about what he said, *I wish I could wave a wand and make everything right for Liz… But she still loves her husband. I know I've got to let her go.*

I like playing the fairy godmother role. It's not entirely altruistic—it makes me feel good to help people. But how can I help? I can't mend her marriage, or make Keith walk again, or change the way he thinks about his disability.

But money has a strange way of sorting out people's 'insolvable' problems.

I let myself into my room. Should I run my idea past Elena first? I weigh it up and finally decide against it. It might not come to anything anyway, and I don't want to get her hopes up. I especially don't want her to let it slip to Liz.

I take out my phone and make a call.

Fifteen minutes later, I hang up, collect my laptop, and sit on the sofa, propping my feet on the coffee table. I have a few hours to work on my book now, so I'd better make the most of them.

Later, I'll be able to catch up with Elena for dinner. I think about her white blouse, and the way her breasts moved in it this morning without a bra. If I undid the buttons, she'd be naked beneath the silky material. It's impossible not to think about last night, and how we were such a tangle of clothing and limbs. It's been a long time since I felt controlled by my passion like that, since I couldn't think about anything else but the woman I was inside. It was incredibly hot.

And… now I have an erection. I blow out a breath. "I have to work!" I scold it, glaring at my crotch. "You got some action yesterday. You're sixty, for fuck's sake. Act your age."

But it refuses to behave, and it takes me several minutes of thinking about cold showers before I'm finally able to put Elena out of my mind and return to my laptop.

Chapter Twenty-Four

Elena

In the morning, when I see how unhappy Liz is, I'm worried that the day is going to be a nightmare, but in the end it passes nicely enough. She cheers up a bit when she realizes she's lost a little weight over the past week despite all the lovely food on the ship, and she buys herself a new pair of trousers a size smaller than what she usually has to wear.

We don't talk much about Daniel or Keith and instead concentrate on shopping, looking at clothing and jewelry, and treating ourselves to a couple of souvenirs. Neither of us is very good at spending money, even though I've made it clear that we have enough to treat ourselves. But we meet another couple of passengers at a little bistro, and we have a pleasant lunch chatting about all kinds of things as we eat a lovely salad with Thai chicken strips and sip ice-cold white wine. Outside, the rain patters on the pavement, but it doesn't bother us, although it does make me think of Nick wandering around Larnach Castle. Is he back by now?

Thinking about Nick inevitably sends memories of the night before floating around my head. It was all so unexpected. I wonder when we'll meet up again? I can't expect the same performance every night! Maybe in a few days' time? I hope it'll happen before we return to Auckland. Even though my body is still a bit tender, I want him again. Having him inside me... it was such a delicious feeling.

I shift in my chair, realizing I'd zoned out. Around me, the other women don't seem to have noticed, thank goodness. They're a group of friends who decided they weren't going to let their single status stop them from going on vacation and enjoying themselves. Despite this, however, they seem to talk about men ninety percent of the time.

"I keep meaning to ask," one of them says. Her name is Fiona, and she's in her late fifties, I'd say, with rather beautiful long, curly silver hair and expressive brown eyes. "The good-looking guy who sits with you at the Captain's table at dinner—is he spoken for?"

I'm so taken aback that I don't know what to say. Is he? Can I claim him as mine?

"Um, no," I end up replying. "Not that I know of."

"Ooh," they all say, and as one they lean forward. Suddenly, it occurs to me that they've singled us out because they want to learn more about him, not because they're interested in a friendship with me and Liz. "What's his name?" Fiona asks.

"Nick Prince," I reply. I suppose I should be annoyed or upset by this, but for some reason I find it funny.

"His wife died a couple of years ago," Liz adds. She glances at me, and I see the twinkle in her eye. She thinks it's amusing, too. "He's the CEO of Prince's Toy Store."

It's comical to watch their jaws drop. "Rich *and* gorgeous," one of the others says. "Oh, Fiona, you've definitely got to make a move on him."

"I will." She gives a little shimmy, and they all laugh. "Tonight's the night, ladies!" She grins. "Full steam ahead!"

I smile, wondering what Nick will make of her. She's not quite the same as the others, who are decked out in gold jewelry and with coiffured hair; she's a bit boho, with a long skirt and hooped earrings. She's not unlike Olivia, actually. I feel my first twinge of worry.

But there's no time to think on it because someone declares the bus is waiting, so we hurriedly pay our bills and head back.

I try not to think about it over the next couple of hours. I take an afternoon yoga class followed by fifteen minutes of meditation, try to find my Zen, and fail somewhat miserably. Afterward, I go for a swim, then come back to my room to read for an hour before dinner. But I keep thinking about Nick, about having his hot, hard body on top of me, inside me, about how he kisses me, and about that look in his eye that tells me he's using his x-ray vision, and I get all flustered. In the end I put down my book and lie on my side, listening to the ship's engines as they start up, announcing our departure as we head toward Christchurch. I think about Fiona, and wonder what will happen when she introduces herself to Nick tonight. Surely he won't be interested? I don't think he will. He's made it quite clear he wants a relationship with me, and I can't imagine him now deciding to go off with another woman. If only she didn't look a bit like his wife…

I haven't thought about Olivia for a while on purpose, but I turn onto my back and look up at the ceiling, and think about the fact that last night I slept with her husband. I know she apparently told Nick she wanted us to get together if anything happened to her, but that's so bizarre it doesn't make it any easier. She was my best friend. She was a strange woman, to be sure—moody, contrary, often in a dream world. I wish she'd told me about the death of her twin sister, and about the possibility of her having a brain aneurysm. But it sounds as if she didn't want to admit it to herself, let alone to anyone else.

I'm not sure I knew her that well at all. I thought I did, but it sounds as if she was a very private person all ways around. I find it strange that she never told Nick about what I confessed to her about Ricky, but maybe she thought secrets were meant to be kept. It's just so unusual. Most people can't keep a secret and feel a burning need to tell someone else.

I'm feeling that need now—I want to go up to that group of women and shout, "Hands off, Nick's mine!" I won't, of course, and not just because it would be crass. I don't know if he is mine. One hot date doesn't mean I own him.

I wear myself out with all my thinking, and within a few minutes I doze off.

When I wake, it's five-thirty, and I feel a bit flustered as we normally meet at six for dinner. Hearing Liz's shower going, I check my phone, and Nick has left a message, letting us know that we'll be joining Daniel as usual. I chew my bottom lip as I pull on a summer dress. The knee-length pale-pink material is covered with a lace layer with darker pink flowers. It's really pretty, and it goes well with my blonde hair. I slip on a pair of flesh-colored high-heeled sandals, brush my hair and spray it, and touch up my makeup with a little pink eyeshadow and some shiny pink lipstick. Lastly, I slot in Nick's diamonds earrings, and I watch with a smile as the hearts sparkle in the light. Then I go out and knock on Liz's door.

"Come in!"

I open it and discover her dressed and slotting in some earrings. She's wearing the new trousers she bought today with a long white tunic, and she looks slim and attractive. I think the day out did her some good.

"Nick has asked us to join him at the Captain's table," I tell her. "I don't know how you feel about that."

Her fingers pause for a moment, then fumble at her ear before inserting the earring. She smiles. "That's fine. We can all be grownups about it."

"You're sure?"

She nods, so I go back out and fetch my bag. By six, we're waiting for Nick's knock on the door, and when it comes, we go out.

He looks gorgeous tonight, as usual, dressed in smart cream trousers and a light-blue shirt with a navy jacket. Damn, I could put this man on a cracker and crunch him right up. He says hello and kisses Liz on the cheek, then turns to me. My heart leaps as his x-ray eyes scan me, stripping me naked in one easy move. Ooh, that zing—it's still there!

"Hey, you," he murmurs as Liz goes back into the room to fetch a wrap. "How's your day been?"

"Long," I admit. "I missed you."

"Me too." He glances after Liz, then quickly leans forward and kisses me on the mouth. I tingle all over. "I've been thinking about last night all day," he tells me.

"Glad I'm not the only one." We smile at each other as Liz comes back out.

"Right then," she says cheerfully. "Shall we?"

"You're sure you're okay with this?" Nick asks as we head off to the restaurant.

"I'm fine," she replies, "but thank you for asking."

"I did talk to Daniel today," he says.

That makes her glance at him. "Oh? Um… what did he say?"

"His actual words? He said he wished he could wave a wand and make everything right for you, but he knows you still love your husband, and that he has to let you go."

Her expression softens. "That was sweet."

"Yeah. Just thought you should know."

I smile and wink at him behind her back, and he reaches out and squeezes my hand. He's so thoughtful. I should have known he'd check on Daniel to make sure everything was okay.

I'm still a little nervous about dinner, but it turns out to be fine. Liz goes straight up to Daniel and says good evening, then deliberately takes a chair a few seats away from him, and Nick and I sit either side of her. Daniel doesn't comment, and a couple of times during the evening he makes sure to include her in the conversation, which I think she appreciates.

As usual, champagne flows freely, and we all have a couple of glasses each. We're just eating our desserts when Nick excuses himself to visit the Gents'. He's on his way back across the room when a woman pushes her chair back and rises, and bumps straight into him. She laughs and rests a hand on his chest as she apologizes, and he stops and smiles at her. It's Fiona. Obviously her 'chance' encounter was engineered.

I take a small spoonful of the cheesecake and eat it, trying not to look at them, and failing miserably. She's talking to him, using her hands expressively, laughing up at him, and he chats back. I've seen him act like this on many occasions. It's part of the reason he's such a good CEO—his friendly manner, and the way he puts people at ease. It's one reason I find him so attractive. I think he likes her. My heart sinks.

But then he checks his watch, and my heart leaps. He's looking for an escape route. He does that at work when he wants to exit a meeting or a conversation, to imply to the person he's talking to that he's busy, and he doesn't have long. I feel a surge of glee. He doesn't want her. He wants to be with me.

He glances at me at that moment. I carefully close my mouth around the spoonful of cheesecake, suck it off, and lick my lips. He blinks, his lips curve up, and then he turns his attention back to Fiona. He ends the conversation and walks away without looking back, leaving her pursing her lips and blowing out a breath.

Liz has left her seat to visit the Ladies' and smiles as she passes him. He sits back in his chair, tucks it in, then leans toward me. I meet him in the middle.

"You little tease," he murmurs.

"Moi?" I have another spoonful of dessert and eat it as slowly as possible.

He watches the spoon slide into my mouth and gives me a helpless look. "I haven't been able to stop thinking about you all day."

"Me neither," I whisper. "I feel all hot and bothered, like I'm coming down with something."

He glances at my flushed cheeks and tips his head to the side. "Maybe you need a cool shower."

"That could work."

"I could scrub your back?"

I open my mouth, but no words come out as the image of Nick under the running water springs into my mind. Naked, soaped-up. Glistening.

I'm saved from replying as Liz takes her seat again, and I return to finish off my dessert. She sips her champagne, listening as Daniel tells a story about some port he visited last year, sending those around him into gales of laughter.

"I think I might go back to our room after dinner," she tells me quietly.

"Oh, are you sure?" I'm a little disappointed. "I thought we might go for a drink."

"I'm really tired, and I could do with a quiet night." She puts her hand on mine. "But you should absolutely go for a drink." She glances at Nick, then looks back at me with a smile. "Make the most of him, Ellie," she says, whispering in my ear. "He's a real catch, and he's crazy about you."

She puts down her serviette, then says her goodbyes and gets up to leave. Daniel stands and says goodbye, but he doesn't attempt to follow her. He watches her walk out, then sits again and stares into his glass before finishing off his drink.

"You must excuse me," he says, "I have some work to catch up on." He rises once more, glances after her one last time, then walks off in the opposite direction.

Nick sighs. "I suppose that was to be expected."

"Such a shame." I've finished my dessert, and I push the dish away. "That was a lovely meal."

He glances around the table. Everyone else is talking amongst themselves; we won't be missed. "Would you like to go for a drink in one of the bars?" he asks.

"I'd love to," I say thankfully.

So we rise and make our way out, and as we pass Fiona, Nick takes my hand. I blush, because I know she sees it, but I feel a rush of exultant joy as we head out and down to the Crooners Bar. Out of all the women on this ship, he wants to be with me. I feel as if I could fly.

Chapter Twenty-Five

Nick

We order a whisky each and sit at a table by the window. Elena sips hers, the hearts dangling from her ears and sparkling in the late evening sunshine.

"These look nice." I reach out and touch one of the earrings. Accidentally on purpose, the backs of my fingers brush her neck, and she shivers.

"They're beautiful." She tilts her head to the side and rests her cheek on my hand.

"Have you had a nice birthday?" I stroke her cheek, then lower my hand.

She nods and tells me what she's been up to today. It's quiet in the bar. I suspect many people are taking the evening off from alcohol after the partying of the night before. The pianist is singing Sinatra's *Witchcraft*, and I look at Elena and feel as if I'm under her spell. All these years I've tried to keep my distance, and now I feel as if she's wrapped me in magical, invisible threads that are gradually tightening with each day that passes. I can't stop thinking about her.

On impulse, I get to my feet and hold out a hand. She blinks, surprised. "I haven't finished my drink."

"We're not leaving. We're going to dance."

She glances at the space in front of the piano. "Nobody else is dancing."

"So?"

"Nick..."

"I want to dance with you." I turn my palm up and beckon her with the tips of my fingers, the same way Laurence Fishburne does to Keanu Reeves in *The Matrix*.

Her lips curve up, and she rises and takes my hand. Her cheeks turn pink as I lead her through the tables to the small wooden floor by the piano, turn her into my arms, and slide my right hand onto her waist.

Slowly, we move to the music. Around us, the people occupying the surrounding tables smile.

"I'm definitely in love with you," I murmur.

I release her for a moment, turn her in a circle, then pull her back into my arms, and she laughs.

"I'm in love with you, too," she says breathlessly.

"I think I have been for many years," I tell her. "But it's been like a bird I've chained and kept in a cage. Now I've opened the door and let it fly free."

"You old romantic," she whispers, but she smiles. "That's a lovely way to put it."

"I'm sorry."

"What for?"

"For making you think I wasn't interested in you all these years."

"It's okay. You had Olivia. It was just one of those things. Nothing was ever going to happen while she was around. I knew that."

"I can't stop thinking about you," I confess. "All day, you've been in my thoughts."

"I'm the same."

"Last night was… amazing. I knew it would be, but it's affected me much more than I thought it would."

"Me too."

"I know we can't right now," I say, "but I want to be with you properly. To take you to bed and go to sleep and wake up next to you. I don't want to be apart from you."

She looks into my eyes and whispers, "Me neither." And we turn to the music for the rest of the song, just thinking about that and what it means.

When the music finishes, I twirl her in front of me, and everyone claps. Laughing, we go back to our seats and finish off our drinks.

"Would you like another?" I ask.

She shakes her head, her gaze creeping up to mine.

I clear my throat. "Shall we head back?"

"Yes, okay."

We make our way through the ship toward our suites, holding hands, not saying much. I'm not sure what to expect. I want to ask her in, but I'm conscious we only slept together last night, and I don't want to be that guy. I don't want her to think that's all I'm after.

We walk along the corridor, and when we get to her door, I stop. Suddenly I feel like a sixteen-year-old again, tongue-tied and unsure.

"Um…" I say, and she laughs. I give her a wry smile. "Don't tease me," I scold, pulling her toward me. "It's not easy, being the fella."

"But you do it so well." She smiles.

"Do you want to go back to your room?"

She gives a tiny shake of her head and whispers, "No."

My pulse picks up a little. I back up to my door, swipe the key card, and let us in.

Maybe she just wants a drink. It would make sense to cuddle up on the sofa and talk for a while. I'm sure she wouldn't mind kissing, and—

The door swings shut behind me, and she immediately places both hands on my chest, pushes me up against the wall, and crushes her lips to mine.

Taken completely by surprise, my thermostat goes from zero to a hundred in seconds. I slide my hand into her hair, tilt my head, and kiss her back hungrily. Our tongues tangle and our breaths intermingle as we move into the cabin, banging into doors and bumping into tables.

"Ouch," I say as I hit my hip on the kitchen worktop.

She giggles, her fingers fumbling at the buttons on my shirt. "I'm determined to do this carefully," she says, but her hands are shaking, and she has trouble popping them through the holes.

"Don't be nervous," I murmur, starting to gather up the material of her dress by her thighs.

"I'm not… I'm excited." She finishes the last button and pushes my shirt off my shoulders, along with my jacket, and they both fall to the floor.

I feel a surge of pleasure at her words. I toe off my shoes, then lift her dress up her thighs, over her hips, up her body, and over her head. I place it on the nearby chair before continuing to walk her back into the bedroom.

Now she's wearing only her lace underwear and her sexy high-heeled sandals. She looks amazing, and my body responds to the promise of what's to come. She undoes my belt, and her lips curve up as her fingers brush against my crotch. She slides down the zipper, and I let the trousers fall, kick them off, and flick off my socks.

Now we're just in our underwear, and she lifts her arms around me and kisses me again, pressing up against me. She's slender and soft, her skin so pale against my darker tan, and I like that contrast. I steer her back to the bed and gesture for her to get on. She climbs on the mattress, and I join her, lying on top of her, and kiss her again.

Ohhh… this is nice, taking our time to arouse each other. I haven't done this in a long time, and it's immensely pleasurable, drawing out our desire and letting it rise slowly, like the tide coming in on a warm summer beach. After a while, I slide a hand beneath her, unclip her bra, pull the straps down her arms, and toss it aside. Then I kiss down her neck to her breasts. They're small and high, perfectly shaped, the nipples an attractive pinky-brown, and I trace my tongue around them, avoiding the sensitive ends, until she groans. Then I cover one with my mouth, and she clutches her hands in my hair and arches her back.

It's her birthday, and I want to give her the best present I can. So I kiss down, over her tummy, and move on the bed until I'm lying between her legs. I pull her underwear down and toss it aside. She lifts her arms and places her hands over her face; I think she's holding her breath. I spread her thighs, slide both thumbs up to part her folds, then bury my mouth in her.

She tastes sweet, and I turn hard as a rock as I pleasure her, taking my time to tease her to the edge with my fingers and teeth and tongue. It doesn't take long before her breathing turns to deep gasps, and it occurs to me then that maybe she hasn't experienced this much before, if at all. I can't imagine her ex was interested in going down on her somehow. It makes me angry, and oddly smug too that I can do this for her, and I slow down my kisses, drawing it out for her until her gasps turn to groans, at which I cover her clit with my mouth and suck gently. She comes immediately, her body tightening with each pulse, and I wait for her to finish before I kiss back up her body to her mouth.

When she finally opens her eyes, they're glistening, and her bottom lip trembles.

"Happy birthday," I murmur.

"Thank you." She watches as I rise and take off my boxers. Finally, I move the tip of my erection into her folds and slowly push forward.

She's well lubricated and it's not difficult to enter her, but she still winces. I stop and look at her. "Are you sore?"

She shakes her head, then admits, "Well, tender. It's okay. It's just from last night. I'm a little rusty."

I smile, but say, "You want to stop?"

"God, no!"

I chuckle, pleased, but I don't want to hurt her, so I withdraw, then turn onto my back and gesture for her to climb on board. Her eyes light up, and she rises and straddles me. "Take your time," I tell her. "There's no rush." At least this way she can control how deep I go.

She lowers down on top of me and closes her eyes as she welcomes me inside her. Her breath escapes her with an, "Aaahhh…" and she waits a moment as she adjusts. "Mmm," she murmurs. "That feels good."

I stroke up her arms, then down to her breasts and brush my thumbs over her nipples. "You guide me," I tell her. "As slow as you like."

So she rides me slowly, rocking her hips back and forth, while I play with her breasts and kiss her when she lowers her lips to mine. Together, we climb the spiral staircase of desire, our bodies gradually speeding up as our breaths become faster. I watch her as she tips her head back, arching her spine, her blonde hair shining in the light, the diamonds in her ears sparkling, and think how beautiful she is, how elegant, how fucking hot, as she lowers her head and lifts her hands to her breasts to play with her nipples. Her eyelids drop to half-mast, and she moistens her lips with the tip of her tongue in a way that makes my blood boil. She's still wearing her sexy sandals, and for some reason that sends my brain into overload.

I slide an arm around her waist, lift up, and turn her onto her back, and she laughs, her hair spreading around her, and her cheeks flushing.

"I love how you do that," she says, wrapping her legs around me. "Ride me, cowboy."

"I don't want to hurt you," I reply, although my hips have already started to move.

"You won't," she whispers. She tilts her hips up to meet my thrusts. "Aaahhh… Nick. Yes…"

Encouraged, I move faster, harder, and she moans with pleasure and digs her nails into my back. Fuck, that feels good. Everything focuses on the point where we meet, and I plunge into her, kissing her too, wanting to be part of this wonderful woman who's gifted me her body and responded to me in a way I would never have thought possible. Oh, that's amazing, and although I try to slow down to make sure she's keeping pace, it's no good, my body doesn't want to do as it's told. Heat rushes through me, I feel the familiar, pleasurable pulsing as my climax hits, and then I come inside her, hot and hard, my hands curling into fists on the bed as, for a few seconds, I become pure sensation, pure pleasure.

She murmurs encouragement in my ear, and I continue to thrust, angling my hips down, and she joins me in less than thirty seconds, crying out as she clenches around me, making me gasp. Ooh, that's almost painful… I think I might actually pass out… Whoa… But then she's done, and we collapse onto the mattress together, gasping.

"Holy shit," she says. "Oh my God."

"I think all the bones have been removed from my body."

She laughs and runs her hands down my back. "You're so heavy!"

"Sorry." But I can't move for a moment. I lie there, limp and immobile, summoning the energy to lift up and roll off her, where I finally fall back onto the pillows.

"Mmm." She rolls onto her side and curls up next to me. "Wow, that felt good. And on a real bed, too! What a treat."

I laugh and smack her bum. "Don't get cheeky."

"I will if it means you'll do that again."

I groan and close my eyes. "You're honestly trying to kill me, aren't you?"

"That would kind of defeat the purpose." She leans her chin on my chest. "I have to admit, this is a bit like an adventure playground. All the fun things I've heard about and read about, and now I get to try them all."

I open my eyes. "Like what?"

"I have many, many ideas, Mr. Prince. So you'd better start eating plenty of steak to keep your strength up."

"If you're interested in keeping certain things up permanently, maybe I'd better invest in some Viagra."

She giggles and strokes me. "I don't think you're going to have any problems there."

I smile, feeling a frisson of excitement at the thought that she wants to experiment, to play in the bedroom. I'd hoped she was interested in a regular sex life, but I honestly hadn't expected this.

"I think I'll book a checkup with the doc when I get back," I tell her. "Make sure my heart can take the strain."

"Not a bad idea," she says, still stroking me. "I plan to wear you out as often as possible."

"Stop that." I take her wrist and move her hand away, then lift it to my lips and kiss her fingers. I adored elegant, organized Elena. Playful, passionate Elena is an absolute bonus.

"Can we meet every night for the rest of the holiday?" she asks. "Even just for a kiss and a cuddle?"

"Absolutely."

"This is the best vacation ever," she says happily, resting her cheek on my shoulder.

I kiss the top of her head and hug her tightly. "Yes, I rather think it is."

Chapter Twenty-Six

Elena

The last four days of the vacation pass in a blur of ports, cities, and happy times.

On the second of January, we arrive at Christchurch. Liz and I have both been to this beautiful city, but it was before the earthquakes that devastated it in 2010 and 2011, and it's changed a lot since then. I'm sad to see how much destruction has been caused, especially of the cathedral, but the transitional, so-called 'cardboard' cathedral is beautiful in its own way. We do some shopping in the city, then visit Hagley Park and have a very touristy trip on a punt down the Avon before catching some lunch in a splendid café in the Botanic Gardens.

The next day, the ship calls at Wellington, but we've decided to stay on until Auckland, so we take one of the shore excursions to the Weta Workshop, where they made the models for *The Lord of the Rings* movies. I haven't been there, despite having lived in the city for twelve years, and we both adore the movies, so it's fun to see how all the models were made, and have our photos taken with Gandalf and a life-sized orc.

Liz enjoys the trips ashore, but after our day in Wellington, she goes into her room to call Carl when we get back, and she comes out subdued and quiet.

"Something's going on," she says. "But he won't tell me what. He was very cagey."

"Like what?" I ask, puzzled.

"I don't know. But when I asked how his dad was, he just said, 'We'll see,' and he told me not to call for a few days because they needed some time to 'sort stuff out.'" She wraps her arms around her waist, her face pale. "I've got a bad feeling about it."

"There's no need for that," I soothe. "If anything, maybe he's making progress. Perhaps Keith has finally seen the error of his ways."

But Liz won't be consoled, and that evening she tells me she's going to stay in our room and have some food delivered, and that I should have dinner with Nick alone. I try to argue that I'll stay with her, but she insists she wants some time to think, so in the end I leave her to it and meet Nick on my own.

"I'm worried about her," I tell him, as we eat spaghetti carbonara and fillet steak in Romano's and sip cold Pinot Gris.

"She's done very well so far," he replies. "She's kept busy and given Keith the space he needs. Maybe now it's time for her to have a good think about what she wants to do going forward."

"She's sure something's wrong at home. Carl told her not to call for a few days."

"I wouldn't worry about it," Nick says, and he sips his wine. "How's the spaghetti?"

"Lovely," I reply, although I narrow my eyes suspiciously. That was his distraction technique—I've seen it often at work. He's adroit at turning the conversation away from a topic he doesn't want to discuss. "What's going on?"

"Hmm? Nothing. Here, have a bite of this steak, it's amazing."

He's obviously not going to tell me, and I figure maybe I'm imagining it, so I have a piece of the steak—which is amazing, he's right—and put it to the back of my mind.

The next day, we stop at Napier in Hawke's Bay. Liz and I are booked for a trip around the National Aquarium, but in the morning she announces she's not in the mood, and she won't be joining me.

"Please don't be upset," she says, taking my hands in hers.

"I'm not upset." I give her a hug. "I'm worried about you, that's all."

"I'm okay. I just need some time to myself. I've got all kinds of things whizzing around in my brain, and I need some peace and quiet to let them all settle. I'll be fine."

I don't want to bully her into going, so in the end I text Nick and ask whether he'd like to join me, and he replies that absolutely he would, and he needs a break from writing. So we go to the Aquarium together, where we see penguins feeding and playing, and sharks and stingrays swim over our heads as we glide slowly on the moving walkway along the oceanarium tunnel.

After that, we're taken on a short wine tour out to one of the vineyards, where we get to taste half a dozen of their wines while we eat platters of meat, cheese, and pickles. We return to the ship slightly tipsy, and when he takes my hand and leads me into his room, I'm more than happy to curl up on the bed next to him and doze for an hour in his arms in the warm sunshine.

The following day, the last of the vacation, we arrive at Tauranga on the west coast of the North Island. Once again, Liz decides to stay on the boat, so Nick and I go ashore and spend the morning walking along the track that goes around the base of Mount Maunganui, an extinct volcano.

It's a beautiful day for a walk, and even though I wear a sunhat and Nick a straw trilby, and we both make sure to use sun lotion, we return with sun-kissed skin, making me feel as if I've really been on vacation.

That night, Nick talks me into taking a night kayaking tour. I'm not really into sporty things like that, but once he hears that I've never gone kayaking, he insists it's time I tried something I haven't done before, and somewhat reluctantly I agree.

We start at the edge of tranquil Lake McLaren with some refreshments—white wine and cheese and biscuits as we chat to the others in the group—and then it's off to the two-person kayaks, while the setting sun turns the river orange and gold. As we paddle up the narrow, high-sided Mangapapa Canyon, the native bush rises around us and forms a dark cave, lit only by the strip of the night sky above us, with the Milky Way clearly visible. And then I discover the main reason for the trip as the sides of the canyon light up with another constellation—this one made up of thousands of glow worms. It's an amazing experience, and although I'm sad that Liz missed it, I'm thrilled to have shared it with Nick.

I love feeling like part of a couple, which is a novelty for me after all this time alone, and I also adore people knowing I'm with him. Not only is he gorgeous, but I also like the way he's the first person to step up when help is needed. When we return and get out of the kayaks and one elderly member of our party slips and twists her ankle, he's the one who lifts her and carries her up to the seating area. While the tour guide assesses the injury, Nick comforts her worried elderly husband. When the tour guide tells her he's sure nothing's broken and it's just a sprain and suggests she see the ship's doctor when she gets back rather than go to hospital, Nick helps her on and off the coach, calls the ship to make sure a wheelchair is waiting for her, and makes sure there's a member of staff waiting to take the two of them to the ship's doctor.

"Hang onto him, dear," the elderly lady whispers before they wheel her off. "He's a keeper."

I smile and whisper back, "I intend to!" before he takes my hand and we head back through the ship to our suites.

Once we're inside his room, I turn to him and slide my arms around his waist. "Thank you so much for talking me into going," I tell him. "I've had such a marvelous time."

"I was as fascinated watching you as I was the glow worms," he says, wrapping his arms around me. "You have a childlike innocence about you that I adore. Don't ever change."

"You either." I kiss him. "I love that you're a man of the world."

He laughs. "I'm not sure that's true."

"Oh, it is, and you know it. You're so self-assured, and you always seem so capable and confident that you can work out any issues."

"That's what having money does for you, I guess. It's easy to sort out stuff when you can throw money at it."

"No," I insist, "or at least that's not all it is. You like being a fairy godmother, don't you?"

"I do think I look good in the dress."

I chuckle. "You know what I mean. You like waving the magic wand and solving people's problems."

"I like to help, if that's what you mean. I don't like to see people worried and anxious when there's something I can fix."

I kiss him again, longer this time. "I'm just crazy about you," I murmur, kissing up his jaw to his ear and nibbling the lobe.

"Mmm. Maybe it's time you showed me how much."

He walks me backward into the bedroom and proceeds to undress me and make love to me slowly, stretching out beside me, and spending ages kissing me while he slides his fingers over my skin and down into the heart of me. Only when his fingers are slipping easily through my folds does he finally shed his clothes and pull me to him, and then we continue to kiss as he moves inside me with long, slow thrusts. It's heavenly, and I'm happy to give myself over to him, to let him guide me through the elaborate pathway of desire, all the way to the end, when blissfulness blooms inside me and sweeps over me like a cool breeze on a hot day. But that's not an end to the delight, because I then get to watch as he continues to move, taking his own pleasure from me, until the moment when he frowns fiercely and his body locks in beautiful ecstasy. I cover his mouth with mine, wanting to drink in his sighs, wishing we could stay like this forever.

But of course everything has to come to an end, and it's not long before I'm kissing him goodbye at the door.

"One day we won't have to do this," he tells me, lifting my fingers to his lips.

I smile, but as usual I feel a touch of worry as I leave. I still have no idea how I'm going to sort everything out. My future is shrouded in mist, and I can't see my way through.

It's late-ish, nearly eleven, and I'm surprised to see Liz sitting curled up on the sofa, a half-full glass of wine in her hand.

"Hey you." I go up to her and kiss her cheek. "What are you still doing up?"

"Waiting for a call," she says, gesturing to her phone. "Carl texted me an hour ago and said Keith wanted to talk to me, and that he'd ring at eleven."

I put down my jacket and bag and take off my sneakers. "That's late."

"I know. I think…" She swallows hard. "I think he's going to say he wants a divorce."

I sink down onto the sofa beside her and take her hand in mine. "What makes you say that?"

"I don't know. It's just a feeling, something about the way Carl sounded."

I stroke her hand. "How do you feel?"

Her bottom lip trembles. "I've spent the last few days thinking about nothing else. Going over and over it all in my mind. I keep thinking about Daniel—not in that way, but reminding myself how I felt like a different person with him because I was happy, and realizing that's how I used to feel with Keith before his accident. I love him, Ellie. I still do. I don't want to break up with him." Her eyes glisten. "But I don't know if he wants to be with me anymore."

As if on cue, her phone does its fancy tone announcing a FaceTime call. I go to get up, but she grabs my hand. "Don't go."

"I'll stay if you want."

"Please. I don't know if I can do this."

I sit back down and watch her touch the answer button on her phone, propping it up on her knee. Ooh, this is hard. I don't want to witness her marriage falling apart, but I'm not going to leave her if she needs support.

A figure appears on the screen. Liz stares at him, and her jaw drops. I move a little closer and look at the phone.

Keith is sitting on the sofa in their living room. Carl must be holding the phone some distance away, because we can see all of Keith, and a good deal of the room. He's wearing a suit and tie. His hair has been cut and neatly combed. He's shaved. And the room is all clean and tidy, the books neatly stacked on the shelves behind him, the table clear of the plates and glasses that normally litter it.

"Hey," he says. I can see instantly that he's sober.

"Hey." Her voice is little more than a squeak.

"Hey Mum," Carl's voice says from behind the phone. "We've been preparing a little surprise for you."

"What's going on?" she whispers.

"I have something to read to you," Keith says. "I had to write it down, so I didn't forget anything." He looks at a piece of paper in his hands. "The last two years have been the hardest of my life. Adjusting to my disability, learning to live in a wheelchair, coming to terms with not being able to work, or live a normal life… It's been real hard. And I know it's been even harder on you."

"Keith—"

"Please, just let me get through this." He swallows. "I know I've been unbearable, and I've taken my anger out on you. It was unforgivable, and I know there's no point in saying sorry, because it can't erase my behavior. But I'm going to say it anyway." He looks up at the camera. "I'm sorry. And, if you'll give me the chance, I'll spend the rest of my life trying to make it up to you."

Liz presses her fingers to her mouth while tears stream down her cheeks. "I don't understand," she squeaks. "What changed? Is it Carl coming home?"

"Partly. He's a good lad, and he's helped me make some changes. But the biggest factor was that a few days ago I had a visit from someone."

"Oh?"

"Yes. Two brothers, actually—Brock and Charlie King."

I stare at him. Wait, what? Brock and his brother visited Keith's house? Why?

"They're doctors," he explains. "They're friends of Elena's guy—Nick Prince."

Liz stares at me. "What?"

"They're cousins, actually," I murmur.

"Did you know about this?" she asks, and I shake my head.

She looks back at the screen. "What did they want?"

"To help," he says simply. "They're partly retired, but they still do some work at Auckland Hospital. They both specialize in respiratory infections, but they also have contacts in other departments and other hospitals. They have a friend who works at Whangarei Hospital." It's much closer to the Bay than Auckland—only ninety minutes away. "They said they could put me in contact with a guy who specializes in spinal injuries, a private doctor who could assess me and see if there's anything he could do. They said Nick has told them he'd pay for any treatment, but that he'd only do it if I was sober."

It's time for my jaw to drop. Holy shit...

"I got angry at first," he admits, "and said I didn't need help, but they didn't walk away, they sat me down and we talked for ages, about addiction and disability. They said they could get me into local AA meetings, and organize transport to get me there. They were such nice guys, Liz. So kind and understanding, but kinda firm, you know? They said I had to want to help myself. And I do want to get better. I just didn't know how to do it."

Liz is crying openly now. She reaches out and grasps my hand, and I squeeze it back.

"The specialist's name is George Martin," he says, "like the Beatles' producer. They took me down to see him—they flew me in a helicopter!"

"Oh my God." Liz's face is a picture.

"He did an MRI of my back and some x-rays. He said he thinks he can do an operation that might lessen the pressure on the nerves. He said it doesn't mean I'll definitely walk again, but with lots of physio, if I work hard, it might mean I have more mobility."

"That's wonderful," she whispers.

"They flew me home again. And then... you're not going to believe this... they took me to meet someone else. His name was Toby Wilkinson. He's a carpenter, and he runs his own business in the Bay. He's semi-retired too, but he makes toys in his spare time, including doll houses, and he said if I'd make some furniture he'd sell it for me in his online store."

That's enough to tip Liz over the edge. She dissolves into sobs, and I scoot along the sofa and take her in my arms.

"That's marvelous, Keith," I tell him, fighting against my own tears. "I'm so pleased for you."

"I need to talk to Nick," he says earnestly. "I need to thank him. Will he be coming back to my house?"

"I'm sure he will."

"He's one of a kind," he says, "a real old-fashioned gentleman. It's… not easy, accepting help, or money. But I've been proud, and look where that's gotten me. I've been so low. The real pits, and it's not a good place to be. I didn't care about anyone or anything, and I'm ashamed about that. But I want to put things right. I'm not saying it'll be easy, or quick, but I'm going to try."

"I think that's marvelous." Tears finally spill over and run down my cheeks. "I'm so happy for you both."

He nods and looks immensely relieved at getting all that off his chest. The phone moves, and it bounces around as Carl joins his dad on the sofa, then reverses the camera to show the two of them sitting together.

"We've worked really hard around the house," he tells us, "getting it all cleaned up and tidy. We're all ready for you to come home, Mum."

Keith swallows hard. "You are coming home. Right?"

"Yes," Liz says. "I'll see you tomorrow."

She says her goodbyes and hangs up, then stares at me. Tears tumble down her cheeks. "I don't believe it," she whispers.

"I know. I can't believe it either."

"Nick must really want to get into your knickers," she says, and we both laugh through our tears. "Seriously though," she says, "Why did he do all that for us?" She looks genuinely baffled, and it strikes me then how cynical and untrusting the world has become, to be confused by a fellow human doing a good deed for someone else out of the goodness of his heart. "Did you ask him for help?"

"No."

"Then… I mean, I'd understand it if it was me he wanted to get into bed. But I'm just your sister."

"It's nothing to do with that," I say, knowing it to be true. "You were both in trouble, and he was able to help. He saw it as his duty from one human being to another."

She shakes her head. "He's a saint."

"No, he's not," I say with a smile. "But he's not selfish, and he's very generous, and that more than makes up for everything else."

Chapter Twenty-Seven

Nick

I'm sitting out on the balcony, feet up on a chair, supposedly reading but in fact lightly dozing, when I hear a distant, gentle knock at the door. I check my watch—it's nearly eleven thirty. I yawn and stretch, then get up and pad through the suite, my heart lifting at the thought that it might be Elena.

It is, and Liz with her. "Hey," I say, seeing their big, wide eyes staring at me. "Everything all right?"

Liz immediately bursts into tears. Elena smiles, though, and puts an arm around her. "She's just talked to Keith," she says.

"Ah." I stand back, and Elena brings her sister through to the living room.

I follow them in and stand before them. "Have a seat," I say, but Elena shakes her head.

"We won't stay. Liz just wants to say thank you. Keith told us how he's had a visit from Brock and Charlie. They took him to see a specialist, and it sounds as if he's going to attempt an operation on Keith's spine, as well as give him some proper physio. And they're going to help him cut back on the booze. She's very touched, aren't you?"

I look at her sister, who's in absolute bits, clearly overwhelmed by the call. "Come here," I tell her, and I pull her into my arms and give her a big hug.

"Thank you so much." Her voice is so high I think it's audible only to dogs.

"I didn't do anything," I reply, "just introduced a few people to other people."

"No," she insists, moving back a bit and wiping her face. "You've done so much for us, Nick. You've changed our lives completely. I'll never be able to thank you."

"I understand," I say gently, a little embarrassed, "but the truth is that I was born into money, and anyone with an ounce of humanity inside them would feel the same way I do—that it would be selfish to keep it to myself."

"It's very self-effacing of you," she replies, "but that's not true. In fact I would say the majority of people are the opposite—if they had money, they'd spend it only on themselves."

"That's not been my experience," I say, thinking of Brock and his brothers, of their children who run the animal sanctuary in the bay, of my boys who are all generous in their own ways. But Liz is shaking her head, and Elena gives me a smile that tells me to take the compliment and leave it there, because I'm not going to change Liz's mind.

"I'm glad it helped," I tell her. "And I hope with the right treatment and aid, Keith is able to turn things around."

"He will," she promises. "He's a good man at heart, I swear."

"I'm sure he is—you wouldn't have married him if that wasn't the case."

She smiles. "I'd better go back, wash my face, and get some sleep, ready for tomorrow. And oh, by the way, Keith wonders if you're coming back with us to the bay? He'd love to see you."

"Yes, I can do that if you like." I'll ask Jock to pick Elena and me up from Kerikeri.

She nods and smiles at her sister. "See you in the morning."

"I'll be back in a sec," Elena promises.

Liz just waves and leaves the room, and the door closes behind her.

I turn to Elena and slide my hands into my pockets a bit sheepishly. "Are you going to tell me off now?"

Her lips curve up. "For not telling me? Maybe."

"I wasn't sure when Brock was going to be able to visit," I admit, "or what he'd come up with. Or even what Keith's reaction would be. I'm conscious of pride being a factor."

She sighs. "Yeah." Then she gives me a mischievous look. "Liz says you must really want to get in my knickers."

That makes me laugh. "Foiled again."

She chuckles and comes up to slide her arms around me. I wrap mine around her, and we stand like that for a while.

"She thinks you're a saint," Elena says.

"Ha! I'm far from perfect."

"That's what I said. I pointed out your many faults."

"I bet that took all afternoon."

She buries her face in my shirt. "I don't deserve you."

I press my lips against her hair. "I felt for Keith when we visited his house, and I also thought Liz deserved a break. I could tell she still loves him, and I admired her for staying faithful to him, even though she had every opportunity here not to. I wanted to help. I didn't do it for you. But I'm glad it made you happy."

She gives a little nod, her nose still pressed against my shirt.

"I love you," I tell her. "Just so we're clear."

She lifts her head and looks at me, eyes wide.

"I know it's early to say that," I add, "and I don't expect you to say it back. But it's not like we only met at the beginning of the cruise. I've known you a long time, and I've grown to admire you over the years we've worked together. And since then, I've had nothing but admiration for you for the way you've taken care of your family, and the unselfish decisions you've made."

A tear rolls down her cheek. "I do love you. I have since the day I met you, I think."

I cup her face and look into her eyes, then press my lips to hers. When I eventually lift my head, she blinks, her eyes shining. "There's something I need you to know," she whispers. "I'm so very grateful for what you've done, but it's not about the money."

"I know."

"I don't want you to think that's why I want to be with you."

"God, Elena, I know that. And if for whatever reason you decide it's not working out, I'm not going to pull the plug on Keith's treatment."

"I know you wouldn't do that."

"Maybe, but it's worth saying. What we're doing for them is separate from our feelings for one another, okay?"

"Okay." She smiles.

I kiss her again, properly this time, wanting to show her how much she means to me, how much I want her in my life. She leans against me, her hands on my chest, her sighs mingling with mine, while outside the silent sea drifts by, and the stars twinkle in the night sky.

SANTA, THE BILLIONAIRE

*

The next day, we disembark early, and by ten o'clock we're in a hire car heading for Liz's house.

She sits in the back, twisting the ends of her new scarf in her hands, her face pale. She looks lovely today, though; she's wearing her new trousers and a pretty pale-blue top that Elena bought her, and she's made up her face carefully, outlining her eyes and wearing a new pink lipstick. She had her hair cut and styled and it's not unlike her sister's now, in a long bob, tucked under at the ends. Despite her nerves, her eyes are sparkling, and she looks a thousand times better than she did when I first met her.

I pull up outside her house and turn off the engine. "Ready?" I say, meeting her gaze in the mirror. She nods, and we all get out and walk up the garden path.

Elena hangs back a little, and she slips her hand into mine. She looks beautiful today in a long green summer dress, and her blonde hair in the sun looks like a halo. I know she's not quite an angel, though. I smile at the memory of the naughty streak in her that I adore so much.

Liz lifts her key to insert it into the lock, but as she does, the door opens, and Keith is sitting there in his wheelchair, waiting to welcome her. He's wearing jeans and a clean, pressed, red polo shirt, his hair is neatly combed, and he's clean-shaven.

"Hello," he says, looking nervous and hesitant, but giving her a big smile. "You look amazing."

She looks up into his eyes. "So do you."

He swallows hard. "Liz... I'm so sorry. Can you forgive me?"

She nods, unable to speak, and then she bends and throws her arms around him, and he gives her a big hug back.

Elena looks up at me and smiles, and I put my arm around her and press my lips to her temple. It's quiet here—I can hear a boat making its way up the inlet, and in the distance the squeals of a couple of children playing in the rock pools. A pukeko walks across Liz's lawn, distinctive with its big red feet and blue body. In the trees above us, a tui bird calls, the white bobble at its throat bouncing up and down. I can smell the lemons in the trees.

In front of us, Liz finally moves back and wipes her face. Keith looks at us and wheels his chair forward onto the porch.

"Mr. Prince," he says.

"Oh God, Nick, please. Mr. Prince was my father."

"Nick." He holds out his hand. "Thank you, sir, for what you've done."

I know there's no point in saying that all I did was give my cousin a phone call. Instead I go up to him and shake his hand. "You're very welcome."

"Have you all had a nice vacation?" he asks, trying hard to be pleasant. I notice that his hand reaches out for Liz's, and she slips hers into it.

"We had a wonderful time," she says. "It was a real rest." She flicks a glance at us, a little embarrassed, and I'm sure she's thinking of Daniel, but of course we wouldn't ever say anything.

"Ate and drank far too much," I say cheerfully, patting my stomach. "Need to go on a diet now."

Elena chuckles. "Well, we're going to get going."

"Oh, don't you want to come in for a drink?" Liz asks, disappointed.

"No, thank you," Elena says firmly. "You two need time to talk, I'm sure, and we need to get back. But I'll come up soon, I promise."

Behind Keith, Carl appears, and he walks onto the porch and comes up to give his mother a hug. He nods at me, a manly gesture of thanks that says a thousand words, and I nod back.

But Liz comes up to me and gives me a more womanly thank you—a big hug, and a kiss on the cheek.

"Let me know how the operation and physio goes," I tell her.

"Of course," she says. "Thank you for everything."

We wave goodbye and exchange promises to keep in contact, and then Elena and I walk back to the car.

We don't say much on our way back to the airport. I hold out my hand, she slides hers into it, and it stays there for the duration of the journey. She looks out of the window, at the palms and ferns, the kiwi and feijoa orchards, and the fruit stalls along the side of the road. I concentrate on driving, content with the comfortable silence and the feel of her hand in mine.

We leave the car at the airport and make our way into the small terminal, which is quiet, its sole gate closed for the next public flight for another hour. Jock is waiting, though, and within ten minutes we're on board and buckled in. Soon we're up in the blue sky heading for

Wellington, and Tim is serving us steaming coffee with a plate of mini muffins.

He retreats out of sight behind the curtains, and now it's just me and Elena, lost in the clouds.

"I feel like we're in heaven," she says, and smiles. She's resting her elbows on the table, and she sips from the mug she's holding with both hands. The thrum of the engines is strangely lulling. I have the sensation of being transported somewhere idyllic, and I realize it's not Wellington but the future—that odd, sometimes scary place that suddenly seems full of promise.

I look out of the window. *I feel like we're in heaven*, she said. For the first time in a while, I think about Olivia. Is she out there somewhere, sitting on a cloud, waiting for me? What happens when you die, if you've remarried? I used to imagine the two of us living in a cloud cottage for the rest of eternity, but what happens if I spend the next twenty or thirty years with Elena?

As I watch the sun peeking over the puffy threads of the clouds, though, and see them lined with gold, as well as silver, I know that everything's going to be all right. Heaven isn't linear and compartmentalized. It's all about love—love for your family, your children, your pets, your colleagues, and those you're closest to. I think it all becomes one in the clouds.

"Penny for them," she says, and I bring my gaze back to her.

"It's that time," I reply.

She lifts her eyebrows. "What do you mean?"

"I said we were going to have 'that conversation' in the near future. Well, it's time."

"Okay," she says softly. "I've been thinking about it. Obviously, things are a lot different than they seemed a few weeks ago. Back then, I felt I needed to be close to Liz to give her extra support. And now I feel it's more important to give her space. It doesn't mean it's all going to be sorted overnight. I think I should be with her when Keith has his operation."

"Of course."

"And afterward, when he's recovering, it could be a tricky time for her. But I'm hopeful they'll pull through it now, and that means in a few months, I should be freer to make more formal decisions about where I live. Is that... okay?"

"Of course it's okay. And I've been thinking, too. It's early days, obviously. We've known each other a long time, but that doesn't mean we don't need to get to know each other properly. There's no rush. So what I was thinking was… how about I rent a place near to Liz's house? You can stay with Liz when you feel she needs you, but I'll come up at the weekends, and maybe we can see each other then and give them both a bit of space."

"That sounds lovely," she says, her eyes shining.

"I have decided, though, I'm going to sell the family home. It feels like the right thing to do. I'm ready. And then in a few months' time, when everything is a bit clearer, I thought maybe we'll buy two smaller houses, one in the Bay, and one in Wellington, and we can share our time between the two places."

"Oh, that would be perfect." She looks delighted. "I have friends in Wellington, and of course you have your family."

"And then we can get away at the weekends or for the odd week to the Bay, like a holiday home."

"I've also been thinking…" she says. "About traveling. I enjoyed the cruise so much. It's a wonderful way to see the world. And I thought maybe we could go away, just the two of us?"

I smile, over the moon at the thought of having a companion as I travel. "I'd love that. Where do you fancy?"

She nibbles her bottom lip, looking thrilled as she considers all the possibilities that have never been open to her before. "I was looking at some cruises online… There's one that goes all the way up to Japan. And I'd also love to see India… and maybe Europe one day…"

She continues talking about the places she'd like to see. I listen, watching her, enjoying the play of the morning sun across her beautiful face, and the light in her green eyes. I adore her gentleness, and the way she cares so much about those around her. And I love her sense of adventure.

The future stretches away from us like the bright blue sky, endless and brilliant, full of sunshine, with the whole world to be explored.

Newsletter

If you'd like to be informed when my next book is available, you can sign up for my mailing list on my website, http://www.serenitywoodsromance.com

SERENITY WOODS

About the Author

USA Today bestselling author Serenity Woods writes sexy contemporary romances, most of which are set in the sub-tropical Northland of New Zealand, where she lives with her wonderful husband.

Website: http://www.serenitywoodsromance.com
Facebook: http://www.facebook.com/serenitywoodsromance

Printed in Great Britain
by Amazon